# THE PATIENT

## BEYOND THE VEIL BOOK 1

### LINDA THACKERAY

Copyright (C) 2020 Linda Thackeray

Layout design and Copyright (C) 2020 by Next Chapter

Published 2020 by Shadow City – A Next Chapter Imprint

Edited by Susan Keillor

Cover art by CoverMint

This book is a work of fiction. Names, characters, places, and incidents are the product of the author's imagination or are used fictitiously. Any resemblance to actual events, locales, or persons, living or dead, is purely coincidental.

All rights reserved. No part of this book may be reproduced or transmitted in any form or by any means, electronic or mechanical, including photocopying, recording, or by any information storage and retrieval system, without the author's permission.

## PROLOGUE
### ONCE UPON A TIME

THERE WERE wondrous kingdoms of men, so great that when they fell, nothing of them remained, as if history itself could not bear the memory of their loss. They survived only in the fantasies of those who do not die, who left our earth long ago for a distant place beyond the Veil. Those who remained, the ones with their finite lives, could only share vague memories to be told around the campfires.

So it came to pass that Avalyne vanished forever into the mists, forgotten in every way save the faint traces of sensation whenever one happened along its places of power. Of the Sacred Three, only Man the Explorer remained. The Immortal elves retreated to their realm, as did the dwarf Master Builders who returned to Tal Shanar and were seen no more. Without the Immortals to teach them, the short memory of Man forgot the stories of what had been. As always, their flames burned bright, but fleetingly.

As time moved on and Avalyne disappeared from their minds for all time, they went on believing themselves alone. They regarded the earth as their dominion, not a home they shared with anyone. Their cities rose and fell. Their empires spread out across the land in conquest and then retreated again until they were conquered themselves. Man's reach spread to all corners of the globe and though they sensed something was missing, they did not know what it was. Still, they longed for the magic that once filled their eyes with wonder.

Avalyne, the golden age of Man, was dead, and no one remembered it.

The glorious kings, like their kingdoms, faded into the ages. Existence became a bitter struggle, devoid of wonder and magic. The sons who followed in the aftermath were a breed apart from those who emerged from Lake Tijon where Sireth gave them life. They were ambitious and driven to master their domain in every manner possible. If there was land, they conquered it. If there were beasts, they tamed them. They destroyed their enemies with such savagery it might have given even the foulest of goblins pause.

It seemed Man's grandest moments often accompanied his bloodiest.

Yet they craved the beauty of Avalyne, even if they carried no recollections of it. In their hearts, they felt its absence and often wondered when the starlight had vanished from their lives. They sought to recreate it in their endeavours, either in reaching for impossible goals or replacing it with myths of their own. Ill-constructed, too often these led to more bloodshed and violence, lacking any actual value. Man concluded there was no such thing as magic. It was a fanciful illusion best abandoned.

Innocence burned away and what remained was indifference.

Once discarded, man continued his existence with a juggernaut of change, not always for the better. An insatiable need arose to conquer all frontiers, and when exhausted, the snake began feeding upon itself, threatening implosion. It was only a matter of time before someone took advantage of this chaos to turn the march of industry into the spiral of Armageddon.

It was the hunt for the very thing lost that allowed this catastrophe to find its root in the present, long after Avalyne's day.

The quest for Magic had birthed Evil.

Behind the Veil separating one world from another, the Immortals lived in a strange sort of stasis.

They enjoyed beauty and tranquillity in a realm unchanged for over a hundred thousand mortal years. For the most part, they were content. Every so often, some took to leaving their enchanted home. Their curiosity of the outside world compelled them to see what had become of Avalyne in their absence. Most returned soon after, others did not return at all. Eventually the stories revealed the same thing. There was no reason to venture forth.

The world was spoiled by men, and it was best the Immortals washed their hands of it.

Instead, they devoted themselves to their own pursuits, removed from the harsher realities of existence in their sanctuary realm. The tragic times of the early ages melted away to a distant memory. After a while, it was difficult to remember they once battled such creatures as Mael, his servant Balfure, and their Primordial armies.

While the Celestials became even more unapproachable with the passing ages, the Elves who shared the Veil with them were a little more grounded.

They remembered with fondness the world left behind and mourned the changes suffered since their departure. They thought well of men, understanding it was unfair to judge a race whose lives were so finite when they possessed all the time there was. Mortals were not evil, they were young, and the nature of their existence ensured they would never live long enough to gain true wisdom. Even when the Immortals roamed Avalyne, they accepted the younger races as children needing guidance. Sequestering themselves behind the Veil for thousands of years did not change this belief.

Perhaps it was because they were so removed from danger and evil, it took them by surprise when it reappeared. Tremors of chaos rippled through their land, not even the barrier separating their realms keeping it away. It was like the sun stealing behind the clouds for a moment, taking with it the heat and leaving a brief interlude of cold. All suffered the chill, even the Celestials. Although they remained ignorant of what caused it, they knew something was emerging, something dark and terrible was taking root in the outside world.

In the aftermath, there were many rumblings of discourse emanating from the High Castle, the mansion of the Celestials. The Immortals held their breaths in anticipation as the Celestials debated what to do. While the cause of the disturbance was unknown to them, its urgency was undeniable. For the first time since the Primordial Wars, the caretaker gods were shaken out of their complacency, though what might cause this was something the Elves could not fathom.

After much deliberation, Enphilim the King God chose his most trusted servant to go forth into the world once more, to deal with the danger capable of consuming all the realms. He set this task to Tamsyn, a seraf who distinguished himself during the downfall of Mael's black servant Balfure. As always, Tamsyn accepted the duty before him without question and prepared for his departure across the Veil.

The warrior prince Aeron offered to accompany Tamsyn on his noble mission, but the seraf declined. The world beyond bore no use for Elves and might not receive Aeron well. Tamsyn suspected Aeron's presence would complicate an already perilous quest, and so he set out through the mists alone.

For a time, the Celestials sensed their agent in the other world, heard his thoughts as he conducted himself on their behalf. Then, without warning, their connection to Tamsyn was severed. From then on, he became as profound a mystery to those behind the Veil as the one prompting his journey. They knew he was not dead, for a seraf's soul would return to his Celestial masters in such a situation.

Wherever Tamsyn had disappeared, he remained lost there for the next four hundred years.

# ONE

# MOSES

It started with a phone. Specifically, *his*.

In the haste to leave work the night before, Doctor Daniel Ellis forgot the cell phone he'd placed in the top drawer of his desk while with a patient. By the time he met up with his college buddy Stuart at a local sports bar and remembered his mistake, it was too late to go back to the hospital. Now he would have to come into work, instead of catching up on a dozen projects at home. Dan swore at himself because failure to keep one's phone within arm's reach in the twenty-first century was tantamount to sacrilege.

To avoid compounding his sin any further, Dan woke early the next morning and drove to Bellevue Psychiatric Hospital where he was a physician on staff. He wanted to get the device, so he did not waste the rest of his day. There was paperwork he needed to catch up on, the football game he'd taped last weekend and, if the weather held out, a plan to wash his car.

Dan left his Dodge Ram in its usual place in the parking lot, not feeling guilty about arriving in jeans, sneakers, and a t-shirt. When he met patients, he wore the respectable white coat over what he considered his grownup clothes. The doctor still thought it annoying he had to look the part when it should be enough that he was a doctor. His gold hair was not exactly long, but it wasn't short either. Despite nearing forty, there were many times Dan was mistaken for someone younger.

The psychiatric ward was busy today.

On his way to his office, Dan noticed the non-violent patients wandering through the hallways escorted by orderlies and nurses. Most appeared lost in their own psychosis, awaiting evaluation before transfer to either state-run or privately funded psychiatric hospitals. Security remained visible, keeping a close eye on them while hospital staff hurried from place to place armed with charts and medication.

It was disheartening seeing so many patients in need when the hospital appeared bursting at the seams. At what point he would become indifferent to their plight was a mystery, but he knew he was not there yet. Dan supposed he was a late bloomer in this regard. He'd never developed the calluses doctors were supposed to grow over their feelings to maintain professional objectivity. The discipline seemed easy enough to achieve in theory, except Dan always failed to do it.

"Doctor Ellis!" Dan heard his name echoing down the hallway from behind him. The voice was familiar to him because he knew most of the people on staff and could narrow down the possibilities.

Dan turned and saw Warren Sheldon, one of the second-year psychiatric residents on staff. It was early morning and judging by the bleary-eyed look on Warren's face, it appeared the kid had been on call last night. Warren was able enough, but Dan was sure his plans after completing his residency would not involve the hospital. The sum of his psychiatric practice would include listening to rich matrons telling him what was wrong with the world, and how breast implants would cure all of it.

"You're still here, Warren?" Dan said with some measure of surprise because someone else should have taken over Warren's shift by now, and the kid looked like he needed the sleep. Warren tried to smooth his crinkled black hair by running his fingers through it, looking more weary than usual. "Shouldn't Doctor Lee be on duty by now?"

"She's got the flu." Warren frowned rubbing the bridge of his nose. "But I'm glad you're here. I wanted to talk to you about a John Doe the NYPD brought in last night."

"Oh no, I'm off today," Dan protested, guessing Warren was about to refer him a case that was too much for the resident to handle. Then again, when could Dan ever say no to a challenge or refuse when a colleague needed the help? "All right, all right, what's his story?"

"Thanks," Warren said appreciatively. "He's an old guy about the same age as Moses. Anyhow, NYPD picked him up last night for causing a disturbance outside the Malcolm Building. He's experiencing severe hallucinations, and it took two cops to get him into a squad car."

"Pretty strong for an old guy . . ." Dan raised a brow, noting the folder clutched in Warren's hand. "Is that his file?"

"Yeah." Warren nodded and handed it over. "We tested him for chemical abuse, and the only thing of note was the amount of nicotine in his system. The guy should have lung cancer by now, but instead he's in fairly good shape for someone that age."

"What about any neurological abnormalities?"

"Nothing." Warren shook his head. "No irregularities whatsoever. It's not the wiring."

Dan gave him a look. "That a professional opinion, *doctor*?"

"I mean, he has all the symptoms of schizophrenia," Warren explained, a little flustered. Dan suspected the hours were catching up with him. "But it just doesn't sit right with me."

Dan studied the file. He could not deny there were gaps preventing them from making an accurate diagnosis at this point. The patient had come in with no identification whatsoever, so there was no way to access any previous medical history. Dan could see why Warren was reluctant to act on his own and needed to consult someone far more experienced than himself.

"You get some rest," Dan answered after a moment. "I'll go see John Doe. Is he lucid?"

"Yeah. When he calmed down, he was pretty coherent, but any discussion about where he came from agitated him."

"Enough to be violent?"

"I'm not sure," Warren shrugged with uncertainty.

"Sounds interesting." Dan frowned, not up for this today. He sighed with resignation because the plans for his day off just got shot to hell. Still, this was his job, and he did it because he enjoyed helping people. There was no caveat he could only do it on his days off. "On your way out, get a nurse to move him into my office. I'll see him as soon as he's ready."

A short time later, Dan stared across the floor at the man designated John Doe.

Now that they were face to face, Dan estimated John was in his late sixties with a scraggly pepper coloured beard. He appeared to have lived rough, with gaunt cheeks and too many lines across his face. His blue-green eyes seemed a little dazed, but Dan expected this after the dose of Thorazine administered the night before. Enough time had passed for the full brunt of the drug's effects to wane so Dan could evaluate his patient and get further information. His previous violent behavior warranted an orderly being posted outside Dan's door just in case John acted out.

Doctor and patient stared at each other for a few minutes as if a mutual assessment were being conducted. Dan sat in his chair with a note pad in his hand, watching the man react to being observed. He tried to picture this old man causing a commotion outside the Malcolm building and could not deny being skeptical that he would try to harm anyone. Something deeper than instinct told Dan the patient was ill, not dangerous.

"May I have a glass of water?" he spoke, his first word croaked into an articulate English accent.

"Of course." Dan poured him a glass.

"I am uncommonly parched," John commented before taking the glass and adding his thanks to the end of his statement.

"Thorazine can do that," Dan offered in understanding.

"I dislike the concoctions you doctors put in my veins," John grumbled, giving Dan a look of annoyance after draining the contents of the glass.

"You were dangerous," Dan explained, not about to apologize for anything. The best way to gain a patient's trust was to be honest. He found nothing worked better - no psychiatric buzzwords or patronizing tones of empathy, just plain sincerity. "We had to give you something to calm you down."

"Yes, yes," the man rumbled, shifting restlessly in his seat, denying nothing. "So, they tell me."

"You don't remember?"

"No."

"Do you often have memory problems?"

"I don't know," John shrugged. His lips quivered as if he were nearing a place he did not wish to be. "The benefit of having memory problems is one does not remember it."

A smile cracked Dan's lips, and he made a mental note to pull back to safer ground for the moment. "Good point. What do you remember?"

"Nothing before waking up in this place." His attention shifted away from Dan as his gaze swept across the room. "Nothing more."

"You don't know what you did yesterday?"

"No," the patient bit back.

Dan could see John was just as unhappy about this as everyone else. His reaction sparked the doctor's curiosity and Dan felt for this patient in his blue hospital pajamas, looking so out of place, not just in his office, but anywhere. There was something about him Dan could not put his finger on, convincing the doctor he wasn't dealing with any run-of-the-mill schizophrenic. If that was what John was. The patient's eyes seemed a little glazed, but that was due to the medication administered.

"You weren't in any condition to give us your name last night." Dan moved on to a safer subject. "Care to tell us what it is? I don't want to keep calling you John during our sessions."

A furrow appeared above those gray eyebrows, and blue eyes stared at him with hesitation. "I don't know what I am called. I told you I remember nothing more than what I have said. Is badgering me with foolish questions your way to help me, War Dragon?"

Dan blinked. "Excuse me?"

John looked back at him just as perplexed. "What?"

"You just called me by a name," Dan pointed out.

"I did?" The old man regarded Dan with disbelief.

"You called me 'War Dragon,'" the doctor reminded his patient. "Who is that?"

"I don't know." John met his eyes and Dan could see the sincerity in his answer, not to mention the genuine puzzlement. "It just slipped out. It seemed...appropriate."

Dan arched a brow at that statement and made a note of it. The patient did not seem violent, but then he was not about to underestimate the effects of 400 mg of Thorazine on a person either. He wanted to see what John was like with no medication because Dan couldn't make a diagnosis from one session alone.

"We will have to think of something to call you. If we are going to continue talking to each other, I think I would prefer to call you something other than John."

"How many of these talks are we likely to have?" John eyed him with suspicion.

"I'm not sure," Dan confessed. "Until we find out what your name is and why being outside the Malcolm Building upset you so much."

The patient's body tensed. Relaxed hands clenched into fists, his back straightened and the muscles of his jaw ticked. He was angry and barely able to restrain himself, Dan realized.

"You seem disturbed," Dan probed, doubtful he would get an answer that made any sense. "Is there something about the Malcolm Building that bothers you?"

"It is a place of darkness!" John snapped, rising to his feet. He seemed to tower over the doctor as his voice altered, becoming deeper and more forceful. It was a voice that made Dan beware, not for his life but because for a brief insane moment, he was almost ready to believe the old man.

"Sit down," Dan ordered, determined to regain control of the session. "Please," he added with a kinder tone.

John looked at Dan with a start, as if he remembered where he was, and the burst of anger subsided, once again replaced by confusion.

"Why do you think it's a place of darkness?" Dan could not believe he was using such a melodramatic term. People used speech like this when describing the plot to the latest George Lucas epic, not a psychiatric session.

"I don't know." John shook his head, his expression strained. "I know nothing. It is just something I sense."

"It's all right, John." A surge of sympathy filled Dan for this old man who seemed so lost. Who was he in the world when he was far away from this place? Did he have a wife or children or even grandchildren? He was old enough for all those possibilities. "You don't have to tell me until you're ready."

"I want to tell you," John whispered. "I think I *need* to tell you. I've been away for a long time, and it's important I come back."

"Admitting you have a problem is always an excellent start." Dan offered him more assurance than was customary, but John appeared to need it. "We'll find the answers together, I promise you. In the meantime, I hope you don't mind if I don't keep calling you John. You're not a person who doesn't exist. You're here, and you're my patient. How does Moses sound to you?"

"Moses?" One gray eyebrow flew up. "You are naming me after a man with a terrible sense of direction and masonry skills?"

"A terrible sense of direction?"

"It does not take an inordinate amount of sense to realise he was wandering on that mountain for forty days because he was lost. Not enough to dedicate an entire testament to his affairs." At that moment, John sounded very much like a cantankerous old man accustomed to waving his cane at young children from his porch.

"All right then," the doctor laughed at that, "you tell me what to call you."

A loud harrumph followed before the patient spoke again. "Moses will do. I suppose under the circumstances I am in no position to take the high ground for sanity."

The ship had appeared out of the mists in the middle of the North Sea almost two months before Doctor Dan Ellis faced the patient he called Moses.

Its arrival went unnoticed because people avoided traveling through the North Sea during the winter months. It was icy cold on a pleasant day, let alone during winter. Hazardous sheets of ice drifted above the black water, pieces of flotsam jettisoned by the arctic pole sure to spell death to any ship unfortunate enough to encounter them. Icebergs, mists, and turbulent waters made the North Sea a most inhospitable place, even for those who spent most of their lives on the ocean.

If anyone had been present, they would have seen a ship not unlike a Roman trireme, with a trio of large sails as gray as the mists it had just escaped. The vessel was crafted from wood, but the skills of the carpenter were unlike any seen in centuries. It was a thing of beauty, crafted not by shipbuilders but artisans. It sailed across the choppy water as if gliding on the waves, trailing a bed of foam as it surged towards its destination. Amidst the singing voices of humpback whales, the ship did not seem real, and anyone who saw it would most likely wonder if they were dreaming.

There were only three passengers on the craft that would seem big enough to accommodate more.

Three was enough, because this was a journey a century in the making. With a galley stocked with enough food and water to reach their destination and back again, so far, the trip had taken place without incident. If anything, it was dull until they pierced through the Veil and sneaked into the world they left behind so long ago.

Once they left the Veil, their trip became a little more exciting as it had been smooth sailing until that point. Where they had been, the sun shone, and the water was still. There was enough breeze to power their sails and keep the air fresh. It was idyllic.

Now they were outside the Veil where the waves could rise almost as high as their masts, where it was gray and gloomy even though they could see the sun above their heads. Wind lashed at the travelers with sheets of rain, and the periodic rumble of thunder and lightning required reacquaintance. It was a stark reminder of how far away from home they ventured. Those left behind had advised against the journey, calling it foolishness to leave a place of safety into an unknown grown more barbaric since their departure.

Aeron stood at the bow of his ship and saw nothing ahead but the horizon of a gray sea against a similar colored sky. The wind was so cold he felt frozen but leaving the open space for the shelter of the craft's innards did not occur to him. It was too long since he had experienced anything as adverse as weather, and he was rather enjoying it. Eden Hallas's perfect weather was so constant he no longer knew how to appreciate it. A few months of this and he would be happy to return home again.

"You should come inside," a voice advised.

The prince glanced over his shoulder and saw his older brother Syannon wrapped in a thick warm cloak, seeing he had also brought him his own.

"Thank you Syn, but I prefer to remain out here a little longer," Aeron said, gratefully taking the garment and slinging it over his shoulders before facing front again.

"How long do you think it will take us to cross this sea?" Syannon asked as he sat down on the deck behind Aeron.

"I do not know. A hundred thousand years have passed since we entered the Veil. Such lengths of time can reshape the world. We sail what was once the Brittle Sea, but we do not go east but farther west than anyone has traveled during our time in Avalyne. We are most likely bound for what was once the eastern coast of the Uncharted Lands."

"Are you sure that is where we must go?" Syannon asked with concern, aware that more than just their quest drove his youngest brother.

"It is the only clue we have to begin." Aeron shrugged, unable to deny the difficulty of their mission. They knew little of where Tamsyn had disappeared to, and they were emerging into a world that most likely remembered nothing of their kind.

"He could be dead," Syannon pointed out. This was a volatile subject to discuss with his brother. However, Syannon and their older brother Hadros had placed themselves at risk, just as Aeron had when they accompanied him on this journey. That earned them both the right to speak their mind and make Aeron aware of the reality of the situation.

"If Tamsyn were dead, his soul would have returned to the High Castle. It has not, so he must still live."

"Aeron, no one wishes to think the worst, but you must prepare yourself for the possibility. Much has changed in Avalyne. We may find the reason there has been no word from Tamsyn is because something worse than death might have befallen him."

"I refuse to believe that." Aeron shook his head, his eyes fixed on the gloomy horizon.

"You may not wish to, but you must at least entertain the possibility."

"I will speak of this to you no more." Aeron stood up to leave, aware he was running away like a child.

"Aeron . . ." Syannon stopped him with a hand on his shoulder. "People die. It is an unfortunate reality of what they are. We must accept it."

Aeron turned to his brother, his features softening a little because he could not deny this truth was at the heart of his pain, driving him to find Tamsyn. "I have accepted the price of immortality is to see the

# THE PATIENT

deaths of all I love. I held Melia's hand when her life slipped beyond my reach, and I sat at Dare's bedside when he passed. I will not be the last of us that still lives, Syannon. I refuse to lose another person. Tamsyn is alive, and I *will* find him."

Syannon could appreciate Aeron's grief for he knew all too well what it was like to care for mortals and be helpless to prevent their eventual demise. He loved Dare as much as Aeron, who was not the only one who lost someone close to his heart. "I understand your fear of losing the last of your friends, but we have all lost. I have seen mortals I loved pass to Sireth's hands."

Aeron saw the sorrow in Syannon's eyes and remembered friends like Arianne. So many of the former queen's words remained with him, even thousands of years after her passing. To this day, her mother Lylea still mourned her. The High Queen of the Elves would light a candle on the day of Arianne's birth, as she had done every year since Aeron brought her the news her daughter was at rest with her king.

"It does not have to be this way for you, Aeron," Syannon continued. "I know Melia is dead, but Sireth promised the race of men does not live one life. They may not have immortality, but they are blessed to return until the End of Days."

"Stop," Aeron warned, not wanting to discuss the open wound that was Melia, his wife.

Syannon's words rang true, however. Even Tamsyn told him once of Sireth's plans for men, who in their own way received a kind of immortality because their souls could return to the world to lead new lives. A hundred thousand years had passed, and Aeron waited, praying his Melia would find her way back to him, and still he was alone, mourning her.

It would never happen, and he had reconciled himself with that long ago.

Tamsyn was in trouble and needed help. The Celestials would send no one else, and Aeron suspected they were reluctant to do so until they knew what had become of him. For four centuries, Aeron waited with growing impatience for his old friend to return, but with another millennium passing, he knew it was time to act. Syannon and Hadros volunteered to accompany him, aware he would go alone otherwise. Aeron intended to find Tamsyn because he would not be the last living member of their circle of friends.

"I cannot abandon him brother." Aeron looked Syannon in the eye. "I refuse to."

"I know." Syannon admired his younger brother's determination if not his stubbornness. Defeated, he rose to meet Aeron's eyes, standing a little taller, before squeezing Aeron's shoulder in comfort. "If he is alive, we will find him, Princeling."

"He is alive," Aeron insisted, smiling at that old nickname used when he was a child. "If I were lost, Tamsyn would find me."

Syannon hoped it would be as simple as that.

## TWO

## WAR DRAGON

Detective Anna McCaughley stared at the body.

It had been floating in the river for some time now, before coming to rest against the embankment. The skin's deterioration had left it gray and mottled. Dumped upstream, it had floated down the river to arrive at its present location. Along the way, rotting leaves, twigs, dead insects, and the detritus of the waterway attached itself to the corpse like a morbid flotilla. The body had reached its latest resting place at the edge of an embankment, found hours later by a family of three.

It had ruined an otherwise pleasant morning.

Anna slipped on the latex gloves as she knelt by the body where it became snagged by reeds at the water's edge. Patrolmen kept the bystanders at bay while remaining at a distance to avoid compromising the integrity of the crime scene until forensics arrived. Anna didn't intend to wait that long. Initializing the voice recording app on her phone, Anna had developed the habit of making audio files when she investigated a scene. It helped when it came time to type the report.

Most of the officers recognized Anna McCaughley. She earned

the reputation as one of the good cops who never handed off unpleasant chores to a patrolman if she could do it herself. She did not mind getting her hands dirty, nor was she squeamish about it.

She'd made detective on her first attempt because she saw details others missed and made accurate deductions with the scant information she perceived. She also had the right pedigree as a third-generation cop. Her father Elroy, who died of pancreatic cancer five years before, retired a sergeant. Her brother Alan, not as fortunate, was killed intervening at a liquor store robbery.

She wore little makeup and kept her brown hair in a neat braid, steel-rimmed glasses framing her blue eyes. Her appearance was fit and youthful, but she preferred not to take advantage of that, dressing conservatively to look the part of a New York City detective She had no need to prove herself to inspire confidence in her abilities. Her record of closed cases accomplished that.

"Detective Anna McCaughley – homicide," she began her narration. "Victim is a Caucasian male, five foot seven, one hundred seventy pounds, medium build with brown hair and blue eyes. His age may be anywhere from the mid-twenties to thirties. The cause of death appears to be a gunshot wound to the head. The facial injuries and the state of the skull appear to indicate a shot at point-blank range. The bullet entered through the bridge of the nose, blowing out the back of the skull. We can't confirm ballistics at this stage, but I'm guessing it's a high caliber weapon, a .45. The victim is wearing a suit and missing one shoe. Whether this is due to the body drifting down the river or the crime is difficult to say. The suit, despite its current condition, looks expensive. I'd say it's an Armani, so whoever he was, he was a professional of some sort."

"Detective McCaughley!" a patrolman called out to her. Anna disabled the app as he approached. She had sent him and several others to canvass the shore along the river in case anything belonging to the victim had ended up there.

She studied the surrounding park, covered in falling leaves and bordered by trees along the river. It was an idyllic place to go for a walk, and the winding path along the edge offered that invitation to locals. She imagined this tranquil setting for sailing model boats with your kids or picnics on the grass. It was too pretty for the macabre discovery of this morning. The patrolman, an officer named Perez, approached her with something inside a Ziplock bag. From the outline, Anna guessed Perez or one of his officers had found the victim's wallet.

"What have you got Sergeant?" she asked as he approached.

"This." He handed her the bag.

"By the river?" Anna frowned. The contents did not appear to have spent any time in the water. In fact, it was in almost pristine condition.

"No. We found it in a trash can along the path. It has a New York driver's license and a Manhattan address."

Anna did not answer for a moment as she reached into the wallet with a gloved hand and went through its contents, hoping to identify the victim. What remained inside had little monetary value, including a driver's license signifying he was an organ donor. The face of the corpse and on the pieces of identification was the same, possessing bland features that would never stand out in a crowd. Just an ordinary person who did not deserve this end.

"His name is Robert Falstaff. He lives on Ninety-Fourth Street, Manhattan."

"I think that address is off Columbus Avenue," Perez agreed. "Wonder how he ended up as fish food on the other side of the river?"

"I don't know." Anna checked the dead man's pockets and found a cell phone. To no one's surprise, the phone was dead after being in the water for so long, but current technology ensured its digital imprint remained intact somewhere in cyberspace. The phone, despite its present condition, was one she recognized from the ads on television, and its presence on Mr. Falstaff's body revealed something glaringly obvious. "This was not a robbery."

"No?" Perez looked at the homicide detective, respecting her hunches from previous cases.

"No." She shook her head. "They made it seem like one, but it isn't. He gave up his wedding ring and his jewelry without a fight. I saw the tan lines on the index finger of his left hand but no scratches to reveal they took it off him. He doesn't look like the type to put up a fight if a mugger came up to him. There's no reason to shoot him through the face when he was cooperating."

"Then why leave the phone and wallet behind?" Perez asked, seeing sense in what she said, though this one point left him at a loss. "I mean if the shooter was doing it to throw us off the scent, why wouldn't he have taken those too?"

"I'm not sure, because you're right. There's no way a robber would leave a phone or a wallet. Look at it..." She turned the wallet over in the Ziplock bag. "That's genuine calf leather. Something like this you buy in Manhattan if you can afford it. Take it to a hock shop anywhere else, and you'll get a hundred bucks for it, easy. A mugger wouldn't leave this or the phone behind. He'd dump whatever isn't valuable to him and keep going."

"Maybe the mugger ain't that smart."

"True, but they're greedy. Robbers wouldn't leave this stuff behind if they could get money for it."

It was sheer impulse prompting Dan to drive past the Malcolm Building on his way home after his session with Moses.

For the rest of their time together, Dan allowed Moses to do the talking. The psychiatrist found Moses to be insightful about his perceptions of the world, what of it he remembered - except for the moments when he tried to remember his past. Then Moses would become agitated, and Dan was sure if not for the residual effects of the Thorazine, Moses might have become violent. Was this motivated by the need to hurt? Or was it the result of his frustration at being unable to remember?

In any case, Dan delayed Moses's transfer for a few days. He wanted more time with the patient.

Dan was convinced some deep trauma kept Moses's memory locked away from him. When he put a call into the NYPD, he learned the cops still had no luck identifying the man. In fact, it might be days before they exhausted all avenues of the search.

Due to his extended session with Moses, there was no point rushing home when his day was shot to hell. Instead, Dan opted to remain in his office, finishing his paperwork at his desk thanks to the Almighty Cloud. As he worked, Dan found his mind preoccupied with the odd phrase Moses had used.

*War Dragon.* It sounded like the name of a video game.

On his way home, Dan used the speed dial on his cell phone to contact the only person who might have access to the information he needed. For all he knew, it could be gibberish produced by Moses's damaged psyche. Still, Dan was working in the dark, so he had to use whatever clue was available, even if it was as slight as this. It did not take long before he made the connection.

"Hey Stu, it's Dan," Dan announced himself to his friend, the college professor who taught at NYU.

"Hi Dan," Stuart returned. Dan heard the clacking of a keyboard in the background and surmised Stuart Farmer was still in his office at the English Lit department.

"You still working?" Dan teased, aware Stuart often spent too much time at work and forgot to have a life.

"Yeah, not all of us like to waste time driving around in our expensive cars harassing friends who do *real* work."

Dan grinned inside his car. "We still up for the game on Saturday?"

"I'm bringing the beer."

"Great." Dan nodded, looking forward to seeing the game and his old college buddy. "Listen, I've got a question for you. You play video games, don't you?"

"Down to my twenty-sided dice."

*Nerd.* Dan thought with a smile.

"Why?"

"A patient of mine used a term today," Dan explained. "Kind of stuck in my head. I thought it might be a video game or something. I'm clutching at straws trying to identify it, and him."

"What was it?"

"War Dragon." The doctor turned his car into the street leading to the front of the building.

"Hmmm, I'm not familiar with it," Stuart confessed, "but I can look it up in the oracle of Google. Give me a minute."

"Thanks." Dan came to a halt at the curb and put the RAM into park.

Beyond the windshield of his car, he studied the towering glass structure officially known as the Malcolm Building.

Though not as tall as the Empire State Building, it was more imposing and had earned the nickname of the "Monolith" for good reason. Like the artifact depicted in the famous Kubrick film, tinted-black glass covered the outer facade of the structure, while black, marble made up its masonry. Against the night sky, it blocked out the stars, as if the space it occupied was some null field where they could not exist.

As Dan stared at it, he could not deny it might seem ominous to a mind already fragile with psychosis. If Moses was being plagued by hallucinations of evil forces, it was understandable why he might choose the place as the source of his anxieties.

"Dan?" He heard Stuart's voice a moment later, snapping him out of his ruminations.

"I'm here." Dan continued to stare at the Monolith through the windshield.

"There is a record of the phrase, but it isn't for a game. It's an obscure reference found in medieval folklore."

That made Dan sit up and pay attention. "Medieval folklore?"

"Yeah, specifically around the Arthur legend."

"The Arthur legend?" Dan exclaimed, astonished. "As in the *Knights of the Round Table,* that Arthur?"

"Yeah." Stuart's voice dripped with sarcasm. "That Arthur."

"Okay." Dan eased back into the car seat, perplexed. "What's the reference?"

"According to popular theory, the Arthur legends are a composite of stories, not about one individual. Before Mallory made it into what it was, these legends were floating all around the place. One of them had to do with a king who started out as something else, hiding his identity until needed, that sort of thing. One of his titles was *War Dragon*, and they incorporated his story into Arthur's."

"So, Moses is some kind of medieval history professor...".

"Who?"

"This patient I have," Dan replied, deciding Stuart deserved an explanation though he was not at liberty to discuss too much about Moses's condition. "He's a John Doe with no identification at all. He sounds like he could be English, but I can't be sure. I think he's suffering from a severe form of post-traumatic stress disorder and while we were in session, he called me War Dragon."

"You think he might be teaching medieval folklore?"

"That's the best lead I have. So, this War Dragon legend is being studied somewhere?"

"No, what I told you is all there is to know about it. I'm not kidding Dan. This is a very remote reference. There isn't even a record of where it might have originated. Your man would have to be an expert in obscure legends to have even heard of it. Unless he met the guy himself."

"You're a real comedian, Stuart." Dan sighed, disappointed. He hoped there would be more, but at least Stuart had given him somewhere to begin searching for his patient's identity.

Without knowing why, Dan was sure finding out the truth about Moses was the key to understanding everything.

The man stood by the glass and watched the world below him with a brief smile of satisfaction.

Even though the tower was not the tallest in the city, it was enough to provide him with a panoramic view of New York. John Malcolm still thought the skyline lost a little without the familiar sight of the twin towers, but so much in mortal existence was fleeting. Buildings, like human beings, had minor staying power. When he first ordered the building constructed, he had wanted to erect something with presence, and that didn't always mean aesthetics. Architects seemed to think buildings should be high, but he preferred to remain grounded.

Malcolm thought the heavens were overrated.

While the building was tall enough for him to enjoy this view, it was its dark facade that pleased him most. Within the "Monolith," John Malcolm ran his corporation like a god ruling his empire. The Monolith was the center of his kingdom, and from here he kept watch over everything.

Leaving behind the twilight city, Malcolm returned to the desk in his private office. He lived in the tower, occupying the penthouse suite with its swimming pool and garden on the roof.

*Fortune 500* called him one of the most powerful men in the world, but the ranking did not concern him. Power was subjective, and only he knew just how much of it he wielded. The tendrils of his power did not confine themselves to the boardroom, but beyond it, in realms most would never even imagine existed. Man's potential was limitless, and Malcolm spent his entire existence on this earth exploiting that boundless resource.

Most of the time, they did not know he was behind the scenes, working things with the expertise of a puppet master. Secrecy was something Malcolm did well, and he prided himself on how far his influence extended. His agents were far and wide, and they worked for him with unwavering loyalty because they knew the price of failure. Still, being rewarded well for their efforts ensured his reach extended into the highest echelons of power. There were heads of state who would be grateful for his attentions.

The public knew nothing of this, and that was precisely how Malcolm preferred it.

*Someone was about to intrude on his privacy.*

The CEO of Malcolm Industries lowered himself into the leather chair before his marble desk and waited. He liked the cool sensation of the black stone and strived to furnish his office with as much of it as possible. The office, despite its ultra-modern appearance of smooth inky surfaces, had a Spartan air due to the lack of personal items. Malcolm had as much use for these as he had for people, which was to say very little. They served him and then they died. It was all so simple. Why complicate things by developing unnecessary attachments to them?

"Sandra," John greeted when the woman walked in. "I don't remember sending for you."

"I am sorry, Mr. Malcolm," the woman, in her dark suit with the high collar, who was his personal aide and confidant apologized.

In her youth, she had been a stunning beauty with flaxen hair, now worn in a bun. Even the emerald fire in her eyes lost its luster when the world took its toll upon her. At fifty, Sandra Collins was still a handsome woman, but she could no longer trade on her looks to get by as she once had.

"I didn't mean to intrude, but I didn't think this could wait." She had sense enough to pause before coming any closer, aware permission was needed before she could approach. He was like an emperor giving an audience, she thought silently.

"I am intrigued." Malcolm gestured her forward.

Sandra had been holding a manila folder under her arm when she entered the room. She reached into it to remove the intelligence it contained.

"We caught this on security cameras last night," she placed the photographs on the desk before him.

The pictures were grainy but held enough definition for him to make out what had caused her such concern.

"He isn't dead. He's alive, and he was outside the building last night."

"Indeed." Malcolm nodded, feeling less anxiety than she did. "I did not expect him to be dead, Sandra. It was always a foregone conclusion he was alive somewhere, but he is in no position to be a threat to me."

"We should resolve this matter once and for all. We have people working for us that could make it look like an accident. They took him to Bellevue after the NYPD picked him up. It would be a simple matter to just—"

"I have told you once, and I will tell you again . . ."

Malcolm rose to his feet and glared at her. His voice sent icicles of fear through her skin and for an instant, she saw everything vile and unholy in the world surface in his eyes.

"He is not to be killed under any circumstances. If his blood is spilled, it will be followed closely by your own. Do you understand?"

Sandra shuddered at the blackness of his eyes and nodded quickly. "Yes, sir."

"Good." Malcolm sat down again. "What you will do is find out who in that hospital has the power to commit my old friend to a nice little asylum, where we can forget him for another four hundred years. That will be all the action taken on this matter, is that clear?"

"Yes, Sir." Sandra nodded. "What if they won't do it?"

Malcolm blinked as if she had asked him something ludicrous. "They'll do it if they want to live."

# THREE
# PHOBIAS

Dan had a restless sleep that night.

When he arrived at the hospital the next morning, he was irritable and bleary, and questioned whether he was in any fit state to see a patient. If it was anyone but Moses, he might have considered canceling his appointments for the day. Yet for reasons that made no sense, he wanted to speak to the old man again. The conversation with Stuart lingered in the back of his mind, offering him no answers but repeating the same question. How did an educated scholar like Moses end up in the state he was in when the NYPD arrested him?

What happened to this man for him to create such a defensive wall against the truth?

*A lot of things*, Dan reminded himself.

Amnesia was a symptom of trauma in a person's past, an incident so repulsive the only way the mind could cope with it was to block it out. Often seen in child abuse cases, the victims repressed the memory until it manifested later down the line when they were adults. Sometimes, the memory remained so buried, it required hypnotherapy for the truth to surface.

Dan knew if Moses's condition did not improve, he might be

forced to resort to such methods. For now, they were in the early stages of treatment, leaving Dan in a dilemma. Under normal circumstances, his authority would extend as far as conducting the preliminary examination necessary to diagnose the patient, before recommending further treatment. Once completed, the patient would be transferred to another facility and into the care of the doctor who would provide a more in-depth therapy for the specific trauma.

It was not unusual for Dan to allow his feelings to cloud his judgement. Though it was a practice discouraged by his colleagues, he never seemed able to avoid it. Some empathy was necessary to help a patient. Yet it was more than that with Moses. Dan's compulsion to draw Moses from the mental limbo in which the old man found himself trapped was overwhelming.

When he left the night before, he'd ordered Moses's dosage of Thorazine reduced. The psychiatrist needed to see just what symptoms Moses would experience without them. Moses stayed under observation with his behavior closely monitored during the night. Before their session began, Dan studied the tapes and noted without the medication, Moses began to hallucinate, carrying on conversations in an unknown language with imaginary persons. During these phantom exchanges, he displayed a range of emotions from grief to outright fear.

When he became too violent for his own good, the doctor on duty prescribed the sedative once more to settle him down for the evening. Dan took a copy of the tape, hoping to determine what language Moses was speaking, if it was a language at all. Some schizophrenics developed speech entirely of their own sounding like gibberish to everyone else. Nonsense or not, the conversation seemed to upset Moses, even if to Dan's ears, it was one-sided.

"You appear to need more sleep than I," Moses remarked, raising a brow in concern as they sat across from each other once again when the session was underway.

Dan rubbed the imaginary grit out of his eye. "You're right. I had a strange night."

"Really?" Moses eased back into his seat. "Perhaps we ought to change places."

"I like the view from here. How are you today?"

"These potions in my veins allow me little recourse but to remain sluggish and complacent. I dislike their effect on me."

"I am sorry about that, but you're not exactly on your best behavior without them."

"Without them I might think more clearly," Moses pointed out.

"I think we need to know why you can't remember anything first, before I gamble on what you will and won't do. I don't want to keep you in a straitjacket, but I need to keep you from hurting yourself or anyone else."

Moses frowned, making a loud huffing noise familiar to ornery old people who thought the price of everything was too high, or that young people should stop playing loud music and get their hair cut. "You make a convincing argument, though I remember little of what happened the night before."

"What do you remember?"

"Fear. I remember fear. It was in my throat and lungs as if I had fallen into an abyss and was trapped. It was most unpleasant."

"I imagine it would be," Dan said. "You seemed to have conversations with people we can't see. Do you remember anything about that?"

Moses fell silent, gazing at Dan with a strange look. For a moment, Dan thought the old man might have remembered something, but the blank mask fell over his face again, and he shook his head. "Nothing. I remember nothing except I sense these people in my heart. Sometimes they are close enough to grasp, but they slip away."

With a loud exhale, he leaned back into his chair, deflated. "When one reaches this age, what else is there but the memories? If I do not have those, then it is better to be dead."

His eyes clouded with sadness, and Dan knew Moses was at the limits of his emotional restraint. He was right, a man Moses's age deserved his memories of a life lived so long. It did not seem fair and Dan wanted to help him regain those lost years.

"We'll find them, Moses, I promise you that. It won't be easy, and it won't be overnight, but we will find out what happened to your life."

Moses smiled at the sincerity in his voice. "I am strangely encouraged by that claim."

"You should be." Dan grinned, sitting back in his chair. "I don't make it often."

"So now what do we do?" Moses let the moment pass to something a little less affecting, which suited both doctor and patient well.

"We'll continue with the therapy. Oh, and I found out what War Dragon means."

"War Dragon?" Moses stared at him blankly.

"Yes, you called me that, remember?" Dan reminded before continuing to speak, noticing Moses's discomfort at the mention of the word.

"I am not about to argue with my doctor," Moses deadpanned with a hint of sarcasm. "Please, I bid you continue since you are bursting with enthusiasm to tell me what you have learned."

"Since you asked so nicely," Dan answered with similar sentiment, "War Dragon was the name of a king in some obscure myth connected to the Arthur legends. It's believed it was the origin for Arthur's own history. There's almost no information available about the character other than this. What they recorded came from myths predating the Dark Ages. It's not the kind of thing just anyone would know unless you were into medieval folklore at an academic level. I think you might be a history expert."

"Arthur was nothing but a mere warlord, one who broke the cardinal rule when possessing a beautiful wife."

"Like what?"

"Never leave her in the company of an equally beautiful best friend. It will always end badly."

"I won't argue with you there," Dan chuckled, finding Moses's cynical wit amusing. "What about you Moses? Do you think you have a wife waiting for you somewhere?"

"No," he replied with surprising certainty.

"Are you sure? You can't remember what you did a week ago, you shouldn't discount the possibility."

"I do not have a wife," Moses repeated himself with a set of his jaw. "I am sure of this if nothing else."

Dan noted that. Obviously, he remembered some things on an instinctual level, if not the details. It encouraged Dan's hope that Moses's past was not as shut off from the rest of his mind as they believed.

"May I ask you something Doctor Ellis?"

"Sure, go ahead," Dan was still fixated on his observations of the session.

"I notice the other patients who arrived at the same time as I did are no longer here. I overheard one of the nurses saying I should be referred elsewhere already, but I remain here, undiagnosed. Is that normal?"

Dan raised his eyes to the patient and lowered his pencil.

"No, it isn't. I suppose I could make a quick evaluation and send you on your way, but I'm almost certain deeming you a schizophrenic or bipolar is incorrect. You have suffered trauma, and your symptoms are a direct relation to that event, whatever it is. I believe if I can find out what forced you to block out those memories, you'll be on the road to recovery. If I must, I'll keep you here as a patient under my care."

"Am I to be your pet project then?" Moses asked with no trace of hostility, merely interest.

"Something like that. It's what I get for being a bachelor with no family to take up my time. It just means I get to occupy myself with interesting patients."

Dan knew he was becoming too personal with Moses even though he had only seen the man twice. Why Moses struck a chord with him was beyond Dan's ability to explain, and until he understood why this empathy toward a near-complete stranger had suddenly developed, he would keep Moses close at hand.

An unexplainable intuition told him there was more going on with Moses than met the eye.

Anna needed a drink.

The detective did not often indulge, and never while on duty. However, after delivering the news to a pregnant wife that her husband was fished out of a river, Anna considered herself justified. Standing at the bar across the corner of the recent widow's home, Anna's hands trembled a little as she raised the mug of beer to her lips. The other officers accompanying her on this duty had gone on their way after Anna feigned some excuse to leave. She wanted to compose herself in private.

As the lead officer in the investigation, it became her duty to stand before Mrs. Falstaff and tell the woman her husband was dead. Worse yet, then having to launch into the unfortunate specifics of how he met his end. Sometimes Anna hated her attention to detail because she did not need to watch Mrs. Falstaff deconstruct before her eyes. Denial, horror and then finally, grief, ran the gauntlet across the poor woman's face. Those tears would be with Anna for quite some time. It was not the first time Anna performed the duty, and it would not be the last, but it still cut to the bone.

Anna lost her brother in the line of duty and knew the price that came with the badge. It did not prevent her from missing him dearly and the job did not make the pain any less, just tolerable. She took a few greedy gulps of beer, letting it settle into her stomach, and lessen the edge of her mental state before pushing it away, half drained. Technically, she was still on duty and now that the unpleasant task of informing the wife was over, it was time to talk to Falstaff's employer, the famous John Malcolm.

Like every other person in America, Anna knew who John Malcolm was.

Malcolm was one of New York's elite, not just because he was one of the richest men in the world. He was also the sole heir to one of America's most elusive dynasties. The Malcolms were private, having learned from the experiences of the Kennedys that being known or treated like royalty was not always the best thing.

Since their arrival in New York during the 1600s, the family had built itself an impressive business empire, escaping the curse of lesser inheritors. All the Malcolms were formidable personalities, with each generation elevating the family fortune to the next level. The latest Malcolm was no different.

After leaving the bar in a more composed state than when she entered it, Anna slipped into her car and drove into town. It took her almost an hour to weave through the traffic to find herself at the imposing structure that was the Malcolm building. Although she saw it in her windshield daily, it would be the first time she ever stepped onto the premises.

Anna took in the sight of the building and could understand why they called it the Monolith. A cold shudder she could not explain ran through her as she took in the sight of the imposing tower. For an absurd moment, Anna thought it looked almost sinister, if not evil.

The uneasiness persisted even after she entered the lobby and identified herself to the security guards at the front desk. The appointment with Malcolm was made as soon as she learned Falstaff was an employee, so her arrival was expected, and she was waved through immediately.

The minute the door of the elevator slid closed to take her to Malcolm's penthouse, Anna's insides clenched.

What was happening to her? There was suddenly not enough space around her, and the need to pound at the doors to get out was damn near overwhelming. Something was wrong. It screamed from every fiber of her being, but it made no sense. The sensation was so unpleasant Anna was on the verge of being physically ill. Its cold tendrils twisted itself around her spine until the doors slid open. Anna bolted past them to get out, and for a few seconds after they closed, she stood in the narrow hall before Malcolm's penthouse, shaking.

This time it was not from delivering some unpleasant news to a widow. It was because for a brief instant inside that elevator, she was gripped with genuine terror. She could not understand why she would feel this way. She was a cop for God's sake! She had been in life-threatening situations before, and none of it caused the level of anxiety she felt during those few minutes. Anna steadied her racing pulse, trying to crush the anxiousness she felt because now was not the time for such weaknesses.

John Malcolm was waiting, and Anna intended to get her answers.

Entering the door at the end of the corridor, she found herself in what appeared to be the workspace of John Malcolm's secretary. The décor of the room was in vibrant reds, and the color was tasteful when it could have been easily vulgar. Earthy red tones covered the surrounding walls, framing the black marble floor and cherry wood furniture. There was a wide set of doors behind the woman's desk, which Anna assumed led to John Malcolm's office.

The secretary seated behind a name plate that read "Carmichael" seemed almost as vibrant as the room. She was a stunning red-haired beauty, impeccably dressed in a suit, and Anna wondered, rather snidely, whether she was an actual secretary or a playmate. Her image did not imply her best talents were typing.

"Can I help you?"

"I'm Detective Anna McCaughley." Anna produced her badge. "I believe Mr. Malcolm is expecting me?"

The woman's gaze swept over her, and Anna had a distinct impression she was being scrutinized. "This way please."

Anna followed her closely, taking time to observe her surroundings, and could not help feeling there was something very wrong with this place. Still, she was grateful the sensation assailing her in the elevator had vanished for the moment. She wanted to be in full control of her faculties when she finally met Mr. Malcolm.

He was waiting for her on the lounge in his office. No doubt he was prepared for this interview the instant he was notified of her arrival. Her first impression was that the magazine pictures did not do him justice. He looked spectacularly good for a man in his late forties, and Anna could just imagine society debutantes jockeying for position to claim this most eligible bachelor. Physical appearances aside, Anna could feel the man's presence even in something as innocent as an introduction. Yet once again, instincts told her almost immediately she could not trust him.

"I checked up on you, Detective McCaughley," Malcolm stated proudly after they settled in. Miss Carmichael furnished Anna with a glass of water before departing the room to leave them alone.

"Understandable," Anna replied. "It would surprise me if a man in your position didn't."

He raised a brow, impressed by that statement. "I am glad that we understand each other."

"I understand it is necessary for someone in your position to check my credentials and the validity of my intentions to see you. However, I do hope you understand my questions are not intended to be invasive, just necessary for the investigation."

"I appreciate your candor detective," Malcolm appeared unperturbed by the recording device Anna had turned on. "Naturally, I am sorry to hear what happened to Richard. He was my senior accountant for over three years and was exceptionally reliable and ordered. Just the sort you would depend on to manage your finances."

Anna absorbed his words before asking, "When was the last time you saw him?"

"I think it was five days ago. You understand Richard worked downstairs and unless he had a problem with our finances or some matter requiring my direct input, I would not have seen him on a day-to-day basis."

"Fair enough." Anna nodded in understanding. Malcolm was the CEO of a conglomerate, and it was perfectly reasonable he would not have daily contact with all his employees. Not when he ruled his kingdom from these lofty heights. "Is there someone I can talk to about finding out when was the last time anyone saw him at work?"

"I took the liberty of acquiring that information for you." Malcolm handed her the folder lying across the coffee table. "You will have all the details of who was the last to see Richard, what time he was at the office, even access to the building's security tapes if you like."

"Thank you very much," Anna said graciously, but she did not like the fact he was feeding her all this information. She would have preferred to interview these people herself before someone else reached them and possibly coached them into corroborating their statements to what was in these nicely typed pages.

"You are free to talk to any one of them," Malcolm continued speaking. "Trust me, Detective, I want to find Richard's killer."

*I'm sure you do*, Anna thought skeptically.

She knew she was being cynical. Malcolm might have just been trying to be helpful, but instinct told her he was hiding something. Unfortunately, she had no way of proving it without further investigation, and Anna suspected Malcolm was a man who knew how to keep secrets.

"I would like to see Mr. Falstaff's office if that's possible?"

"Certainly," he replied amicably, "but, I thought this was just a mugging."

Anna's mask of calm held. "It was made to look like a mugging, but the murder was execution-style. They shot him in the face at point-blank range and took his jewelry but left his phone and wallet. Mr. Falstaff isn't the type to give a mugger much trouble. Furthermore, a mugger would not waste time dragging the body to the river. His first instinct would be to run. I believe Mr. Falstaff was dumped to destroy any physical evidence. This makes me believe it was premeditated, so if you don't mind, I would like to see his office. It may give me a clue as to a motive."

She hoped her words might rattle him a little, but Malcolm seemed to take what she said in stride. "Detective McCaughley, I am impressed. No doubt with you on the case, it will be only a matter of time before you find Richard's murderer."

"It is my job to notice the details." Anna was unswayed by his compliments because she was used to criminals trying to deflect suspicion by doing just that.

She gave Malcolm a polite show of thanks before Ms. Carmichael showed her out of the office and pointed her toward the names on the list Malcolm gave her. Although it was a foregone conclusion that she would find nothing more than what was in their written statements, Anna was compelled to try. She even braved using the elevator again, and while the sensation was not so acute this time, she could not help experiencing the same feelings of dread once more.

Anna did not know what was wrong with her and wondered if she was developing sudden claustrophobia until she remembered it first started when she was staring at the Monolith.

From the *outside*.

## FOUR
## THE NEW WORLD

THIS JOURNEY WAS BECOMING MORE COMPLICATED than anything they imagined.

While they remained on the known territory of the Brittle Sea, they were relatively in control of their circumstances. But soon, they saw more and more things beyond their comprehension as they slipped further from the Veil and the familiar mists of home. As they left behind the cold seas where the water was warmer and the waves less turbulent, they saw other vessels. Caution forced them to keep their distance, but the encounters revealed men had evolved considerably since the time of the Elves in Avalyne.

Whether this evolution was good was still a matter of debate.

At first, they could not conceive of the thing sailing across the waves as a ship. It had no mast to speak of and it was made entirely of iron. The size of it was enormous beyond belief, and yet it somehow remained above the surface instead of sinking into the depths as something of that size should. It remained afloat with a mechanical keel, thrashing rapids of foam behind it as it journeyed westward. In comparison, the craft they occupied was tiny and could be crushed without the behemoth being aware of it. The vessel's construction of iron inspired in the Elves the black memories of Syphia's Chasm and Mael's Pit.

However, the iron leviathan did not accost them, merely continued across the ocean, oblivious to those whose awe it had captured for a time. It was not the first of these vessels the elves would sight during the journey to their destination. Not all sailing craft were like the titan they encountered, but their construction confused the elves. Iron seemed like such a heavy material to construct a sea-going vessel. Wood was so much lighter and straightforward.

Still, even in the days of Avalyne, little about mankind was simple.

Sometimes, they heard noises in the sky and saw what appeared to be a winged bird soaring through the clouds, but its construction was once again of metal. The elves wondered what was behind this worship of iron that inspired men to create everything from it. The sound of it moving through the air was like the low rumble of thunder, and the speed in which it crossed the sky would have put even the great griffins to shame. While some of these things were marvels, others concerned Aeron. It was clear man's world had changed beyond anything they ever dreamed.

He was right, it seemed, because soon after they sighted land, they were intercepted by a vessel of similar size to their own. Aeron would have preferred not to engage anyone until they found Tamsyn, but the ship gave them no choice. Crafted from iron, the vessel could sink them with ease if it rammed them. As it approached, a voice materialized out of thin air, speaking an unfamiliar language. Aeron had believed they would be able to converse with men using the Old Tongue, but the language spoken was unknown to any of the three brothers.

"They mean to board us," Syannon watched the craft narrowing the gap between them.

"I do not wish to place my fate in the hands of men," Hadros declared. "We have no idea what has happened to them since our departure."

"I do not think we have a choice in this matter. They will come aboard whether we give them our consent or not. Cover your ears, they need not discover we are not one of them," Aeron stared across the bow at the fast-approaching ship. Adjusting their hair somewhat, they disguised their ears before being boarded.

"You surely do not mean for us to go with them?" Hadros gaped at him with incredulity.

"I think perhaps we should determine their intentions before we assume the worst. Much has changed since our departure. We know nothing of men or their ways. Perhaps we should adhere to their ministrations for the time being."

"They are using sorcery," Hadros reminded. "A voice spoke to us out of nothingness!"

"I have seen iron birds that fly, and ships as large as cities that should not be able to float in the past few days. I believe much of this is invention. In our time, you saw how clever they were. They built devices of remarkable cunning. A hundred millennia has passed for them while we were in the Veil. What we perceive as sorcery could be their more elaborate creations."

Aeron based his reasoning on the lack of danger he sensed from the approaching craft. If they were creatures of darkness meaning to harm Aeron and his siblings, the elves would have surely felt it by now. As it stood, their elven senses did not perceive any sinister intent, just the need for caution.

"I must agree with Aeron, brother," Syannon weighed in. "We should know what they wish of us before we act. For all we know, we may have wandered into their territory without permission."

"True." Aeron had not thought of that.

Their father Halion was determined Eden Halas was free of trespassers before the days of the evil god Balfure's destruction. With Tor Iolan, one of Balfure's fortresses, sitting at the edge of Halas Green, such measures had been necessary to protect their people. No kingdom left its borders unguarded, so perhaps this was what was transpiring here. If so, Aeron hoped a simple request to travel to the Uncharted Lands was all that would be necessary. No matter how reasonable he might appear, nothing was going to stop Aeron from finding Tamsyn.

The vessel came to a halt off their bow. Aeron, Syannon and Hadros had a closer view of the ship. Though it was fast descending into the evening, the craft shone with a myriad of lights that did not appear generated by flame. It reminded Aeron of the light Tamsyn cast using one of his spells. Once again, that strange voice spoke to them, and its intensity told Aeron it was a warning. The elves decided the best course of action was to respond, hoping perhaps (though highly unlikely) someone on board understood Elvish.

While it did not appear that the humans comprehended a word they said, their inability to communicate seem to diffuse the situation. The humans boarded wearing their strange clothes and carrying oddly shaped pieces of metal at their hip, where swords should have been. They overtook the Elven ship like a swarm of locusts, examining every corner of the craft and growing more confused at every discovery.

"I dislike those things they are pointing at us," Hadros grumbled as several humans surrounded them, pointing the strange metal objects in their direction.

"Is that a weapon?" Syannon questioned, noticing their speech was raising more brows from their captors.

"I would say it is," Aeron remarked, more curious than he was afraid. "Notice they are all from different races?"

"Yes," Hadros nodded. "These are of Carleon, Astaroth and some I have never seen before. Perhaps they have matured enough to unite into one people."

"Or one has conquered the others," Syannon pointed out.

"They have women among them." Aeron noticed one of the searchers ransacking their ship was female. "If this is a combat vessel, why do they have women on board?"

It was a question no one could answer through lack of knowledge or of language. The searchers continued working for another hour or so before the leader among them attempted to communicate. The man was tall and reminded Aeron a little of Braedan, the warrior of Sandrine who was a friend to both him and Dare. Braedan had perished before Dare embarked on his campaign to free his kingdom from Balfure's occupation. This version was, by the look of him, an experienced man of the sea, for his hands and his sun-dried skin bore the marks of a seasoned mariner.

He tried speaking to them, but their language was so foreign, Aeron recognised none of it. It almost sounded like gibberish. Aeron, who was one of the last to leave Avalyne, bristled at being unable to understand him at all. Still, a hundred thousand years could change language as much as the land, making any communication between the elves and their human captors impossible. When no headway was in sight, the leader ordered them off their craft into his own.

They went without incident, taking note their ship was towed instead of destroyed, contrary to their fears. The inside of the human craft was an odd construct of steel, wood and other materials Aeron could not identify. After boarding, their captors locked them away, but if it were a dungeon, then it was the cleanest one they had ever known. While the brothers worried about their situation, they were fascinated by the strange objects inside their prison. For instance, the privy worked with such efficiency that the twist of the handle could produce water so clean it could have been drawn from a pool in Eden Halas. Not at all like the kind drawn from the rivers of men, filled with silt, sediment, and waste.

"What is that?" Aeron asked when he emerged from the cubicle and saw Syannon staring at the thick pane of glass facing the room. It resembled a mirror, but its black glass obscured any reflection.

"I cannot say," Syannon ran his hands over the dark finish. "I see no purpose in it."

"What are those things along the side?" Hadros asked as he sat on the bed, wanting to be anywhere but indoors. The elf had taken to staring at the sea and sky beyond the window.

Syannon ran his fingers over the largest of the small protrusions and pushed. The sudden sound it made, not to mention the image that flashed on the glass, sent all three elves retreating backwards, startled.

"Oracle!" Hadros shouted as the three elves stared mesmerised at the image before them.

"That is not an oracle," Aeron protested. "I have seen one, and I know they do not look like that."

"What is it?" Syannon asked, studying the images moving across the dark glass. A beautiful woman was running along a shore, wearing almost nothing. She seemed to jog slowly, allowing the trio a rather tantalizing view of her body's movements before she leapt into the ocean.

"That is not decent," Hadros frowned. "She is almost naked!"

"Men always possessed a capacity for decadence, but this is debauchery." Syannon continued watching the picture displaying her swimming beneath the waves.

"And yet you two have not moved your eyes away from her." Aeron grinned.

"Is this sorcery Aeron?" Syannon asked. "I know of only oracles and seeing pools capable of such visions."

"It could be, but if they are sorcerers, they have not treated us harshly, even if they have taken our ship. I am uncertain what to make of them or their intentions."

"Aeron we cannot remain in their custody," Hadros said. "Just because they have treated us well so far, we cannot perceive what they will do later. I sense we are a mystery to them, which is why we are being handled so cautiously. That may change if they discover what we are."

"I agree, but we should wait until darkness before we escape. I would prefer to do it when we are close enough to port so they cannot pursue us into shallow water. We must retrieve our weapons and the gold we need to trade."

"Are we even certain they still use gold?" Syannon asked as he cast his gaze over the room. "They seem to prefer iron."

"We have to take the chance gold is not out of fashion. It matters little. We do not have a choice; it's all we have."

---

Their escape was relatively simple, mostly because their captors did not believe them dangerous. When the craft neared the shoreline in the twilight, creating a commotion brought one of their guards into their prison to investigate. After that, it was a simple matter of skill and agility to overpower him and make their way to their own ship. It would not take long for the humans to discover their departure, for their escape plan was not elaborate enough to prevent it. After sneaking stealthily onto their vessel, the elves retrieved the canoe attached to the hull and paddled to shore.

A watch on the bridge sighted them but by the time the alarm sounded, the canoe had reached shallow water and the large craft could not pursue. By the time the humans mobilized, the elves reached the trees beyond the shore. Once there, they concealed themselves easily. Even in this strange land, the forest was the same, and they were each experienced woodsmen capable of disguising themselves when needed. At night, they could cover much ground, following the same stars as Tamsyn when he began this quest.

"The air smells foul," Syannon complained as they made their way through the trees.

"It reminds me of Astaroth." Aeron remembered how the air had smelled when they stood at the Burning Plain during the last days of the war. It was heavy with ash and other things that he could not identify. While this was nowhere as bad, it deepened Aeron's concern at what other changes had taken place in the realm of men since their departure.

"Those who visited these lands after the last of us left Avalyne, spoke of a dark age," Syannon reminded. "Perhaps the loss of the Old Tongue is because of that."

"It is possible."

Centuries in Eden Halas after his retreat behind the Veil, Aeron knew of elves who explored the world beyond, to see what became of Avalyne. They brought back stories of Carleon's demise, along with tales of the kingdoms of men that had fallen into ruin. Some humans were once again scrambling to survive with stone tools, with none of the craft the elves taught them. It was like listening to the news a beloved child had died. It broke the heart of all who considered men their friends.

Aeron remembered his own anguish thinking of how hard Dare fought to rebuild Carleon into something that would endure as a beacon to all mankind. To know all of it would crumble into darkness the way Sandrine, once the seat of man's power, had disintegrated, would have broken the proud spirit of his noble friend. Aeron was rather grateful Dare lacked the immortality to see it.

"They will search for us," Hadros commented over his shoulder along the path they took through the woods.

"I do not doubt that." Aeron intended to go on despite the risks.

"Aeron, this quest of ours may not be possible." Syannon voiced what both he and Hadros had been thinking since their encounter with men. "We thought the terrain would be unfamiliar, but this is beyond us. We cannot make our way in this world without being noticed. You saw how they looked at us. If we did not conceal our ears when they found us, I doubt our escape would be as easy as it was."

"Do you think I am blind to this? We cannot stop until we find Tamsyn, not for his sake but for ours as well. Do you think they will let us go if we turn back? If there is one thing that remains constant in the race of man, it is their propensity to fear what they do not understand. There has been nothing like us in their presence for millennia. If we were to reveal ourselves, and what we are, none of us will leave this place. If Tamsyn is still alive, he may be able to help us."

Syannon or Hadros did not speak, because for the first time, Aeron revealed his doubt of whether Tamsyn still lived.

Dan saw his last patient for the day and looked forward to having a quiet night at home when he heard a knock on his office door.

Glancing at the clock and noting the time, the doctor wondered who would call on him at this time of day. The lack of sleep the night before was catching up with him, and Dan was looking forward to a good night's sleep. Hoping whatever business his late caller had would not take too long, he called out for them to enter. Dan expected to see a colleague or a nurse coming through the door with some new problem. Instead, a tall blond woman he did not recognise, in a smart business suit and a briefcase, entered the room.

She was in her forties, but she was still a spectacular beauty with the look of a lawyer or someone from corporate. She offered him a smile as she entered, extending her hand in greeting, but Dan could tell it was an obligatory gesture.

"Doctor Ellis, I am pleased to meet you. My name is Sandra Collins. I am an associate of Mr. John Malcolm of Malcolm Industries."

"I know of Mr. Malcolm," Dan returned, somewhat confused at why she was here. "What can I do for you?"

"May we sit down?"

Dan saw no reason to deny the request. He was still puzzled at why someone from Malcolm Industries would wish to see him but supposed she would eventually state her business.

"So, what's on your mind, Ms. Collins?" Dan asked once they settled in.

"I understand you are treating the man who caused a disruption at our premises two nights ago?"

"Yes, I am." Dan nodded and wondered about her interest in Moses. He suspected she knew perfectly well Dan was treating him if she came all the way from the Monolith to talk to him. "He is still undergoing evaluation."

"Mr. Malcolm would like to provide the best care possible for Mr...?" She gazed at Dan for a name.

"We haven't identified him yet," Dan revealed, surprised by the interest a corporate giant like Malcolm Industries would have in Moses. The patient did attempt to vandalize the place for being some kind of supernatural threat. "I am calling him Moses for the moment."

"How sweet of you." She smiled, and it struck Dan how devoid it was of any actual warmth or emotion. "I see he is in the best hands possible. Mr. Malcolm would like to offer financial help for any medical expenses 'Moses' may incur. Perhaps we could facilitate his removal to a private sanatorium where he can get the preferential treatment he would lack here."

"He is being given the best treatment here," Dan stated, somewhat offended by the insinuation Moses was receiving anything less than his utmost attention. "I am treating him."

"I meant no offense," she apologized quickly, trying to compensate for the slight. "However, your role here if I understand it, is to evaluate patients for transfer to other facilities for specialized care. I didn't think you were allowed patients of your own."

"You understand it correctly," Dan answered, becoming more annoyed by the minute at this woman's presumptions.

True, it was irregular for him to keep patients there to treat himself, but not unheard of. To keep him on staff, hospital administrator Jim Hancock was more than willing to extend him some liberties. Jim knew Dan could have quite the career if he chose to set up a private practice and only remained at the hospital because he liked the work.

"I do, from time to time, take on patients as I have done with Moses. Now might I ask why John Malcolm is so interested in a transient? Do you know him? Is he a friend of Mr Malcolm?"

"Not at all," Sandra returned, but Dan was an able enough student of human behavior to know she was lying through her teeth.

"My employer feels sorry for this old gentleman and wishes to help him any way he can."

"Well, the best thing for him right now is to remain here where I can continue treating him." Dan tried to keep things cordial. "Something terrible has happened to Moses, Ms. Collins, something he needs to remember to regain his identity. Switching doctors will not help him. He needs a face he can identify with and confide in. I believe I've established that level of trust with him, so I am not about to upset his progress by transferring him to another physician. Now, if you wish to fund his removal to a sanatorium, you are free to do so, but I will still continue to treat him as a patient."

"I see." Her lips thinned, and she gave him a deep, meaningful look. "I suppose nothing I say can convince you to relinquish your claim on the patient?"

"Relinquish my claim? The patient is not a piece of property, just an old man with severe memory problems - and his name is Moses."

"He is not *your* responsibility." Sandra shot him a look convincing Dan she ran on pure ice water, not blood. "All he is, is a human tragedy walking the streets, like so many others. You waste your time and effort in attempting to salvage something from the wreckage."

Dan could not believe he was having this conversation.

"He is a patient, and he needs help. I am a doctor, and I treat people like him. I don't consider him wreckage and if he was such a nonentity, then why has Malcolm sent you here?"

She did not answer but reached instead into her briefcase. What was she up to now? Would she cite some jurisdictional nonsense all these corporate types used as a fallback position? She produced a heavy brown envelope and handed it to him.

"If you cooperate, what is in that envelope is yours." She still wore that infuriating expression of smug triumph. "All you have to do is sign Moses over to me and you won't be troubled by either of us again. Mr. Malcolm would consider this a close personal favor. It's always helpful to have friends in high places."

Dan glanced into the envelope and felt his breath catch. Inside its confines was more money than he could imagine. It stared at him in thick piles of green, all in thousand-dollar bills. He could not even count how many were in there, but it was more than he made in a year. He raised his eyes at her in question, astonished by what he was seeing.

"What is this?"

"Your fee for cooperating," she answered, confident the money would end his resistance.

"This is a bribe?"

"I would not put it quite that way." Sandra laughed. "Consider it a bonus."

"Who *is* he?" Dan surprised her by asking instead. "Who is he that you're doing all this?"

"That is none of your concern." She glared, all traces of humor draining from her face. The beauty Dan admired vanished and in its place was a mask of cold malice. Dan realized he was seeing the *real* Sandra Collins. "The time for games is over, Doctor Ellis. Understand if you turn me down, the next request will not be as cordial. We want custody of your patient, and if you do not help us, then we will acquire him ourselves."

"The hell you will," Dan snapped, thrusting the envelope back into her hand. "I don't respond to threats, and if you try to strong-arm me, I'll make further inquiries why you're so interested in him. Maybe the police might be just as curious."

"That would be a mistake," she warned, her eyes blazing. "I don't think you appreciate your situation. Perhaps I should leave you with a day or two to consider your options."

"Is that a threat?"

"We do not threaten Doctor," she replied, turning to leave. "We *never* threaten."

A little disturbed by his meeting with Sandra Collins, Dan was glad to leave the hospital for the night. He never thought a woman could ever unnerve him, but Sandra's words were disconcerting. The old story about the corporation with dirty dealings was a cliché Dan did not want to believe, but Sandra's threat didn't sound empty. Whether or not it was her intention, his encounter with Ms. Collins made him more determined than ever to learn the truth about Moses.

When he arrived at his apartment, Dan discovered a note slipped under his door after he stepped inside. Unfolding it, he stared at the plain, crisp white paper with its brief message.

*Call Stuart.*
S.C.

Dan pulled out his phone immediately, dialing his best friend's number. She was just trying to rattle him, Dan told himself, but his heart was pounding with anxiety as he waited to hear Stuart's voice. The number rang for a few seconds before someone answered it. But it was not Stuart who spoke. The voice on the line belonged to Maggie Brent, Stuart's secretary.

"Maggie," Dan exclaimed, puzzled at why she was answering Stuart's phone. "Why are you on Stuart's number?"

"Oh, Doctor Ellis," she burst out. "I had his calls diverted to my number. It's so awful." She broke down in tears, sending a surge of fear through his heart. "I'm here with the police. Doctor Farmer was just involved in a hit-and-run accident. He's *dead*."

# FIVE
## UNTIMELY RESCUES

Dan drove back to the hospital, numb.

Thoughts of Stuart Farmer, his best friend since college, filled his mind. He remembered the all-night keggers and the girls they dated. During their first year of college, Dan made it his business to loosen up the tense English lit major. Stuart was one of those people who left notes on everything. Against the fridge door reminding you to buy milk. On the wall above the trash, so you remembered to take it out. A dozen texts telling you he was coming in late that night. Dan could not even remember the number of arguments during their four years at college about the edibility of day-old pizza stored under beds.

He drove trying to see through the windshield as tears filled his eyes. His best friend was dead, and he might well be responsible for it by refusing Sandra Collins. The woman stated she did not threaten and with Stuart's death, she proved she hadn't lied.

It was a lesson he would have preferred to learn without Stuart losing his life. Now he knew without doubt, if he did not allow them to take Moses, worse would happen.

Dan wanted to go to the police, but he had no proof the woman orchestrated Stuart's death other than a veiled threat.

A hit-and-run accident did not prove Malcolm Industries' guilt in the eyes of the law, and millions in New York had the initials of S.C. Through Maggie's deluge of tears, he learned a black sedan came out of nowhere and ended Stuart's life with a loud thud while he was en route to his Chevy. He died instantly, Maggie said. As if a speedy end made it any better. Stuart's life ended without his even knowing why.

He and Dan shared that much in common.

They wanted to get Moses and would stop at nothing to make it happen. If Dan permitted it, he would never find out why. In the space of a few hours, Stuart's death had shredded his safe and comfortable reality. Instead, a shadow realm where corporations erased people from existence had taken over his life.

The simplest solution to regaining his lost security would be to cooperate with Ms. Collins and let Malcolm Industries take charge of Moses. No one would blame Dan if he surrendered the old man to the tender mercies of the corporate giant. Moses was his patient for only two days. Ms. Collins promised Moses would receive the best care at a proper facility. To walk away and let Moses be someone else's problem, he only needed to sign the release.

It would be the smart thing to do. Dan almost considered it. However, he also remembered the promise he made to his patient, to help Moses regain his memories and the connection Dan defended with such determination to the menacing Ms. Collins. He could not do it. Dan refused to betray Moses and let him fall into the hands of Malcolm Industries or allow Stuart's murderers to go unpunished. The safer solution might be to let them have Moses, but Dan would never be able to look himself in the mirror again if he did.

All these points ran through his mind as he drove back into the city, determined to deny Malcolm Industries their prize. His grief now became anger, and while a plan of action eluded him, one thing needed to be done before anything else. Ms. Collins believed killing Stuart would scare him into obedience. Instead, it got him mad. Maybe he was just a psychiatrist, a powerless nonentity they thought they could intimidate by taking away his best friend.

Dan intended to show them the error of their arrogance.

The hospital slipped into the evening shift as Dan strode down the quiet halls of the psychiatric ward. Most of the staff had already left for the day with only a handful remaining on duty. The head duty nurse at her station, Brenda Watts, glanced up at him from behind her book.

"Doctor Ellis." She gave him a smile. "What are you doing here? I thought you went home for the evening."

"Something came up," Dan answered, not really in the mood for pleasantries but feigned the sentiment for her benefit. "Brenda, I want you to get an orderly and have Moses ready to leave."

"Leave?" She stared at him. "You're discharging him?"

"I'm taking him to Gracie Square. Malcolm Industries wants him transferred. By the time you get him ready, I'll have the papers ready for processing."

Brenda, an experienced nurse, raised a brow at the irregular request. Still, as the head of the psychiatric ward, Dan had the authority to make it. Brenda returned to her station to carry out the task, the suspicion on her face barely concealed. Mindful of her doubt, Dan retreated to his office to fill out the papers to release Moses into his custody. He did not doubt the request might fall under scrutiny by hospital administration if Brenda queried it, but right now, Dan had more significant concerns. John Malcolm wielded sufficient influence to use the bureaucracy to get his hands on Moses if Dan didn't remove him from the hospital first.

When Dan emerged from his office, he sighted Moses already waiting in the lobby. He paused at the pharmacy long enough to requisition some supplies, including the drugs he would need to treat Moses's condition. While Moses remained medicated, the old man was manageable. Without it, he might become more than Dan could cope with, and neither of them had the luxury of that complication right now.

"He's ready, Doctor Ellis," Brenda announced. She still appeared a little confused by the transfer. Carl, the orderly who helped Moses get ready for his departure, showed similar hesitation.

"Thank you, Brenda," Dan said, ignoring the confusion in Moses's expression for now. "I know this is all very unusual, but I believe the patient's life might be in danger. I'd appreciate it if you left it for an hour or two before you queried this, Brenda."

She opened her mouth to object but fell silent when she noted his serious expression and realized he was not exaggerating about the urgency of the situation. "Are you in trouble Doctor Ellis?"

"No," he said, owing her the honesty. "But I think our patient is, and if I'm going to help him, I have to get Moses away from here while I still can. I'm asking a lot, but I need you two to trust me."

Carl, who often sat with Dan at the cafeteria where they talked about fishing and sports, answered first. "You do what you have to Doc. I won't say nothing until they ask me."

"I trust you Doctor Ellis." Brenda, a long-time colleague, admired the man for the care he gave to patients most would not bother with. If he really thought a patient was in danger, she believed him. "You do what you have to, we'll do what we have to on this end."

"Thank you," Dan answered and then turned to the patient. "Come on, Moses, we're going."

Moses's bewilderment at the whole scene showed on his face, but he remained silent until they neared the elevators. His tattered old clothes, no doubt from some surplus store, looked a little more respectable after being laundered during his stay at the hospital. Dan wondered fleetingly just how long Moses suffered this condition. Years perhaps? He shuddered at the thought this man might have been wandering around the streets for decades with a hole in his memory and no idea a life awaited his return.

Only when they had cleared the main doors of the hospital with the night sky above their heads, did Moses deign to speak.

"Is this an aggressive form of therapy?"

"No," Dan replied as they crossed the parking lot to his car. "I just needed to get you out of there."

"Not that I am ungrateful to escape that wretched place, may I ask why the sudden urgency?"

Dan did not reply until they shut the doors of the RAM and drove out of the hospital parking lot. Once on the street, Dan realized he had no idea where to go, mostly because he never imagined he would get Moses out. Now that he'd overcome that hurdle, Dan realized taking Moses home was impossible. It would be the first place they looked once they discovered his actions. For the moment, Dan just wanted to put some distance between them and the hospital. He would figure the rest out later.

"Someone from Malcolm Industries came to see me today," Dan spoke after his nerves settled.

"Did they now?" Moses's demeanour shifted from a frail old man to someone formidable and in control of his situation. "Please continue."

Once again, the same sense of foreboding gripped him as surely as it did Moses at the mention of Malcolm Industries. It occurred to Dan that perhaps John Malcolm had something to do with the state in which Moses found himself. Their determination to retrieve the old man proved he possessed something they desperately wanted. More than ever, Dan realized the key to this mystery was Moses's hidden memories.

"A woman called Sandra Collins came to see me. She said she was an associate of John Malcolm."

As Dan spoke, a surge of hatred bubbled inside him at the memory of the mercurial female who most likely ordered Stuart killed on behalf of her employer. "She wanted me to release you into their custody. Gave me some bullshit story about paying all your medical expenses and sending you to a private sanatorium where you'd get the care you needed."

"I take it you refused."

"I did." Dan shot him a brief glance from the wheel. "You're my patient, and I promised to help you. I take that responsibility pretty seriously."

"It may cost you dearly."

Dan didn't look at Moses when he spoke again, his voice wavering a little.

"It already has. When I got home this evening, I found a note from Sandra Collins under my door. She told me to call my friend Stuart. We've been buddies since college. He's my best friend. Stuart is dead. I found out from his secretary he died in a hit-and-run accident tonight. It happened not long before I called."

"Oh Dan." Moses let out a heavy sigh of sympathy. "I *am* sorry."

"It's not your fault," Dan declared, sucking in his breath because saying it out loud brought the anguish to the forefront once more. For the duration of this mess, Dan wanted no part of it. To get to the truth, Dan needed to maintain focus despite the grief in his heart. "You didn't kill him." Dan threw a quick glance at Moses to show he meant it.

"Neither did you," Moses countered, proving to be just as kind. "I am sorry I brought this on you, however."

The old man fell silent again, choosing to stare at the bodies moving up and down the pavement along the darkened road. Anonymity in the flotsam of human tragedy was possible. It might serve the doctor trying to help him if he disappeared into it. Moses hoped Dan could help him because even if he remembered nothing about his past, his instincts were still intact. His emotions were just as capable of aiding him as his lost memories.

From the moment he met Dan Ellis, the doctor's presence comforted and assured him. Moses was convinced it had little to do with the doctor's healing and everything to do with Dan himself. Moses did not know why, but he sensed Dan would never disappoint him if he entrusted his life to the doctor. Still, Moses had no wish to be the harbinger of doom for him, either.

"Perhaps you should just let me go, Dan," Moses whispered, no longer thinking of the man who risked himself as just his doctor but as a friend. "Let me go before it becomes any worse for you."

Dan shifted his gaze from the road long enough to show the old man his incredulity.

"No." Dan shook his head, not needing to think about it any further. "I will not let you disappear hoping they won't find you. I will not walk away just to make things easier for me."

"You've already lost your friend. I do not wish you to lose your life."

"Bullshit!" Dan snapped, feeling a burst of anger spill out of him at the statement and the situation. "My life is already in danger! And it's not up to you. It's my choice, Moses, because I want to know what is so goddamn important it's worth Stuart's life just to get to you! I think they're terrified of what's in your head and they're doing everything they can to get their hands on you to make sure I don't find out first."

"I wish I could tell you. I sense things even if I cannot remember them. My instincts tell me we mean a great deal to each other, though I cannot understand how. When you speak the name of John Malcolm, I am filled with fear and loathing. I cannot explain it to you any better. I wish I understood why my memories remain as elusive as my name. Each time I try to remember it, my mind rebels against the desire and I am plunged into an abyss. I am sorry for your friend. I wish more than anything I could have prevented it, but I cannot even help myself."

The sorrow in Moses's voice touched Dan and prompted a surge of guilt in the doctor for raising his voice. Moses was as much a victim in this as Stuart and it was Dan's choice not to cooperate with Sandra Collins. Moses had little to do with that decision. The psychiatrist understood he was displacing his anger, taking it out on his patient. The person he should be angry at sat in a penthouse at the Monolith, a place Dan was starting to believe was evil.

"It's not your fault, Moses. I don't blame you and I sure as hell don't want you to deal with them on your own. I said I wanted to help you, and I still mean it. Except now, I also want to help you because I need to understand why Stuart died. I need to know so I can do something about it."

"It is a dangerous path you seek to travel with me, but I am grateful for the companionship."

The man's words affected Moses more than he cared to admit. Moses suspected he spent too many years in the wilderness, and to have companionship, even if it was fleeting, was not unwelcomed.

Who knew how long he had been alone?

The Immortals concluded one thing when they traveled once again through the world of men: mortals were incapable of leaving anything alone and unspoiled.

For most of the night, they moved without pause, determined to put as much distance between themselves and their captors. Aeron had only the stars to guide him on his quest to find Tamsyn, and even that small benefice was centuries out of date. It had been the place of Tamysn's last known whereabouts, and it was more than likely that Tamsyn, if he still lived, had moved on a long time ago. Although Aeron refused to admit the seraf could be dead, the things they were encountering were giving him an excellent reason to change his steadfast opinion.

There were things in this world with more cunning than sorcery.

Aeron knew on some level many of these were devices. Men shared one common trait with dwarfs, and this was their love of invention. The machines were more elaborate, and some of them functioned in a manner no elf could even conceive, but they were still devices. Such power at the hands of a race so young and foolish was a dangerous thing.

For once, Aeron did not know if Tamsyn could acquit himself against it.

At the edge of the wood, it became necessary to emerge into the open, a situation that gave none of them comfort. Beyond the tree line, the paved roads seemed endless. There were structures everywhere, and Aeron concluded while mankind had progressed since the days of Avalyne, his eye for architecture was lacking. The buildings they encountered were ugly and gray, covered in facades of glass, but they resembled towers one might find in Astaroth. Aesthetics appeared to have little importance now.

Cloaked in darkness, the three elves remained close to the shadows along the street, trying to fade into the background because their strange appearance drew attention. So far, they remained unaccosted, though they received some rather odd looks from the people they encountered. Syannon's observation earlier about men being unified was not incorrect. As they walked through the paved streets, they noted there were many races which also explained the loss of the Old Tongue in this amalgamation of cultures.

He also noted that there were two different paths. One was wide, with lines of white running through the middle. The other was smaller and resembled the stone pathways of home, flanked by grass and bushes. Like Sandrine of Carleon, the illumination of the lamp posts framing the street used a source of light unknown to them since it was not flame.

"Where are their horses?" Syannon questioned as the number of people they were seeing increased.

"Horses?" Aeron looked at his brother and realized it was a valid observation. They had seen none since arriving.

"Yes, we have traveled an interminable distance and have seen no horses. How do these people travel?"

"Perhaps they do so on foot," Hadros suggested, noting two adolescent females staring at them and bursting into a full set of giggles before going on their way.

"We *must* change our clothes," Aeron remarked. "We look too different."

"At least our ears are covered," Syannon smirked, "though I wish my sense of smell were diminished. I do not know what these people have done to the air, but they have a great deal to answer for. I do not think even the stench from Astaroth was as terrible as this."

Twin orbs of bright light blinded them as it approached,

piercing through the night. The glare was so sharp it forced them to turn away, squinting. A low rumble accompanied the brilliance, not unlike the mechanism powering the craft that brought them to shore. As the source closed in, all three stared in awe as the metal beast sped past them, expelling noxious gas from its innards with a human sitting inside it. Its presence explained why no one walked on the black road and revealed how humans travelled.

"Well, now you know why they have no horses. They have carriages that do not require them," Hadros stated.

"I had no idea they were *this* creative," Syannon spoke with some awe. He was still staring after the mechanical beast as it disappeared into the darkness, the red lights behind it flashing as it drew further away into the night.

"Creative?" Aeron snorted. "What is exuding from that thing is poison. Did you not notice?"

"I have given up using my nose in this place."

"How long are we to travel in this manner?" Hadros tore his gaze away from a single-story building with a transparent glass facade. Judging by how the items of clothing were being displayed, this was a market. Though many of the shops were closed, the ones still trading exuded aromatic flavors of food. The scent made the elf's stomach rumble. In their haste to escape their captors, they only packed the essentials, which did not include food.

"I do not know," Aeron frowned. "We must seek shelter, but I do not know where we could find it in this place, or how to even ask anyone for guidance."

"We should at least eat," Syannon pointed out. "My strength to continue on foot would be a good deal better on a full stomach."

"I cannot disagree with you," the youngest prince of Halas agreed. "It would be interesting to see what passes for a decent meal in this place."

"If it is anything like what they consider clothing, I shudder to think," Hadros frowned. "I still cannot believe that fetching woman allowed herself to be displayed in such a manner. She was exquisite and yet indecent."

"Perhaps they are uninhibited by their bodies," Aeron explained, trying to be fair regarding mortal customs.

Hadros, however, was not listening. His nose was leading him to one shop because of the exotic aroma of food coming from it. It was a scent laced in spices and with the faint essence of meat. For three elves who had eaten nothing in almost a day, the aroma was tempting. As they entered the premises, the food was prepared and waiting at the counter operated by a dark-skinned mortal of Nadiran descent, much like Aeron's beloved wife, Melia. The human regarded the new arrivals with a raised brow and spoke to them, no doubt inquiring of them what they wanted. The language of shop owners was universal, even if the words sounded different.

Their presence in the establishment captured the attention of other patrons and made the elves feel very self-conscious. Aeron hoped barter was still in existence because he knew of no other way to communicate what he wanted. Producing a gold coin once used as currency in Avalyne, he handed it to the puzzled owner of the shop. The man stared at Aeron for a moment, but his eyes spoke volumes when it widened at the sight of gold. He examined the coin by biting into it, a practice Aeron was familiar with despite being away from the business of trading for almost a hundred millennia.

Apparently, their offering was acceptable to the owner, for they were soon seated and served whatever food they pointed to. Their presence was still a matter of fascination to the other patrons of the establishment, but Aeron did not expect it to be any different. At least they knew gold was still a valuable commodity that would help them survive in this alien world.

"Be careful with that. If I recall correctly, the Nadirans like their food spicy," Aeron advised Syannon as the elf was about to dig into their meal. Fifty years married to a lady of that land left him with an indelible memory of Melia's cooking. He loved the woman, but she was never *that* good a cook.

The bottle of cold, dark fluid in his hand preoccupied Aeron as he inspected it. Cold vapors rose out of its narrow mouth, and it rather amazed Aeron at how icy it felt against the skin. It seemed to be a favored drink because the other diners were also partaking of it. He held it to his lips and was surprised by the tingle against his tongue. Even the cold seemed to complement the experience.

"You are right." Syannon savored the taste, finding it pleasant.

"Try this," Aeron told his companions as he drained the bottle in his hand.

"You ought to take care," Hadros remarked with a grin. "You know how useless you are with spirits."

Aeron shot him a look. "This does not appear to contain spirits of any kind, but it is pleasing."

Despite their presence being a source of interest, they were left alone to dine on their exotic meal. Aeron took the time to look about the place and noted hygiene had improved since the age of Avalyne. Aeron admired humanity's ability to endure. They had survived the Dark Age following the Immortals' departure from Avalyne and created this grand civilization. Sireth made them hardy as a substitute for immortality, with the fierce need to endure at all costs. It pleased Aeron that they had reached some measure of prosperity, though their urbanization seemed to have gotten a little out of control.

The opening of a door drew his gaze as two men entered the premises. Their faces were grim as they made their way towards the owner and something about their manner made Aeron tense. He glanced at Syannon and Hadros and noted his brothers felt the same suspicion. Aeron reached for his bow discreetly as the men stood at the counter, appearing unarmed. Yet Aeron remembered the size of the weapons brandished against them on the high seas and decided it was easy to conceal them.

The shop owner seemed to have similar concerns, and he approached the new arrivals nervously. Though Aeron did not understand the words, the elf gathered the owner was asking the duo what they wanted. Their reaction, though abrupt, was predictable.

As expected, one pulled out a weapon, pointing it to the helpless shopkeeper's face and barking his demands. The second man pulled out a longer version of the weapon, aiming at the patrons. Its appearance provoked cries of fear from the children and the women.

Hadros's first impulse was to attack. Both Syannon and Aeron could see him wishing to. However, Aeron ordered him to stand down, wanting the situation to play out a little more before they decided how to act. Meanwhile, the thief at the counter discovered the gold coin Aeron used to pay for their meal amongst the other earnings the shop owner was forced to relinquish. It did not take him long to determine its source, and when the man shouted orders at his companion terrorizing the patrons, Aeron knew he would come towards them.

He was right.

Within seconds, the second thief marched up to Hadros and demanded the rest of their gold. Aeron rose to his feet, keeping his bow concealed beneath the table for the moment, poised to act. The man was shoving his weapon into Hadros's shoulder, and both Syannon and Aeron could see the firstborn of Halion was fast losing his temper.

"Can you take him?" Aeron asked his brother.

The thief shouted at him, but since Aeron could not understand a word he was saying and did not care to reply, the elf ignored him.

"If you can deal with his companion, I can take him."

Their conversation seemed to infuriate the man. He lashed out with his weapon, striking Hadros. Syannon moved towards his brother, but the thief trained his weapon on the elf to restrain him. With speed most mortals had not seen in an age, Hadros was on his feet. He gripped the weapon and shoved it towards the ceiling, away from his brother's face. With his other hand, he threw a punch into his attacker's jaw, using the man's disorientation to wrestle the weapon away.

The first villain, seeing his friend attacked, aimed his weapon at Hadros. While Aeron did not know how it worked, he was in no hurry to see it used. Without thinking twice, Aeron loaded his bow with lightning speed and let one arrow fly. The bolt tore into the thief's shoulder, forcing the human to drop the weapon to the floor with a loud clattering noise.

"Are you all right?" Syannon asked Hadros with concern as he noted the ugly bruise forming against his brother's pale skin.

"It is nothing that will not heal in time." Hadros handed Syannon the strange weapon and searched for something to restrain the fallen man at his feet.

As he did so, the establishment burst into loud cheers and applause as the other patrons expressed their admiration at the elves' handiwork.

While Aeron would have liked nothing better than to soak up their adulation, this attention to their presence was unwise. The need to depart became urgent, and it was best to do so while they could. Aeron approached the subdued man with his bow, hearing the human curse a litany of words whose meaning was clear enough. Leaving the arrow where it was, Aeron bound the man's wrists together with rope to ensure he would cause no further mischief after they departed. Syannon did the same to his companion.

"We should go," Aeron advised, even though the shopkeeper was shaking his hand with a smile on his face, offering them thanks for their help. He also returned the piece of gold sparking the thieves' interest. Aeron refused its return but helped himself to several bottles of the brown drink, a sacrifice the shop owner was more than happy to make instead of the gold.

The trio emerged into the night once more but advanced no further after hearing a loud screeching noise speeding towards them. There was a moment of pandemonium before they were facing two mechanical beasts, the bright glow of their orbs like eyes glaring at them. These were unlike the carriages seen earlier. A spinning red light perched on top of each vehicle, like a beacon.

The purpose of the crimson light was a mystery lost when the sons of Halion found themselves surrounded with nowhere to run.

# SIX
# SWEDISH

THE INVESTIGATION WAS NOT GOING WELL.

Every instinct Anna possessed told her John Malcolm had something to do with Richard Falstaff's death. Yet theories made a poor witness in a court of law. She needed evidence, and so far, none had surfaced to support the idea Malcolm had anything to do with it. As expected, when Anna interviewed the staff in the financial department where Falstaff worked, their stories differed little from the statements Malcolm had prepared for her. Whatever the truth about Richard's death, she would not get it from them.

Anna suspected Falstaff was not just a senior accountant. She knew this even before she searched his office. When she conducted her examination, little was discovered to justify his murder. Except the office appeared too spartan, like a showroom, not a place a corporate accountant would use to manage the financial complexities of a company like Malcolm Industries. The idea made her inspect the furnishings closer, and she spotted the indentations and drag marks in the plush carpet. With a start, Anna realized they had put this together for her benefit. This office never belonged to Richard Falstaff.

After pondering her options and concluding that pushing the point would only provoke John Malcolm's suspicions, Anna retreated for now.

Instead, she visited Victoria Falstaff, now in a better state of mind to answer some questions. Now the widow had a few days to recover from the shock of her husband's death, Anna needed to interview her properly.

Once the interview began, it became clear Mrs. Falstaff had no idea what her husband did for Malcolm Industries beyond his role as the Chief Financial Officer. In fact, she seemed reluctant to say anything at all about him. When Anna insisted she try to remember, Mrs. Falstaff reminded Anna she had a child to raise. The income coming from her husband's insurance policy was being held by a subsidiary of Malcolm Industries.

Anna sat at her desk in the precinct, wondering if she would end up relinquishing this entire matter to unsolved cases. There didn't seem to be any other avenues to pursue. She supposed she might try pulling up Falstaff's bank records, searching for any large deposits or to determine what kind of salary the man earned. It might help to prove Falstaff carried out more than accountancy for Malcolm Industries. Few accountants wore Armani suits unless they performed more than bookkeeping duties. Even less showed up at a part of town known to be an easy target for muggers – if his murder was a mugging at all.

It struck in her craw she could do nothing to give justice to a man who lost his life, but with no fresh leads, she had no other alternative. Refusing to work herself into a state of depression at being stymied in this investigation, Anna left her desk bound for the Starbuck's across the street. She needed to take solace in a Frappuccino to nurse her out of her annoyance. Suspects ushered by cops, pushed past her through the front desk of the station.

Out of nowhere, shouting erupted.

*Well, there was something you didn't see every day.*

Like everyone else in the vicinity, Anna gaped at the three men being escorted by a handful of cops. The trio looked like Robin Hood and his effeminate merry men. No, not effeminate, she recanted, handsome, almost beautiful. They seemed just too pretty, with their shoulder-length hair and their sculpted features. Their fashion sense clearly originated from the Middle Ages, with clothes made from leather and thick wool, in earthy tones one would expect of people accustomed to the outdoors.

Brothers, she decided, just by looking at them. Same features, with mahogany brown hair hanging against their shoulders in curls. They possessed the same blue eyes and upswept eyebrows, with cheekbones so sharp they could cut like a knife. Roughly the same age except for one. Anna put him in his mid-thirties. They scrutinized everything with a mixture of fascination and awe and looked positively out of place.

The youngest of the three glanced her way, and when their eyes made contact, his jaw dropped in astonishment.

"ARIANNE!"

For a second, Anna didn't realize he'd called out to her since she had no idea what he'd said. As he jabbered to his companions in a language she did not understand, pointing at her, Anna watched them turn to her struck by the same shock.

"What is this?" Anna asked the arresting officer, a rather brutish looking man named Idzikowski, a good cop who moved through life impersonating Dennis Franz.

"We picked up these guys on an INS warrant," Idzikowski replied as the rest of his comrades ushered the three towards processing. "Coast Guard picked them up off the coast near Long Island. On the way to shore, they escaped. No identification papers, nothing. Can't even tell what language they're speaking. INS figured they might be Swedish. Anyway, we're s'posed to hold them until INS get here."

"Swedish?" Anna ran her eyes over them.

Even while being escorted towards Central Booking, the trio kept turning in her direction, trying to see her. Somehow, she captured their undivided attention, and Anna wondered why.

"Arianne!" the youngest one shouted again, and Anna became convinced the cry was intended for her. The desperation in his voice troubled her as if what he needed her to hear might be vitally important. It unnerved Anna a little, but then everything affected her more acutely these days.

"Looks like you made a friend," Idzikowski observed with what Webster termed as your classic shit-eating grin.

"Not the worst thing to happen to me today." Anna shrugged. "Can't we get a translator in here?"

"We can't even tell what language they're speaking. I mean, if you ask me, these bozos look like some performance art fags from the Village."

Anna winced at the description. Wanting to spare Idzikowski a session at a cultural sensitivity seminar, she gave him a look to imply what he just said was *not* okay. "The correct term is 'gay', sergeant."

"Whatever. Ain't gonna mean shit when they hit lockup."

These men being placed into a cell even for a day did not sit well with Anna. As they headed into processing, she noticed they continued to keep her in their sights, as if they still did not believe their eyes. The one calling out to her had fallen silent, yet like his siblings, he continued to gape at her in wonder. Watching him disappear into the next room, Anna found that for the first time in days, her mind lingered on something other than Malcolm Industries and John Malcolm.

The Frappuccino she intended to get faded from her mind. Instead, she stayed close by, watching the officers remove the strangers' baffling personal effects. Speculation ranged from them being circus people to crazed method actors. Someone even suggested they might be from California.

While they were being fingerprinted, Anna examined the strangers' belongings. Their curious arsenal consisted of swords and bows and arrows, like the weapons found in the Medieval section of any museum. Anna had to admit this collection surpassed those in beauty easily. The leather pouch, so soft and delicately stitched, clinked loudly when she picked it up. Anna unfastened the leather cord holding it closed. She tipped it over and stared at the veritable fortune in gold coins accompanying their small arsenal.

The coins clanked against the wooden table as Anna emptied the pouch. She leaned forward for a closer look, marvelling at the pieces of gold glittering under the harsh illumination of the precinct room's fluorescent lights. Maybe Krugerrands or doubloons? She admired the craftsmanship of the beautifully elaborate design across the gold face on either side. Currency, perhaps? As the intricate patterns of gold reflected in her eyes, they spread out like a blooming flower in her mind.

The room spun so fast; Anna did not realize her knees buckled under her even as the surrounding faces melted into a blur of color.

Once again, the same paralyzing disorientation as in the elevator at the Malcolm Building gripped her. Except this time, the sensation seemed more intense. Images crowded in on her in a kaleidoscope of colors, like being trapped on an inescapable merry-go-round. While she did not experience the mind-numbing fear of earlier, something heaved inside of her. Something clawing its way through a mire of unease ever since she laid eyes on the Monolith. Bewildered, Anna had little time to process the insanity of everything happening to her before she lost complete control of her senses.

Faces appeared, fleeting images leaving enough traces to form memories. The faces of the three strangers flashed before her, and they engendered a sense of familiarity. She stood among them, like the idealized fantasy princess all adolescent girls wished to be in their youth. Anna only ever wanted to be a cop, so to see herself this way was laughable, except something about it felt familiar, though she couldn't imagine how. She stood with the three men, surrounded by a garden just as idealized as the rest of this daydream sweeping her along so vividly. Laughing with them, a surge of affection spread across her chest, like she'd known them all her life.

This is crazy, Anna told herself, until she realized something else, with just as much clarity. Someone was missing.

And his absence felt like a hole in the universe of her heart.

Something smelled terrible.

Anna pulled away from the stench as the fog lifted from her mind. The pungent smell assaulting her nostrils awakened her senses, and she turned her head, trying to escape it. When she blinked, faces were looking down at her with concern. Sergeant Idzikowski stood over her, waving an ammonia ampule under her nose. She brushed him away, her face scrunching up with distaste. When he retreated, she stared about in confusion and realized she was lying on the floor. She sat bolt upright and immediately regretted it. A wave of dizziness swept through her but did not linger long this time.

"You fainted, Detective," Idzikowski explained, gesturing someone to hand Anna a cup of water.

"Fainted?" Anna balked before she took a sip. "Bullshit, I don't faint!"

"You're on the floor. Looks like fainting to me."

Anna got to her feet, brushing off Idzikowski's efforts to help her up because the entire situation was mortifying. "You mean I just fell over?"

"Well, you kind of went spacey first, holding that thing in your hand."

Anna dropped her gaze to her open palm and noticed the coin still there. Once again, the images from that fantasy world flashed in her mind. What the hell? Why did seeing those three men do this to her? Somehow, they knew her and even as she resisted the possibility of it, she suspected otherwise.

All her life, she'd gotten as far as she did because she possessed an intuition allowing her to predict, without evidence or prior knowledge, how a situation would unfold. From the moment Anna laid eyes on the strangers walking through the precinct, something tugged at her and connected her to them in a way she didn't understand.

"Must be a long day." She feigned nonchalance and then regarded the officers standing by in concern. "Thanks everyone, I'm okay."

"You sure?" Idzikowski looked dubiously at her. Anna could just imagine him thinking she had lady troubles or something equally feminine related.

"I'm sure." She handed the coin back to him. "What happened to those three you brought in?"

"Well, they're in lockup." Idzikowski took a moment to reply after she jumped tracks on him. "We tried fingerprinting them, but it didn't work."

"Didn't work?"

"Yeah," he frowned. "They must have done something to their hands to keep us from identifying them because they didn't have fingerprints. Not one of them."

Anna stared at the items in the impound room a short time later, trying to make sense of everything she was seeing.

Swords, bows and daggers, pouches made of leather. Who even used these things anymore? The gold coins stared at her, charging her to solve the riddle of their origins. She read the report from the Coast Guard. They picked these men up off Bay Shore on a replica sailboat from the Middle Ages, with enough rations in the hold for an extended journey. So how far had they traveled? Even the commanding officer of the cutter, a Commander Wallace, was at a loss to explain the entire affair.

The European maritime agencies contacted offered no insight into the mystery. There was no record of any sailing craft matching the one towed into New York harbor. Wallace claimed it looked like something out of an old Viking movie. He seemed almost relieved they had jumped ship to become someone else's problem.

If not for their timely intervention in an armed holdup at a local Indian restaurant, they would still be at large instead of in NYPD custody.

*He'd called her "Arianne."*

What did that mean? He'd said it with such emotion after his initial stunned reaction became happiness. He seemed overjoyed to see her! Anna did not even want to think about her fainting spell at the touch of one of those engraved coins. She was a rational person who believed in science and reason, yet she could not deny the number of times she depended on instincts that relied on neither of those.

The images of what she saw while unconscious were too vivid to ignore. They seemed to be the latest in a list of strange incidents of late, ever since she returned from the Malcolm Building. She did not know how she knew those men in the lockup below, but she felt something for them that was difficult to explain. The mystery about them was deep enough, with their inability to speak a recognizable language or the fact that none of them seemed to have fingerprints. Where there should have been whorls and loops and arches on their fingertips, there was only smooth skin with no pattern at all.

Officer Donaldson, who had tried to fingerprint them, believed they'd burned away their prints. Yet Anna didn't have to be an expert to know self-mutilation of this type left behind scars. On closer examination, there was nothing of the kind on any of the trio's hands. It looked like a natural omission of their genetics, which only made the entire thing more bizarre.

Her ruminations were leading Anna down a path she did not wish to go. What was forming in her mind might jeopardize her badge, her career and perhaps her assurance life was a solid bedrock, not the shifting sand of a desert. The more she mulled over her experience, the more the sands shifted, until she sank through the grains.

Damn, Anna thought as she stood up from her desk, her mind made up, unaware she'd been pondering the question for an hour.

She'd be lucky if they didn't throw *her* in lockup for what she was about to do.

"It is impossible!" Hadros exclaimed with exasperation at Syannon as they sat inside their latest prison.

"It is not impossible!" Syannon burst out just as vehemently. "Aeron believes it and so do I! That was Arianne!"

"She *resembles* Arianne," Hadros conceded but was less

determined to believe as his younger siblings. "But the woman out there was human and our cousin, however she lived out her life, was elvish!"

As Aeron listened to his older brothers arguing, he tried to wrap his mind around the possibility. When he first saw her, there was no doubt in his mind, but having reflected on it, he was nowhere as confident. The woman they saw before being brought into this cell was the spitting image of Arianne, daughter of High Queen Lylea of the Elves. If Aeron didn't know better, he would have thought it was destiny allowing their paths to cross.

"She may have been elvish, but her soul did not return to the High Castle," Syannon insisted. "We know the souls of mortals are different. Sireth allowed their souls to go beyond. What if it was to live other lives? What if he did not grant them immortality as much as he granted them the power to reincarnate?"

"Syannon, I agree with you. She resembles Lylea's daughter. Yet we have no way of knowing the similarities between them run any deeper than skin!" Hadros fought to remain calm before the exasperation at his brother's stubbornness taxed his patience beyond its limits. Most of the time, Syannon wore his heart on his sleeve in contrast to Hadros, who liked to keep his emotions restrained.

Aeron had not weighed in with his opinion because he was still reeling in shock. Once his outburst died, other possibilities entered his mind.

Once upon a time, he loved a human even though everyone told him it was folly. After fifty years together, Melia died as all mortals did, and he was never the same. He mourned her, and though Sireth's promise of men returning in other lives lingered in his mind, he never dared to believe it could be true. Melia's loss nearly killed him. Aeron was sure he would never survive the anguish a second time.

"She is Arianne." Syannon refused to entertain any other possibility. "I know in my heart that woman is our cousin, reborn in mortal flesh."

"Whether she is, is beside the point." Hadros reminded them they had more significant concerns to deal with at present. "It does not change the fact we must escape this place."

The dungeons differed from any the elves had experienced in their lifetime. It was far cleaner and well lit. Harsh white light glared at them from overhead. There were privies and bunks for prisoners. The steel bars allowed the inmates to see each other, removing the sense of isolation. When they were shown to their cell, the other prisoners jeered and heckled derisive words whose maliciousness none of the elves doubted.

"I think we face a greater problem," Aeron examined the ink stains on his fingertips. "Their concern our fingers bore no marks was considerable."

"Even more so because we all bore the same trait," Hadros agreed. "I doubt telling them we are Immortals will illuminate the situation for them."

"That is for certain." Aeron frowned, staring through the bars at the few prisoners who were still staring at them, trying to understand what they were. "I fear the next time we see them, they will wish to examine us more closely and I do not relish the experience."

The dungeon suddenly came alive with the raucous hoots and jeers that could only come from unruly men in the company of a woman. To his surprise, Aeron could only stare as Arianne - no not Arianne, the woman who resembled her - walked toward their cell, being bombarded with all manner of disrespect.

Perhaps there was reason to hope.

"Are you sure about this?" Idzikowski looked at Anna.

"Yeah," Anna nodded. "I spoke to the INS. It was all a misunderstanding. It seems the Coast Guard didn't search their ship enough because they had papers on board, and it's taken this long to translate them. They're supposed to be performers for some cultural shindig at the Met next week. Anyway, everyone is pretty embarrassed about it and they'd like me to get these boys to the Swedish Consulate."

"Okay, but you sure you don't want me to assign a squad car to handle it?"

Idzikowski thought this entire thing felt strange, but Anna McCaughley was a good cop, and he trusted her enough to dismiss his concerns. Besides, there was something spooky about the trio and he was glad to see them gone. It was not his place to debate the matter with a detective and a lieutenant, nor was it his badge in jeopardy if anything went wrong.

"Nah," Anna replied, questioning herself for the hundredth time what in the hell she was doing. "They're pussycats."

"You're off by *one* word."

Anna gave the men a look once the door to their cell slid open. They stared at her, puzzled, but remained silent.

Anna gestured them to come forward and though their faces showed their uncertainty, they obeyed. With only hand signals to cross the language barrier, Anna was rather pleased with herself when she communicated her intention well enough for them to follow her down the corridor. Once again, the sense of familiarity struck her even if it made no sense. At least they seemed to understand what she was attempting to do, which helped convinced Anna despite the loss of her mind, that she was doing the right thing.

Anna had waited until most of the officers left for the evening and the night shift was on duty. She retrieved their belongings from impound, including their weapons, and for some odd reason, several bottles of Coca Cola. Once Anna secured their release, all she had to do was get them out of the station before someone asked questions. Anyone querying her actions received the same story she'd provided Idzikowski. This was a delicate matter to save the face of the US Coast Guard and the INS.

If these men jumped and murdered her as soon as they left the precinct, it would be her own fault.

Fortunately, they seemed to know their departure required stealth and played their parts by remaining docile until out of the precinct. A visible change overtook them once they were outdoors.

The tension and grim demeanor gave way to ease. Whether this was because they were free or out in the open, Anna could not say for sure.

She led them to her car she'd returned home to retrieve, gesturing for them to get in. The vintage T-bird convertible was left to her by her father and usually spent its time in the garage. However, for what she intended to do, it was best she used her own vehicle instead of one issued by the department.

The three seemed reluctant to enter the vehicle at first, staring at the car as if it were a menace. Anna climbed in first and ordered them to get in. While they did not understand the words, her tone was unmistakable, and they soon settled into the wide back seat, still appearing anxious.

"All right . . . " She turned to face them from the driver's seat, not really expecting them to comprehend a word she was saying but feeling compelled to try. "I don't have a clue why I just risked my career on you three Game of Thrones rejects, but if you try anything, I will shoot you." Just to prove her point, she showed them the gun she was carrying. Their wide eyes told Anna they understood her meaning.

"Anna." She pointed to herself, deciding introductions were necessary since she just broke them out of jail.

"Arianne," the one who had called out at the station repeated. Now that he wasn't shouting it out loud, Anna realized she could not place his accent at all, but it was melodic.

"No Arianne," she grumbled and tapped her chest again. "Anna."

He frowned, unhappy to yield the position. "Anna."

"And you are?" She pointed to his chest, hoping he would reciprocate in the exchange.

"Aeron," he answered after a moment.

"Aeron." The word rolled off the tongue and had a lyrical quality about it, which Anna found she quite liked.

"Hadros, Syannon." He pointed to his older siblings, one after the other.

Strange names, but once again the sound was pleasing, like something out of a storybook.

"It's nice to meet you," She smiled.

They were still staring at her in fascination, unable to reciprocate her words, but Anna guessed that wasn't necessary by the smiles on their faces.

"Sit tight," she instructed before turning on the ignition.

All three jumped in fright, one leapt out of the car, and the jabbering that followed told Anna one thing for sure.

They were definitely *not* Swedish.

## SEVEN
## AGGRESSIVE THERAPY

THIS WAS DANGEROUS.

Hypnotherapy should always be a last resort, something psychiatrists used when conventional therapy did not yield results. If time permitted, Dan would have preferred to apply those methods to help Moses regain his lost memories. But with Malcolm Industries forcing his hand by prompting him to release Moses into his care, Dan had no other alternative. He needed to discover the truth trapped in the old man's head because it was the only weapon they possessed against the enemy.

Although familiar with the practice of hypnotherapy, Dan didn't relish using it on Moses. So much of Moses's condition remained an unknown and prudence demanded they approached the tampering of his subconscious mind with caution. Despite the risks, the urgency of their situation required Dan to attack the old man's condition with a more daring form of treatment.

After leaving Bellevue, doctor and patient hid in a motel in Brooklyn, while Dan tried to decide what to do. Moses seemed content to let him make all the decisions, and Dan would not have minded this if he had had some idea of what they should do next. If he involved the police, it would avail him nothing. The nature of his enemy made going to the authorities impossible.

John Malcolm was part of a dynasty almost as prominent as the Kennedys. An accusation against the family needed airtight evidence, or else it would be tantamount to sacrilege. Dan possessed nothing of the sort.

Everyone believed Stuart died because of an accident. Only he thought otherwise, and he doubted the note supposedly from Sandra Collins would impress the cops enough to act. The initials on the card could belong to anyone. So, Dan had to improvise, by forcing Moses to remember what threatened Malcolm Industries so much they had killed to leave it buried in his mind.

"How are you?" Dan asked as he sat before Moses nestled comfortably in an armchair inside their motel room.

"Rested," the man muttered somewhat dazed.

"Good." Dan's voice exuded calm. With the drugs administered to Moses during his hospital stay, putting him in a suggestive state posed no difficulty. The old man trusted him. Trust played an enormous part in the exercise when attempting to open someone's innermost psyche. "There's a flight of stairs where you are, you need to climb them."

"Stairs." Moses nodded. His eyes blinked with drowsiness.

"Are you walking up those stairs?" Dan prompted, setting the stage for Moses to unlock the memories his conscious mind barred from him.

"Yes," he spoke dreamily. "I'm walking up the stairs."

"There's a door waiting for you, Moses."

"I see it." Moses's eyelids fluttered a little. "I fear it."

"Don't be afraid," Dan assured him. "I will be right there with you, and I won't let anything happen to you. You can trust me, Moses."

It surprised Dan how much he meant it.

"That is without question," he nodded. "I always trust you, Alasdare."

Dan blinked, thrown by the word. This was new. Moses called him War Dragon once, but this sounded more like a name than a title.

"Who is Alasdare, Moses?"

"You are. Alasdare, the War Dragon."

Dan moved on. He didn't wish to waste time with curiosities when more important questions needed answering. The doctor filed away the conversation for future reference and continued with the procedure. "Moses, you need to go through that door."

"I need to go through that door," he repeated in his stupor.

"When you go through, you will step into the past. You will remember everything about that past. If you experience any discomfort, you just have to tell me. We'll leave together. Okay, Moses?"

"Yes, Alasdare," he muttered again, "together."

"Are you through the door?"

"Yes."

"Where are you?" the doctor asked, noting every action displayed by the patient.

"On the street, it is freezing," Moses replied, his teeth chattering a little as he spoke. He removed the hands resting on the armrests of the chair and folded them over his body as if shielding himself from the icy weather in his mind. "There's a mission where they serve warm soup at the next block. I want to go there."

"Okay." Dan let this play out for the moment, wanting to see where it went. "How long have you been living on the streets, Moses?"

"A long time," he replied. "So long, I cannot remember when it began. I think I have been like this for many years."

"Why do you say that, Moses?"

"Because I remember when people still rode around in carriages, with horses pulling them wherever they wanted to go. One wandered the streets without worrying about being run over or noisy horns screaming at you to leave the roads. In those days, the roads belonged to everyone, not just the wealthy or the influential. Even the displaced walked the paths like masters of their own journey. It was a more civilized age when the air smelled sweeter, not full of chemicals and poisons that came with automobiles. I remember when I saw the first one and thought it would never catch on, but I have been wrong before..."

Dan paused a moment to consider Moses's words. Delusions, he decided. Moses might look old, but he was not wandering the streets as a derelict before cars were invented.

"Moses, we'll go back a little further now." This phase of Moses's life told them nothing. He resisted asking the patient his name because instinct told him the moment wasn't right for the question. During their sessions, Moses's extreme behavior always resulted from probes into his identity and Dan wanted to collect more information before making the attempt. Whatever trauma brought about Moses's amnesia, it was connected directly to the man's sense of identity.

"I want you to go back to a time before that, before you took to the streets. When you first met John Malcolm."

Moses twitched, making Dan regret asking him the question. His eyes moved faster behind his eyelids. Dan saw their movements even in the dim light of their motel room. Moses returned his hands to the armrests once again, gripping them so hard his nails dug into the fabric. The muscles of Moses's neck tightened into chords, and his jaw clenched as if fighting to restrain himself.

"I saw him." Moses's voice smoldered with contempt.

An unexplainable chill ran down Dan's spine. For a moment, the doctor swore the shadows in the room became more ominous. The place no longer appeared dingy but cavernous, as if transforming to fit Moses's grim mood. It was not the first time that Dan experienced it, and when he looked at Moses, his patient no longer appeared old or frail. His voice took on a quality of command, demanding respect from those listening.

"Tell me about it," Dan nudged gently even though his insides knotted with uneasiness.

"He stood at the foot of that terrible place, like a god about to take possession of his kingdom. I was not far wrong, though no one would believe it if I told them the truth. He has a new body now, but it is Malcolm whatever face he wears. I have become accustomed to his changes. He surrounds himself with devout followers to ensure his secret does not escape and those who discover the truth without permission, die."

Dan's heart beat a little faster at Moses's chilling words as he debated how much of this was a delusion and how much of it was real. "What do you mean by Malcolm having a new body?"

"Exile depleted much of his power," Moses continued to speak. "When they banished him, they destroyed his ability to take corporeal shape, but he has escaped that limitation. All he needs to continue in a new body is to infuse his wicked soul into an infant still slumbering in its mother's womb. Once he no longer has use for his present receptacle, the body dies, and he is born again, as heir and successor to his own empire."

Dan listened, even if he refused to believe any of it to be real. This was Moses' delusion. With dismay, he realized the truth might have become lost in the fantasy Moses concocted around John Malcolm. Malcolm wasn't a supernatural creature, living out countless lives in new bodies like a parasite. If this was what Moses stored in his head about John Malcolm, then Sandra Collins had embarked on a fool's errand for nothing. Then again, there had to be another reason, surely. Why else would Malcolm Industries be so determined to get their hands on Moses?

Dan considered the history of the Malcolms. He knew little about the prominent family in American culture who occupied the same role of royalty as the Kennedys, the Rockefellers and the Vanderbilts. Somehow, the Malcolms remained respectable, avoiding the scandals and sordid affairs dogging all those families, gleefully spread out across the media for years. The only time the press received any access to the family was when a marriage or birth announcement needed publicizing.

If there was anything odd about them at all, it was just that there weren't many members of the family. It remained small and out of the public eye, and it was the chairman of the board, always a male, who represented the face of Malcolm Industries. Then again, if one believed Moses, the person inheriting the Malcolm fortune for the past four centuries was the same man.

"Moses, why do you believe this?" Dan asked, hiding his disappointment that Moses revealed no useful information, just a rather outlandish story. "How can you be sure John Malcolm isn't just another man?"

"Because it was my duty to find out the truth. They sent me here to find the source of darkness. We all felt it, even behind the Veil. We sensed his awakening. During the Primordial Wars, I fought against him and aided his defeat. Enphilim thought I could do it again."

Once again, Dan concluded this story was some elaborate construct of Moses's damaged mind and supposed hypnotherapy was always going to be a long shot.

"Who are you?" Dan finally asked, because he had no other choice now. He needed something tangible to trace Moses's origins, not this fanciful story Moses's subconscious mind conjured up to keep him away from the real trauma causing his amnesia.

Moses touched Dan's cheek the way a father would do to a favorite child. "You know me, Alasdare. We have been friends since you were a boy when Halion pondered what to do with a child of Carleon. You and I have seen evil empires fall and light prevail. You know my name."

"No, I don't. Tell me Moses. If I'm going to help you, I need your name."

"All right then." Moses frowned as if the question was annoying and a waste of his time. "My name is..."

He screamed.

It was a cry torn from someone in excruciating agony. Moses toppled out of the chair as he convulsed, his hands flying towards his head, howling so loudly it cut through Dan's skull. Occupants in the adjacent room pounded on the walls, demanding silence. Dan opened his mouth to bring Moses out of his trance when the walls started shuddering around them.

An earthquake in New York?

Light globes glared brilliantly until the filaments burned out entirely and they shattered, spraying glass in all directions. Inside the bathroom, faucets burst free from ceramic, with jets of water spraying forth from broken and exposed pipes. Furniture rattled around the room, chairs and lampstands toppled over, while larger pieces like beds and tables shuddered across the floor. Dan's eyes widened in astonishment as glasses shattered. Picture frames clattered to the carpet, broken loose from their hooks, joining the growing pile of debris.

Throughout the pandemonium, Moses continued to howl as he lay on his back, writhing in agony. Dan recovered his senses enough to move. He was at Moses's side as everything around them continued to tear itself apart. Dan ignored the calamity around him for now because he needed to extricate Moses from whatever terrible place in his mind the old man had entered to produce such agony.

"Moses!" Dan cried, pulling his patient to a sitting position, not an easy feat while Moses was still clawing at his hair. "Moses, find the door! Find the door in your mind! Listen to my voice, Moses. It's me, Dan. Follow my voice back to the door!"

Moses struggled a little more before the convulsions slowed, with Dan continuing to speak, leading him away from the memories causing him so much pain. "Just listen to my voice. You're leaving it all behind. There's only the door in front of you. Go to it, I'm there on the other side."

"Door," Moses muttered, his convulsions becoming less violent by the second.

"Come through, Moses, come through and shut it behind you." Dan tried to sound calm even though his voice was cracking.

The tremors and the shuddering ceased. Furniture hit the floor in mid-quake, creating a last explosion of sound. The room remained in darkness, with the only light coming through their window from the moon outside. As things settled, Dan surveyed the damage, still a little dazed himself. In the background, he heard the hiss of water spewing from damaged pipes. Moses had all but stopped shaking now, and Dan stood up, heading to the window to survey the destruction outside.

But when he reached the window, he could do nothing but stare.

Outside, everything was calm. There were no sirens from emergency vehicles rushing to deal with the disaster. People weren't hurrying in and out of buildings, appearing frightened and shaken. The streets were devoid of the usual damage in the aftermath of a quake, especially one as violent as this one. On the walkway outside, he saw a man in a robe making his way to the ice machine, with no sign of any tremor bothering him. Everything was normal.

Whatever just happened was only confined to *this* room.

"Jesus Christ," the doctor whispered, even though he knew God had nothing to do with this.

"Well, this is it." Anna opened the door to the house her father left her after his death.

It was an old colonial, much too big for one person. While Anna could get a reasonable price for it if she ever sold, a part of her could not bear it in someone else's hands. She and Alan grew up in this house. The notches on the doorway marking their growth spurts were still where her father etched them so proudly. It was a home filled with memories Anna was unwilling to let go. Her mother had died of cancer when she was ten, and her father lasted a year longer than Alan. He never was quite the same after her brother died and all Anna had left of their precious years as a family was this house.

Even as she led her unexpected guests into her home, Anna wondered if she had taken complete leave of her senses. This question repeated itself in her mind ever since she rescued these men from lockup. Anna did not understand why she was risking her career for three strangers she met only today. Yet her gut told her she was doing the right thing. Anna felt compelled to help them, and though she could not explain why, she also knew they would not harm her.

The three men followed her into the living room, studying everything with utter fascination. Anna wished she understood what they were saying because it looked almost as if they were seeing everything for the first time. During the drive home, Anna noticed their apprehension at being forced to ride in the vehicle. It was only towards the end of the trip when they realized they would not die in her beloved T-bird that they relaxed.

Even though they tried to communicate, Anna could not even fathom the language they were speaking and was convinced she wouldn't find a translator for them. It was frustrating being unable to talk to them because her curiosity about their origins was overwhelming, especially after how she reacted to them in the precinct room.

All three men spread out across her living room as if they were visitors to a museum, studying everything. She noted two of them pausing in front of the mantelpiece, examining the framed family photographs with deep interest.

"That's my brother." Anna walked over, noticing how they were staring at Alan's picture.

They looked at her blankly, not understanding. Anna decided she would have to find some other way to explain herself. She thought for a moment before coming up with an idea.

"Brothers." She tapped them both on the chest in quick sequence before repeating the action on the photograph. "Brother."

Syannon nodded in understanding and tried the word on for size. "Ber-oth-er."

"Brother," Anna repeated so he could hear the subtleties of the word's pronunciation.

"Brother," Syannon spoke, getting the pronunciation right.

"That's right," she beamed before hearing the crack of the lid being twisted on one of the bottles of Coke these strangers were carrying. Anna turned to the source of the sound and froze.

Aeron was tilting his head back, draining the contents of the Coke bottle. His brown hair fell away from his ears, and Anna's eyes widened in shock as she saw them for the first time. She strode across the parquet floor, away from Syannon and Hadros, to reach Aeron.

Aeron stared at the woman approaching him with puzzlement. She stopped in front of him and reached out. Suppressing the urge to pull away, Aeron realized Anna was reaching for his ear and cursed himself for not taking more care to conceal it. It was too late now. She had seen it. Her expression showed her confusion as she touched him, her fingers tracing his ear where it tapered to a point. When she reached the tip, Anna withdrew as if scalded.

Her hesitation lasted only briefly, because she was soon scrutinizing his other ear just as carefully. When the same sight greeted her, Anna turned her attention to Syannon and Hadros, wondering if they were the same. His older brothers understood the time had passed for concealment, and brushed the hair away from their ears, confirming her suspicions.

"Oh my God," she gasped. "You're Vulcans."

# EIGHT
## VULCANS

"I THINK we should have waited to reveal ourselves."

"We did not show ourselves." Hadros shot Aeron a glare after Syannon's comment. "Someone who shall remain nameless chose a most inopportune time to expose himself like a child."

"I did not think!" Aeron fumed, setting down the bottle responsible for all this trouble. "Besides, I do not believe it is fair to hide from her what we are, considering we owe her our freedom."

"It has upset her though." Syannon studied Arianne's reincarnation with concern. Even if she bore a striking resemblance to the former Queen of Carleon, Anna was not the same person.

"I doubt men even remember who we are."

Hadros's brow disappeared into his hairline when Anna downed the swill in her glass like a Sandrine drunkard.

"I wish she understood us. She could help us find Tamsyn if only she understood a word we were saying." Aeron stared at her with frustration.

"We will have to learn. How hard can it be? Their speech was always simple, and we were the ones who taught them to speak to begin with."

"That is fortunate. . . ." Aeron stared at Hadros. ". . . since there is little we can teach them about humility."

Anna downed the scotch she kept in the house for occasions like this, although in all truth, she couldn't recall the last time she invited three men with pointed ears home.

*Men,* she snorted. They weren't men. Okay, so they weren't Vulcans either. Vulcans did not get picked up off the coast of Bay Shore by the Coast Guard or carry weapons straight out of the Middle Ages. Fairies? No, these guys were not Tinkerbell's cousins, and she was certain fairies came with wings. She didn't see any wings on them either...

Anna decided she was rambling.

Elves! Were they elves? She couldn't believe she was having this internal debate. What did she know about elves?

Other than their origins in Teutonic mythology, Anna remembered little about the subject. In high school, world mythology fascinated her and she recalled Teutonic folklore where elves were servants of the Norse god Frey and lived in a place called Alfheim. That was just one story since the legends were vague and difficult to pin down to any single culture. They appeared in Celtic, Germanic, and Scandinavian myths. In the Dark Ages, Anglo-Saxon Christians considered elves dangerous creatures capable of harming humans. Despite their varied descriptions, one characteristic remained constant.

Their pointed ears.

"This is insane. I have elves in my house. What next? Leprechauns?"

The three looked at her, sympathizing if unable to offer any words of comfort.

"If you're magical beings, how come you can't understand a word I'm saying?"

She was unsurprised when they stared back at her, bewildered.

Until her phone started ringing.

All three men jumped, displaying the same startled reaction to her Joan Jett ringtone as they did to her car.

"CALM DOWN!" Anna shouted, gesturing at them wildly as she hurried to her phone before it got smashed to pieces with the business end of a sword.

"Hello!" She snatched it off the table with one hand, while waving at the three men present to be quiet with the other.

"Detective McCaughley?"

Anna recognized the voice belonging to junior detective Ken Harper. "Harper? Is that you?"

"Yes, ma'am," Harper's voice politely responded. "You asked me to run a financial check on Richard Falstaff?"

"Oh, yeah." Anna blinked to remind herself that despite the bizarre events of her day, there was still the matter of an open murder case to solve. "I remember. Did you find anything?"

"I sure did. I got a friend of mine to pull some strings, and she got a copy of his bank records from an account I don't think his wife knows about. It seems Mr. Falstaff was making a $500,000 salary. Too much, I think, for a senior accountant."

"I knew it!" Anna burst out in triumph, ignoring her guests' puzzled expressions. "I think I need to go talk to Mr. Malcolm again. Thanks Harper, I'll talk to you later."

Anna ended the call, rather pleased there was now something tangible to confront John Malcolm with. Their next interview would not be as cordial as the first. She would deal with it tomorrow. Right now, a more pressing problem awaited.

"Okay, first things first . . . " She put down her phone. "Let's lose the weapons."

She gestured at them to lower their arsenal, wanting them to relax since they all looked poised to do battle with her cell phone.

"Second. . . " She intercepted the Coke bottle Aeron was reaching for. ". . . stop drinking this stuff. You'll rot your teeth."

*This was a mistake,* Dan told himself, but was helpless to keep away.

The rain came down hard on the cemetery lawn. The wall of water created a sheathe of gray, turning the landscape into watercolour images bleeding into each other on the canvas. Despite the weather, a sizeable gathering appeared for Stuart Farmer's funeral. A flotilla of black umbrellas surrounded the plot intended for his ultimate resting place.

The mourners included family, teachers, and students, sharing their mutual grief for the deceased. The preacher commanding his audience carried out the ritual of ending for the benefit of those left behind. When Dan saw the Dean of the University orating the eulogy, he felt a surge of anger at being robbed of the duty.

It should have been Dan who delivered it and no one else.

From behind the refuge of a tall, moss-covered obelisk, Dan listened in tears to the service. He wanted to join the mourners because he needed to feel the kinship of those who would miss Stuart as much as he. What would life be like without his best friend? Once again, Dan cursed Malcolm Industries for taking Stuart's life and himself for being the reason it happened. If he imagined this outcome when standing his ground, he might have reconsidered his actions. No sooner than the thought crossed his mind, Dan knew it wouldn't have made a difference, even if the outcome was wholly disproportionate to his act of defiance.

The rain soaked into his skin and the chill bit Dan to the bone, but he insisted on staying until the service ended. It was the least he could do for Stuart since Dan was the reason the professor was dead. When he left Moses at the motel, the old man questioned the prudence of his decision to go. Moses was right. It *was* dangerous, but Dan's guilt refused to let him do anything else. As a psychiatrist, he recognized the folly of blaming oneself for things out of one's control. Yet he couldn't forget his actions provoked Sandra Collins into killing Stuart as a lesson to him.

*Stop it.* There was no way he could have predicted that his refusal would cost Stuart his life.

Now that he was aware of why they wanted Moses so badly, Dan consoled himself knowing he did the right thing. Once he brought Moses out of his hypnotic state, Dan bundled the old man into his car and fled the motel before anyone discovered the state of the room, especially since it seemed impossible that no other room in the motel registered the slightest tremor despite the whirlwind that had torn theirs apart. Although part of him argued there had to be a reasonable explanation for what took place during the session, Dan knew better. There was no such thing as an earthquake so localized it confined itself to just one room.

Moses *made* it happen.

As a psychiatrist and a trained analyst, he thought he'd seen everything.

Never did he imagine he would see a patient's mood manifest into a physical force capable of affecting the surrounding environment. He knew what telekinesis was beyond its portrayal in pop culture. Although once considered nonsense, it was gaining legitimacy because of the mounting cases incapable of being explained away as hoaxes. Some people bent spoons, set fire to things and shattered glass. Moses's talents surpassed those and more. He could have been some parapsychologist's life's work if Dan believed Moses was just telekinetic, which the doctor did not.

Whatever Moses was, Dan sensed he was in way over his head.

Wiping away the moisture from his eyes, Dan saw Stuart's family, wishing he could offer words of comfort. What must they think of him for his absence? It didn't matter, he couldn't stay. If they were searching for him, this would be the best place to trap him. Sandra Collins knew what Stuart meant to him. The woman would assume he'd want to be present for the funeral. If what Moses said was true, then John Malcolm would never stop searching until he found them both. It may be necessary for Dan to take Moses and leave the city.

Strangely enough, abandoning Moses to Malcolm never crossed Dan's mind.

Things would be so much simpler if he could. Yet something inside of him refused to take the easy path out of this mess. Not when he kept hearing the names Moses called him in his dreams, names of people whom Moses trusted. Who was this War Dragon? Was it even a person? Even though "War Dragon" sounded like a video game, Moses had used it as if it were a shield capable of protecting him from harm. Perhaps if they could discover what *War Dragon* meant, it might reveal what happened to Moses.

Better yet, bring an end to all this, whatever "this" was.

When the sea of umbrellas dispersed, Dan decided it was time to leave. He crossed the manicured lawns of the cemetery using the worn cobblestoned pathway through the gravestones. During the service, Dan had come up with an idea of where he could take Moses and wanted to get back to his patient as quickly as possible.

Dan's grandfather had left him a place upstate in Goshen near Bear Mountain. As a child, he'd visited the old man at the cabin, and they'd gone fishing. While Dan didn't fish as much in recent years, it was a place to go when he needed to get away from it all. It was hardly luxurious but remote enough to serve as a sanctuary while he decided what to do next.

Sandra was waiting for him the minute he stepped out from behind the tall headstone. With her were four men in suits who bore the look of private security. Even if Dan didn't see the guns they carried, he knew those smart jackets concealed them. His first impulse was to run but appearing through the rain across the cemetery at almost every exit point, were more men.

Moses was right. They were waiting for him.

"Doctor Ellis, you are a hard man to find," Sandra gloated.

Dan would have been happy to wipe it off her face with a hard right across her jaw, even though he was not one to hit women. In fact, he was not one to hit anybody, but he would gladly make an exception for Stuart's killer. Instead, he spat at her, feeling some satisfaction at her revulsion when the spittle hit her skin. Their very public location kept her entourage from beating him senseless, but they still managed adequate vengeance to the insult delivered. Dan's face stung with the punch to his jaw and a jab to the abdomen.

"Well, I suppose we can dispense with the pleasantries. Take him to the car." Sandra wiped the spittle from her skin.

"I won't tell you where he is."

"You will," she threatened. "Before the night is over. You will."

Anna drove to the Monolith, determined to interrogate John Malcolm now that she knew Richard Falstaff was no mere employee.

Armed with the evidence gathered from Harper, Anna intended to confront Malcolm about his lie and rattle him enough to get the truth about what Falstaff did for him. Perhaps then she might unravel why the man died. While she didn't yet understand the level of Malcolm's complicity in Falstaff's death, he had lied to her, and his efforts to hide it provoked her suspicion. How he reacted to being caught would be telling.

Meanwhile, Anna contacted the INS to apologize contritely for losing the three prisoners who escaped her custody. Although she expected this would have consequences for her professionally, it was better than telling the INS the truth. Fortunately, after the bizarre report filed by the Coast Guard, the INS didn't seem surprised by their escape. They didn't even admonish her too severely for allowing it to happen. To the INS, these men appeared experts at escaping the clutches of government officials since their arrival in the United States.

Once in her car, Anna confessed to being glad to get out of the house. There was only so much she could take before naming everything for her guests made her want to reach for her gun. Although they learned English fast and expanded their vocabulary in a matter of hours, Anna could only tolerate so much before it got on her nerves. She still had difficulty accepting they were elves, even if their actions proved it more than their ears. It seemed they knew nothing of the modern world, from her clock radio to the contents of her refrigerator. By midnight, Anna gave up trying to explain everything using hand signals and turned on the TV, allowing six hundred television channels to do the teaching for her.

Hey, it worked in *Splash*.

After parking her car on the street facing the entry to the underground garage of the Monolith, Anna tried to think of the best way to approach John Malcolm. Gray clouds covered the top of the tower when Anna looked at it through the windshield of her car. It was a gloomy New York day, with the low-level cumulonimbus unleashing a heavy rain across the city. Large droplets of water pelted the canvas roof and splattered across her windshield. The sound soothed her and eased her anxieties about being anywhere near this building.

The appearance of a long black limousine descending the ramp into the lot prompted Anna into starting the T-Bird's engines. If Malcolm were in the vehicle, it would save time if she could talk to him outside the comfort zone of his office. Anna hoped the surprise might lead to Malcolm giving something away. Turning the ignition, she brought the T-bird to life and followed the limousine down the ramp after a few seconds to avoid giving away her presence.

At this time of day, the parking garage was empty, with most of the building's staff gone for the evening. The limo driver, occupied by the business of finding Malcom's reserved spot, didn't notice Anna's car behind him. After sighting where it stopped, Anna proceeded to the spaces for the visitors and parked the T-Bird out of view before heading back towards the limo.

"Get your hands off me!"

Anna froze in mid-step.

The acoustics in the parking garage ensured the angry voice echoed across the entire structure, so Anna heard the scuffle following the outburst. Without thinking twice, she reached for her gun, and advanced stealthily, prepared for trouble. More voices spoke, and the substance of them implied an attempt to contain an escalating situation. When the limo and its occupants came into sight, Anna darted behind the cover of a concrete column to assess the situation.

Sandra Collins and the suits working for her, all of whom

appeared to be ex-military or private security, were shoving the odd man out. Unlike the others, he wore jeans and a long-sleeved tee-shirt. Anger was etched across his handsome features as he struggled to break free of his captors. The bruises and blood on his face were clear indicators that whatever was going on here, he was not having any of it.

Thanks to him, Anna now had probable cause to act.

"Restrain him!"

The goon holding Dan produced a Browning and pressed the muzzle against his head at Sandra's demand after his latest failed escape. It was all the warning the psychiatrist needed to give up any further attempts to break free. Dan surrendered to his situation, aware struggling would only result in a bullet to the brain.

"Doctor Ellis." Sandra stepped in front of him. "We are doing this with or without your cooperation. If you know what's good for you, you'll tell us what we need to know, and we'll avoid any further unpleasantness. Otherwise, we will resort to more persuasive methods. Make no mistake, you will not be leaving until you tell us where your patient is."

"You're such a goddamn cliché, and you better be prepared to kill me, because I am not telling you shit!"

Sandra lashed out angrily in a burst of temper, striking him across the jaw.

Dan shook off the blow and glared at her with defiance.

"I know what Malcolm is! Moses thinks he's an immortal supernatural monster. Is that why you're so hell-bent on getting your hands on him? So, you can keep Moses from telling people Malcolm can jump bodies every few decades? Is that why you want him so badly, because someone might *actually* believe him?"

Truth or not, Sandra's stony mask faltered at that revelation, and she struck him again, this time with more venom and rage. "You had your chance to come out of this alive, Doctor. You should have taken it. It doesn't matter what you tell us now, you'll tell no one about Mr Malcolm."

"You know," Dan returned with more courage than he felt. "I thought Moses's story was insane, but seeing how terrified you people are of anyone hearing it makes me wonder if maybe Moses is telling the truth. Maybe Malcolm *is* some kind of creature."

"Kill him!" Sandra roared. "He's no use to us and too much of a liability!"

"EVERYBODY, FREEZE!"

The voice came out of nowhere and to Dan, it might as well have been heaven sent.

A woman approached with a 9mm Glock leading the way, eyes fixed on them. With a leather jacket over her collared shirt and blue jeans, it was the gold shield clipped to her belt that removed any doubt of her authority. She wasn't just a cop. She was an NYPD detective. He'd seen enough of the badges during his time at Bellevue to know the difference.

"Detective McCaughley." Sandra turned to his savior. "You have the worst timing. If you know what's good for you, you'll walk away from this. This is not your concern."

Detective McCaughley ignored Sandra and addressed the goon holding Dan hostage. "Let him go."

"Or what?" Sandra eyed the woman with skepticism.

"Or I'll blow his goddamn head off."

The gunman flinched, but Sandra didn't. "I don't think you will."

She fired.

Unlike Sandra, Dan could sense that the detective wasn't bluffing. The bullet whizzed past his ear and the grip on his arm slackened, freeing Dan as his would-be executioner fell to the ground, clutching his bleeding shoulder.

His rescuer shifted the barrel of her gun to another target. Sandra.

"Sir, walk towards me."

Dan obeyed Detective McCaughley immediately, grateful to do so. He would rather take his chances with this cop instead of Sandra with her threats of torture.

As he approached the detective, Dan saw her silent message. It was telling him to be ready to run at a moment's notice.

He would not hesitate.

Whatever Anna stumbled into, there was no way in hell she was allowing anyone to get gunned down in the middle of an empty parking garage.

What the hell did this guy do to warrant such an act of cold-blooded murder? Even if this was Malcolm Industries' bastion of power, it was an extremely reckless action. Had she stumbled into something worse than Richard Falstaff's death? Eyes still concentrated on Sandra, she dug into her pocket and retrieved her car keys as the man approached. Having seen her shoot one of them, Sandra's henchmen were not as eager to open fire when she had a gun aimed at their boss.

Still, this detente would not last long.

"There's a blue T-Bird parked behind me." Anna tossed him her keys when he was close enough. "Get in and start the engine."

Dan caught the jangle of keys with one hand. "What about you?"

"Just get going!" she barked, shifting her gaze from Sandra to him for a split second to show him just how serious she was. "NOW!"

It was a split second she could ill afford. No sooner than she took her eyes off Sandra, the goons drew their guns, taking the gamble to open fire now her attention was elsewhere.

The first shot hit the column behind her. Anna squeezed off a round, directing the shots at Sandra who went running for cover behind the limousine. Sandra's men hesitated, fearing John Malcolm's most trusted aide might become caught in the crossfire. It gave Anna the opening she needed to run because she had no desire to get into a firefight when she was alone without backup.

"Come on!"

He took cover, reluctant to leave but uncertain of what to do either. She admired his loyalty if not his sense.

They sprinted across the concrete floor as fast as possible with Malcolm's men falling into pursuit, Anna taking the lead as she hurried to her car. Once again, she admonished herself for coming here without reinforcements, but she never expected to enter this situation either. She envisioned her encounter with Malcolm to be an interrogation, not a shoot-out.

Upon nearing the T-bird, the revving of engines from elsewhere in the structure told Anna their pursuers were not about to let them escape, either by car or on foot.

"You drive!"

"Are you sure?" Dan looked at her when they reached the vehicle.

"Do you want to be the one to shoot?"

"I'll drive." He jumped behind the wheel.

Anna climbed into the passenger seat, feeling a sense of momentary disorientation at having someone else behind the wheel of her car. It didn't last long because she soon sighted three of Sandra's men running towards them, armed to the teeth.

"Get us out of here, now!" she barked before firing at them through her open window.

"What do you think I'm doing?!"

Dan slammed his foot against the accelerator as a barrage of bullets drove their pursuers to take cover. Two tons of good old-fashioned American steel roared forward with more speed than he could control. One of the pursuers flew towards the windshield, making a blunt thud against the smooth finish of the metal. He clung there as the T-Bird swung around in a tight circle, forcing him to lose his grip before he went tumbling across the concrete.

A gunshot shattered the back window of the car and Anna cursed before discharging another couple of shots. She was not aiming to kill, just discouraging them from maintaining the chase. In the meantime, the T-Bird was roaring up the sharp incline of the parking garage ramp. The loud screech of the limousine echoed through the structure as Anna saw the vehicle surging towards them in pursuit.

"Where are we going?"

"Police station!"

"Thank Christ! If you hadn't come along, I don't think I would have gotten out of there alive!"

"Who the hell are you anyway?" Anna grabbed one of the extra clips she kept in the glove compartment and reloaded. She sensed she would need the extra ammunition.

"Dan Ellis," he stuttered as the car made its bumpy re-entry into the outside world. "I'm a doctor."

"What, did you overcharge them or something?" she asked, focusing on the limousine in pursuit. Other cars carrying Malcolm Industries goons might accompany the stretched vehicle if the T-Bird didn't get out of sight soon.

"I'm a psychiatrist." Dan tried to remember where the nearest police station was in this area. "They want a patient of mine."

"Why?" She glanced at him before her eyes moved to the rear-view mirror.

Dan paused, unwilling to tell her the truth because she would think he was insane. For now, he avoided telling her his tale because the limousine behind them was trying to catch up. Through the glare of headlights, he could see the figure half hanging out of its window carrying a gun that looked like an Uzi.

"Get down!"

The order came a split second before the shooter opened fire. Dan turned sharply, trying to avoid the bullets before jamming his foot harder against the accelerator, forcing the T-Bird to weave dangerously through the traffic on the road.

The limousine sped up to match their speed but could not maintain it. It didn't matter because Anna caught sight of two other vehicles overtaking it to keep up the pursuit. The T-Bird was racing through the rainy streets, trying to avoid collision with other cars. Before they killed someone, she put the dashboard siren against the window, praying it would warn pedestrians to get clear. Anna leaned out of her window debating whether she ought to fire or not. There were just too many civilians on the street.

Her dilemma ended however, when new sirens were heard and

as she looked out the window, saw other squad cars joining the chase, probably alerted by the dozens of 911 calls resulting from their car chase.

"Hey, the cavalry is here!" Dan cried out over the sound of the siren blaring inside the car. He saw the other sirens through the rear-view mirror and felt a surge of relief when the cars in pursuit began to fall further back.

"Thank God," Anna sighed, grateful for the assistance.

"Do we stop?"

"No." Anna shook her head, not wishing to explain all this to her fellow officers when she had no answers herself. "Not yet. I think we need to talk."

Anna intended to find out what Doctor Ellis knew about Malcolm Industries that was so important it was worth killing an NYPD cop.

## NINE
## CHASE

"For what it's worth, thank you for saving my life."

Anna turned to Dan, still finding it odd he was driving her beloved car. However, after the night's excitement, she wanted to get home quickly, without wasting time stopping the car to exchange drivers.

"Just doing my job." She offered him a little smile. "Besides, I have a feeling I might have just put it off. I don't think those goons are done with us."

Dan didn't doubt it.

"I know. I just wanted to thank you in case I didn't get the chance later, Detective McCaughley, was it?"

"Yeah, Anna McCaughley." She smiled at him in greeting. "So why do they want you?"

"You'll never believe me." He glanced at her quickly before facing the road again. "It's pretty crazy."

She gave him a look and laughed. "After the week I've been having, crazy is a matter of perspective."

"True," Dan was the first to admit it, before he let out a sigh.

"They won't stop until they do. Sandra Collins ordered Stuart murdered because I wouldn't cooperate and give up Moses."

News of another murder captured Anna's undivided interest. "Who is Stuart?"

"My friend. They wanted me to turn over Moses, and when I wouldn't, they killed him just to show me what would happen if I didn't cooperate."

Anna had more questions, but the sadness in his eyes made her hold back. His grief was too fresh, and this wasn't the time for an interrogation. "You should never blame yourself for murderers doing what they do."

She was right of course, but Dan refused to let them hurt Moses, not when he saw firsthand the power the old man possessed but he needed help and something he couldn't explain told him this woman might be able to provide it.

He nodded and then straightened up in his seat before glancing at her again. "I got a story to tell you Detective McCaughley and I hope you don't think I'm crazy when I'm done."

John Malcolm's glare burned into her skin as Sandra stood before him in his office.

Their association had existed long enough to know he could make her burn for real if he wished it. Although suffering no significant injuries from the limousine crash, her inability to take part in the rest of the search did not impress her employer. Worse yet, telling Malcolm of Dan Ellis's escape was nowhere as incendiary as revealing the man knew what his patient had buried inside of him for so long.

"So, you are telling me he is now with Detective McCaughley and has most likely told her what he knows?" Malcolm stared at her impatiently from across his desk.

"Yes." Sandra nodded slowly, able to see the fury in his eyes despite his outward calm. "It will not take long to find them. We are locating where Detective McCaughley lives even as we speak. We will have our people there within the hour."

"I trust you will dispose of him a good deal more efficiently than you disposed of Falstaff?"

"That was a mistake." Sandra blushed with embarrassment, unable to shake the anxiety from her voice. Malcolm did not take failure lightly, and while he might not kill her, his punishments might make her wish otherwise.

"You seem to make many of them lately. Richard was a valuable employee, and while I have no interest in your sexual proclivities, I do object when you tell him more than you should while *in flagrante delicto*."

Sandra flinched, remembering the punishment for that mistake.

Forcing away images of the spiders set loose upon her bare skin, she tried not to shudder. Somewhere in the Monolith was a room with restraints on the floor. Sandra remembered the clutter of spiders crawling on her skin, unleashed in a swarm across her body. She couldn't even scream for fear they would crawl into her mouth. Her stomach heaved at the memory of those spindly legs running across every inch of her flesh.

"I paid for that mistake." She stared back at him once she had composed herself.

"You paid for the error. The mistake lives on. I found you because I know your soul. You served me and mine once, and you had certain successes, though I am sure you remember little of it. However, I am not as forgiving or as weak as my servant was. Disappoint me, defy me, or worst of all, challenge me, and I will see you burn in a hell that will make Dante's depiction of it positively pleasant."

"Yes, Sir." Sandra nodded. She turned on her heels to leave when Malcolm stopped her in her tracks.

"There is one other thing. Detective McCaughley. I want her alive."

Sandra paused and looked up at Malcolm in confusion. "Alive, Sir?"

"Yes." He nodded, "Alive."

"I don't understand." She met his gaze with growing confusion.

"Detective McCaughley is trying to connect Richard's death to us. We should eliminate her."

"Thanks to your incompetence in this matter, it may be necessary for me to vacate this body sooner than I would like." Malcolm stared at her hard. "If that becomes necessary, I will need a receptacle to host my rebirth. Detective McCaughley will furnish that need adequately, so you *will* capture her alive. Is that clear?"

"Yes, perfectly." Sandra knew better than to debate the issue with him. He would do what he wished anyway, and after Anna McCaughley delivered his child, she would cease to be anyone's problem.

Like all the others.

# TEN
# FAILSAFE

Anna questioned the sensibility of bringing Dan back home with her. Yet after he told his story, she didn't have much choice. If she guessed right, then Malcolm's men would be on their way. Although she had difficulty taking his patient's claim about John Malcolm being an immortal monster seriously, her houseguests at present were *elves*. It was difficult to take the sanity high ground under such circumstances.

As it was, Anna was grateful Dan did not consider her insane or delusional after explaining how the elves found her. She supposed with an incredible story of his own, it just felt nice to have a kindred spirit. While he did not appear ready to believe there were really elves in her house, he gave her the benefit of the doubt. After what he told her about his patient, it seemed they were both in the company of some rather peculiar individuals of late.

Besides, now they had escaped the peril of the earlier car chase, Anna had the chance to study Dan Ellis.

He didn't look like a psychiatrist. Psychiatrists were stodgy old men with thick glasses perched on their noses wearing dull tweed coats. Dan reminded her of a frat boy with his jeans and sneakers, looking as if he just strolled off a college campus. Still, he projected compassion, and that probably helped him gain his patient's trust.

"Here's the plan," Anna explained, walking through the door. "I'll get my guests, and we'll pick up your patient before heading out of the city. You said you had a place upstate?"

"Yeah," Dan nodded, looking around Anna's home once they stepped through the door. He admired how warm and comfortable it looked even if it was more appropriate for a family, not a career-minded single woman. Without having to ask, he suspected she didn't have much time for a social life either. "It belonged to my grandfather. We used to go fishing there all the time when I was a kid. It's in the mountains, in a town called Goshen near Bear Mountain."

"It will do. We need to stay out of sight while we figure out what to do. Once we get there, I'll put a call in to my precinct, fill my boss in on what's going on."

"Hello!" Anna sang out to her guests, wanting to give them some warning she had brought home a visitor.

One thing Anna had learned about these elves since their entry into her life, it was that their sense of hearing was better than bat sonar. When they didn't immediately appear, she guessed they were probably in front of the TV. She wondered whether introducing them to the device responsible for dumbing down modern man was such a wise idea. The night before, they spent most of their time in front of the screen, absorbing programming like sponges. Perhaps she should have disabled TLC and the talk show channels first.

CRASH!

She and Dan jumped at the sound of glass shattering. Anna almost went for her gun at the sudden noise, while Syannon and Hadros jumped to their feet, gaping at Dan in unmasked shock. It was Aeron emerging from the kitchen who dropped the glass in his hand, gripped with the same disbelief. It took Anna a second to realize they were reacting to Dan the same way they had when they first saw her. Except the effect seemed more profound on Aeron. Anna swore his eyes were glistening with tears.

After their shock subsided, both Syannon and Hadros strode over to Dan, their faces beaming in delight. Syannon reached Dan first before wrapping the confused doctor in his arms to deliver a heartfelt embrace. Hadros, slightly more restrained, patted Dan on the back, grinning at him like they were long-lost friends.

"They're friendly." Dan stared past the elf's shoulder at Anna, looking bewildered.

"Yeah, I noticed." Anna shrugged, not understanding the reaction herself.

"Syn?" She tapped the elf's shoulder for an explanation.

"Dare!" He grinned at Anna as if that explained everything, before pointing at Dan again. "Dare!"

"No, I'm Dan," he corrected before the older of the two men embraced him just as warmly. While the affection seemed genuine, like most heterosexual males of his time, Dan found the entire display uncomfortable and confusing.

"Dan, Dare." Hadros dismissed the mortal's attempt to make the distinction. It made perfect sense, Hadros decided. If Arianne lived in this time, why not Dare? Not even time had the power to shatter the links between these two soulmates, even after centuries of separation.

"They did that to me too," Anna sympathized but could offer no explanation. "I can't tell what language they're speaking, but they keep calling me Arianne."

Something sparked in his mind, something he did not even remember until this moment when Anna mentioned these elves associated her with someone else. What did Moses call him?

"Alasdare."

The word made the elf who had dropped the glass react sharply.

Recognition and hope flooded his eyes, and suddenly Dan's heart rate jumped. As the elf Anna called Aeron stared at him, Dan imagined he stood on the brink of some truth that could possibly turn his world even more inside out than it already was. Ever since meeting Moses, Dan was drawn headfirst through the eye of a singularity whose end would change everything he understood about himself.

"You," Aeron spoke, using the word for the first time. "You, Alasdare." He tapped Dan's chest.

Everything about this mortal reminded Aeron of his dearest friend. It made perfect sense Dare would be here. His heart never lingered far from Arianne, not since they laid eyes upon each other so long ago in Avalyne. When Dare's latest incarnation spoke the word "Alasdare" with no idea what it meant, Aeron's heart took flight. Next to his wife Melia, the mortal Aeron loved most in Avalyne was Dare or Alasdare, the beloved King of Carleon and Aeron's best friend. They had been more than friends to each other, they were family.

"No," Dan repeated. "I'm Dan."

"You," Aeron repeated the gesture and spoke with more insistence, "Alasdare."

These elves recognized him, and Dan realized it the instant they saw him. Just like Anna. It took Dan a fraction of a second to remember Alasdare was not the only thing Moses called him. During their first session, Moses spoke another name, a name he asked Stuart to research for him. With a pang of grief, Dan now realized it was the last conversation he and Stuart would ever have.

"War Dragon." He said the words with a halting breath.

"Yes." Aeron nodded slowly and placed a hand on Dan's chest. "You, War Dragon."

"Who the hell is War Dragon?" Anna asked, unable to comprehend what was going on. Just when Anna thought she had run the gauntlet of how much more bizarre all this could get, the goalposts shifted. Before leaving that day, Anna had taught the elves a few words, including "dragon," and now they were using them in the most shocking way.

"I think I am." Dan finally allowed himself to admit it. "I don't see how that can be, but they're sure of it. Just like they see you as this Arianne. This makes no sense."

They did not have time for this, Anna decided, realizing that if they began debating this now, they'd still be there when Malcolm's men arrived with an arsenal.

"Alright . . ." Anna gestured for silence from all four men. ". . . we can deal with this later. Right now, we have to leave."

Dan agreed wholeheartedly. One life and death situation were all he was prepared to accept today. "No argument here, but we have to get to Moses first. Maybe they might have some idea who he is, too."

While Dan collected whatever provisions she had in her kitchen, Anna had the elves help her load a small nondescript chest, secured with a padlock, into the trunk of her car. Although she did not tell them what was in it, she successfully conveyed to them they were not leaving without it. After their encounter with Malcolm's goons, Anna didn't intend getting caught unprepared. Their enemy came well-armed, and she intended to be the same at their next confrontation.

Once they were ready, the five left the house and drove towards the Washington Heights motel where Dan left Moses. He was glad to get back to the old man because he had been out of touch since going to Stuart's funeral against Moses's advice.

There were so many unsettling questions Dan did not wish to deal with right then. Moses said so many times he trusted Dan, and until now, Dan supposed it was the trust of a sick man towards his doctor. The possibility never even occurred to him there might be another reason, one so unbelievable he still had difficulty accepting it.

"Are you sure this is a smart idea?" Anna questioned as they walked to his motel room.

"Look, this whole situation is crazy, but I've seen things in the last twenty-four hours that tells me I need to keep an open mind and trust my instincts. Moses is connected to your friends here. I don't know how, but I'm sure of it. All I know is this is too much of a coincidence to be anything else but true."

Anna wanted to disagree, but she conceded Dan had a point. In her police career, she had witnessed the very depths of human ugliness and deception. She recognized liars and cheats because it was necessary for her professional survival. This situation challenged everything she knew with no suitable explanation for anything. At some point, one had to take a leap of faith.

"No," Anna whispered softly. "Damn I wish it were a hoax. I wish we could explain this away, but I can't."

"I'm just as lost as you are. Moses started out as just a patient, but he's more than that now. I don't know what happened to him, but if he's right, John Malcolm has been creeping around our world for God knows how long. That scares the hell out of me."

Anna had to admit, he wasn't alone.

"Okay." Anna took a deep breath, deciding she would follow this rabbit hole no matter how deep it went. "I'm with you on this, all the way."

"Good." Dan smiled at her, inordinately pleased by her company. He looked at her and realized how easy it would be to let himself become lost in those blue eyes of hers. She was easily the most captivating woman he ever met in his life, not simply because she was beautiful, but her courage left him in awe. If they got out of this mess alive, he promised himself not to let her slip out of his life.

Arriving at a door towards the end of the corridor, Dan knocked once. "Moses, it's me."

Anna noticed the elves tensing. Their faces became grave as if there was something in the air giving them concern. Aeron pushed his way next to Dan as the door opened, which confused the doctor. Since their meeting, the elf seemed very reluctant to let Dan out of his sight.

"Dan?" Moses's voice returned as the door swung open.

"TAMSYN!" Aeron exclaimed with a surprised gasp. The elf's blue eyes widened in astonishment as the reason for their quest to this strange world suddenly materialized before them.

"Who?" Dan questioned as the elf dropped to one knee in reverence before the old man. Behind him, Syannon and Hadros did the same. It stunned all three how after four centuries of worrying about their friend, he now appeared before them as if conjured by a wizard's spell.

"Is that his name?" Dan demanded excitedly and then cursed at not being able to communicate to get a more accurate answer. There were several questions Dan wanted to ask, and it was frustrating to be unable to do so because of the language barrier. Instead, he directed his question at Moses. "Moses, is that your name?"

Whether it was or not, Moses did not seem happy to hear it.

The patient reacted poorly to the unfamiliar faces around him. He recoiled when Aeron called him by name as if the sound of it affected his psyche like a physical assault. His eyes darted frantically to Dan, conveying the fear rushing through him. By now, Aeron had risen to his feet, trying desperately to communicate in that alien language neither Dan nor Anna understood. Yet even if the words themselves eluded Dan, the emotion behind them did not. Aeron's face displayed nothing but joy at the sight of Moses before him.

"Aeron . . . " Dan grabbed the elf's arm, restraining him because his presence was distressing Moses.

Aeron grasped Dan's meaning before glancing at Tamsyn again. The seraf who fought at their side during the Primordial Wars, and aided their campaigns against Mael and Balfure, appeared terrified by his presence. What had happened to the wizard? Tamsyn was the most powerful emissary of the Celestials. Who had turned him into a frightened old man devoid of his ancient memories?

"Something had been done to him." Aeron retreated and glanced over his shoulder at his brothers.

"Yes." Syannon concurred with Aeron's assessment when he saw Dan attempting to calm the wizard from his fearful state.

"Moses, it's okay." Dan ushered him back into the room.

Aeron, Syannon and Hadros remained a few paces behind Dan to avoid crowding Moses. Behind them, Anna entered and locked the door behind her. Of all of them, she understood the situation the least but refrained from asking questions because things were confusing enough.

"You don't have to be afraid Moses. They're just as worried about you as I am."

"Who are they?" Moses retreated into a wing chair, staring past Dan at the elves with clear apprehension.

"Friends," Dan answered, not knowing what else to say. "Yours."

"I do not remember them!"

"Can you try Moses?" Dan pressed a little. "This is Aeron, Syannon, Hadros and Anna. Concentrate and see if you can remember any of them. I'll be right here with you."

Moses looked past the elves at the lovely face behind them. He stared at the woman for a long moment, a wealth of information pounding the walls of silence inside his mind. A trickle of memories escaped through a crack, but not the ones Moses needed most. Still, as he took in the sight of her, a word surfaced in his mind like a drowning man learning to swim at last.

"Her name is Arianne."

Anna's jaw dropped in surprise.

"You remember?" Dan asked gently.

"I do not wish to speak of this! There is something inside me that will not allow me to remember. It gnaws at me!"

"Tamsyn," Aeron spoke in Elvish, hoping it would spark a memory within the mind of the seraf. "Calm yourself, old friend!"

"No!" Moses screamed. "I do not wish to listen to your words, Prince of Halas!"

Both Dan and Anna shot Aeron a look of surprise before Dan faced Moses again. "Can you understand him, Moses?" Dan stood between his patient and the elf. "Do you know what he is saying?"

"Yes!" Moses nodded. "He says that I am a friend, but I do not remember him!"

"But you can understand him?" Anna did not know how any of this was possible, but at least she no longer doubted the insanity of all this.

"Yes," Moses nodded, his body relaxing as if Anna's question gave him focus. "I understand him. I cannot say how, but I do."

"What language is he speaking?" Anna asked again. Moses's ability to communicate with the elves could answer some important questions.

"It is the language of the Immortals. The First Tongue, for the first race of the world."

"Moses, is your name Tamsyn?"

As the word escaped Dan's lips, Moses uttered a shriek of agony, like a wounded animal about to die. As before, the old man clutched his skull in pain, his fingernails digging into his skin as he writhed and bellowed. The violent reaction threw Moses from his chair to the thin carpet, leaving everyone save Dan in stunned horror. Their silence would not last because Dan braced himself for what came next. As the thought crossed his mind, the walls of the hotel room shook once again as the same calamity repeated itself.

"What the hell?" Anna exclaimed at the vibrations under her feet.

Every piece of furniture in the room began shuddering. Objects clattered off surfaces, picture frames broke free and plunged to the carpet. The wing chair Moses occupied tipped unto his back and a cupboard flew open spilling out its contents. Hadros gripped Anna's arm, steadying her as she struggled to remain on her feet. The mirror in the bathroom shattered and fixtures became deadly projectiles flying across the room before crashing into the wall tiles. Jets of water sprayed in mini geysers as pipes bursts. Overhead, a light fixture broke free from the roof and smashed into the ground next to Syannon, who caught the spray of glass across his back.

"Moses!" Dan scrambled to the old man who continued to scream, muttering incoherent words of agony. Meanwhile, the surrounding room tore itself apart. "Moses, listen to me! Try to listen to my voice. Try to come back from wherever you are by focusing on my voice!"

This time, not even Dan's soothing words rescued Moses's mind from the terrible place trapping him. His agony deepened the intensity of the tremors until the walls fractured. Mighty cracks ran across the brick, splitting wallpaper and paint. From above, fragments of sheetrock broke free and fell around them. Aeron scrambled next to Moses, trying to help Dan settle him down, but Moses was beyond hearing anything.

"We have to get out of here!" Anna shouted at Dan.

"No!" the doctor shook his head. They would get nowhere with Moses in this state. "Get my bag!"

Anna surveyed the room and spotted the black doctor's bag. She darted forward, keeping her head down while she sidestepped falling debris and upended furniture. Dust covered the bag along with fragments of a broken table. Snatching it up, Anna scrambled back to Dan, handing him the leather case.

"Tamsyn," Aeron tried desperately to reach the wizard who was always the one to save their lives with his magic.

"NO!" Dan shouted. "Don't use his name!"

Aeron stared at him blankly, not comprehending.

"Moses," Dan stated firmly as he produced the items he needed from inside the case. "Not Tamsyn!"

To ensure Aeron understood, Dan shook his head when he uttered the word, hoping the elf would realize what he had discovered only in the last few seconds - these violent episodes were being triggered by any mention of Moses's correct name.

"Do not use his name Aeron!" Syannon replied, grasping what Dare was trying to convey. "It is his name that makes him this way!"

"How can that be? He is a seraf!" Aeron burst out, unable to accept what power could do this to Tamsyn. Save the Celestials themselves, serafs were the most powerful beings in existence.

"There should be nothing capable of harming him." Hadros appeared just as mystified. "Until we discover what that might be, we must listen to Dare! I believe he speaks the truth!"

Aeron needed no further convincing as he struggled to maintain his grip on Tamsyn, trying to keep him from harming himself. While he did not know what Dan was doing, he guessed it had something to do with the vial of medicine he was preparing. Tamsyn - or Moses -

was unleashing all his power, and if they did not help him, he might well bring down the entire building.

"What is he doing?" Hadros questioned when he saw Dan piercing Tamsyn's arm with a sharp needle.

Aeron did not answer because he was just as curious.

Tamsyn's seizure eased as Dan's potion took effect. As his strength waned, so did the chaos taking place around them. The powerful forces Tamsyn unwittingly manifested subsided with his looming unconscious state. The walls ceased to shake, and the tremors faded into nothingness, leaving the room in ruins.

"What did you do?" Anna asked as the old man drifted into unconsciousness.

"I knocked him out with 50 cc's of Thorazine." Dan let out a heavy sigh. "He will sleep for a little while."

"Thank God." Anna swept her gaze across the room, somewhat dazed. Whatever lingering doubts she had about Dan's story ended for good with this latest episode. No matter how shaken she might be right then, denying what she just witnessed was impossible. "What the hell just happened?"

"He's telekinetic." Dan tried to explain the best he could, but this was a difficult proposition when he did not understand himself. What ailed Moses was beyond psychiatry. In fact, the doctor suspected helping Moses might well be beyond any of them.

"We have to get out of here," Anna pointed out, not wishing to explain this room to anyone who came to investigate. After the ruckus they just caused, she wouldn't be surprised if someone called 911.

"Yeah." Dan nodded, surveying the damage. "I don't think I'll be getting my deposit back for this room, either."

With the same urgency as before, Dan and his companions took Moses and hurried out of the motel room before the destruction within it brought others. Thankfully, the T-Bird could seat all of them, even if it was a bit of a squeeze. Moses remained unconscious throughout most of their journey out of town. This time it was Anna who took over the driving duties while Dan kept a close eye on his patient. He also tended to Syannon, injured during the worst of Moses's episode. It had been years since Dan had done a medical rotation, but he still knew how to treat simple wounds.

"What?" Dan noticed Aeron looking at him with a bemused smile as he removed a small shard of glass that had pierced skin through Syannon's clothing.

"You." Aeron smiled with warmth. "Dare."

"I think it might have been your nickname," Anna suggested as she took them out of the city. "Alasdare sounds like a mouthful."

"I still have trouble believing all this." Dan shook his head as he cleaned Syannon's injury with an antiseptic wipe.

"Any more difficult than believing your patient is telekinetic?"

"Telekinesis I can deal with, but reincarnation? If that's what we're talking about."

"Listen, I don't presume to understand any of this, but ever since I came within sight of that damn Monolith, something has been happening to me. I've always had intuitions - strong intuitions. It's helped me size people up on the job for years. But since I walked into that place, my senses feel dialed to one thousand or something because the minute I saw these guys," she tossed a quick glance at the three elves, "I was sure I could trust them. As impossible as it is to believe, I can tell they mean us no harm, and we mean something to them. In the absence of any evidence, you sometimes have to take a leap of faith."

Dan could not disagree with her when his instincts told him the same thing.

"Yeah, I can relate," Dan admitted. "The night before they killed Stuart, I dreamed I was someone else. Ever since Moses called me War Dragon, I've had this strange sense we've met before. I've heard of hypnosis bringing back memories of past lives, but I'm a psychiatrist, I am trained to think there should be other explanations. But like you, I believe him when he says I'm this War Dragon person because I can feel it in my gut. It scares the hell out of me, but when I dream, I can almost remember it."

"So, War Dragon, Alasdare, Dare," Anna flashed him a smile. "If we ever work out how to talk to our friends here, I will have to ask which is which."

Dan laughed softly before casting a look at Moses, who was still very much unconscious. "I figured out one thing about Moses, though."

"What is it?"

"John Malcolm did this to him."

"Malcolm?" Aeron shot him a look.

"Too long to explain," Dan said, and it was true. Hand gestures would not do when conveying anything about John Malcolm.

"Maelog?"

Did Dan just refer to Maelog? Once again, Aeron cursed the inability to communicate because he wanted to know why Dan mentioned a word that sounded very much like the evil Celestial Maelog or Mael. Tamsyn left the Veil in pursuit of a darkness so powerful its presence penetrated the Veil between worlds. Maelog possessed the power to do that.

"No." Dan shook his head. "Malcolm, John Malcolm."

Aeron pressed him no more, but the elf's expression troubled him. Dan was learning to read Aeron very quickly, and the look on the elf's face told him Aeron had suspicions he had no way to communicate.

"You were saying?" Anna prompted him to continue. She wanted to know why he suspected John Malcolm was responsible for Moses/Tamsyn's condition.

"It has to be Malcolm considering everything else we know. John Malcolm can resurrect himself," Dan reasoned out as he placed a clean bandage over Syannon's wound. "What if Moses knew about it? Moses spoke to me about being alive when carriages were still on the roads. What if he has been around for as long as Malcolm?"

"He sure looks old enough," Anna agreed with the possibility. It was surprising how easily this outlandish theory seemed entirely plausible once she accepted there were elves in the world. She supposed it was only a hop, skip and a jump to believing there were immortal people roaming the streets of New York.

"That's why I called him Moses."

"Clever." Anna rolled her eyes. "Go on."

"Okay. If Moses has been around as long as Malcolm, he might know how Malcolm was reincarnating himself. Moses told me they sent him to stop the evil, to stop the darkness they felt even though they were a world away."

"So, Moses came from wherever these guys are from."

"But he's not an elf," Dan declared, having just thought of that.

"True but if they sent him here to stop evil, then perhaps they made him come looking like one of us. You know undercover, so he wouldn't draw suspicion," Anna reasoned, helping Dan with his hypothesis.

She was right, Dan decided, and continued, "I think Moses came to stop Malcolm and Malcolm couldn't kill him, but Malcolm could make him forget. If he could affect Moses's memory, he might've put in a fail-safe to ensure Moses could not remember the truth."

"Like sending him nuts if he ever heard his name," Anna suggested.

"No, it's worse than that," Dan whispered. "If he ever *remembered* his name."

## ELEVEN
## COSMIC TURNTABLES

By the time Sandra Collins stepped into Anna McCaughley's home an hour later, the detective was long gone.

The silence greeting them after her people kicked in the front door told her as much. No doubt the detective suspected they were coming here after she and Doctor Ellis eluded capture earlier. Sandra crossed the foyer and paused in the middle of the living room. By the disarray, she guessed the policewoman's departure was a hasty one and most likely extended. While her security spread through the house, Sandra conducted her own investigation. She needed to find where the detective might have fled, taking Doctor Ellis and Moses with her.

Anna McCaughley and Dan Ellis had one frustrating thing in common. Neither of them possessed any attachments. Aside from the lack of leverage, it meant fewer alternatives for sanctuary in the event of flight. During the investigation, Detective McCaughley figured in Sandra's mind as a minor annoyance. In the wake of Richard's death, she had expected it. The woman gave Sandra no reason to place her under surveillance when Sandra was far more interested in Doctor Ellis. Now this miscalculation might cost her because the duo had vanished, taking Moses with them.

Sandra moved through the house at a leisurely pace in contrast to her security who were carrying out a more robust search. From where she stood in the upstairs hallway, yanked drawers squeaked in protest while doors opened and closed like irregular heartbeats. A picture of Detective McCaughley in plain clothes uniform, flanked by two men in similar clothing, showed the family's close association with the NYPD. Both family members were dead. One in the line of duty, the other from grief. Meanwhile, the older pictures revealed the same family with its deceased matriarch.

Judging from the photographs, the house had changed little since Mrs. McCaughley's day. Sandra suspected it remained so as homage to the family now buried in the ground.

"Anything?" Sandra asked as one of Malcolm Industries' security consultants, a bear of a man named Barry, who never wore a suit well, approached her.

"No." Barry shook his cropped blond head. "They're gone and by the looks of it, in a hurry. They cleared the kitchen of supplies before they went."

"Supplies?" Sandra gave him a look. "What supplies?"

"They took food with them. The upstairs closet in the hallway looks like someone went through it, possibly for pillows and blankets."

Sandra frowned. "They're trying to go to ground."

"What are your instructions?" Barry asked, subtly implying that continuing the search was futile. Their quarry had eluded them.

"I want to go back to Ellis's apartment." Sandra's eyes rested on another picture of McCaughley and her brother Alan.

"Yes, Ms. Collins. I'll get the others moving."

"Not yet." Sandra stopped him before he moved past her. "I want you to meet me there after you finish up here."

"Finish up?" Barry looked at her, puzzled. "There's nothing to find here. McCaughley won't come back. Not if she's smart."

"It doesn't matter," Sandra stated coldly, "but if she does, I want her homecoming to be memorable. So, burn it to the ground, Barry. Burn it all."

It had been ages since Anna visited a place as lovely as this.

It was easy to forget there was a world beyond homicides and vice, drive-by shootings, drug dealers and liquor store robberies. Beyond the walls of the concrete jungle was a simpler world, and half the time, it was a pleasant place to be. For a brief period before succumbing to the family business, Anna considered escaping its boundaries to see what lay elsewhere. She wanted to travel and experience a little of life's beauty before she witnessed its ugliness from the other side of the badge. It was a flight of fantasy, amounting to nothing, and Anna had enrolled at the Academy, just as destiny dictated.

Anna regretted none of the choices she'd made, standing on the porch wrapped in the old flannel robe she hadn't had the heart to give to Goodwill after her brother died. She nursed a steaming cup of coffee while admiring the resplendent beauty of Bear Mountain at dawn, wondering about the paths not taken. Her life was the job, and since her father passed, it seemed the only part of it she did not neglect. Until now, she'd never realized the depth of her isolation.

After Alan and her father died, Anna admitted she withdrew into herself. Devotion to the job seemed less exhausting or emotionally draining than caring for people who would only leave you when you least expected it. Yet in recent days her isolation appeared more acute since unfamiliar faces had entered her life seeking help. The compulsion to risk everything for elves, an insane old man and a psychiatrist was beyond her.

Even if she found Dan a little compelling.

She liked him. In the past, her relationships with men seldom survived the revelation of her career. While dating men on the force would solve that problem, she feared it harmed her professionalism to date colleagues. Since her brother's passing, Anna avoided the subject entirely, choosing to focus on her career instead. Besides, she rarely found any man who piqued her interest enough to go to the trouble.

Unusual circumstances brought Anna and Dan together. They formed a kinship in navigating some rather strange waters. As a psychiatrist, he was nothing like what she expected of one. Anna couldn't deny she was a little biased about the profession. She only encountered them at required departmental evaluations and at court, where they sometimes facilitated criminal behavior by justifying horrific crimes with insanity pleas.

However, Dan's devotion to Moses impressed Anna. Most people would be scared off after the murder of a best friend, but Anna suspected Sandra Collins had miscalculated. It only made Dan more determined than ever to protect Moses. He possessed a moral code far more substantial than all the threats Malcolm Industries could muster.

"Good morning."

"Morning." She glanced over her shoulder as the subject of her ruminations appeared on the porch, before returning her attention to the rustic scenery.

"How did you sleep?"

"After the day we had?" She crooked a brow at him. "Like a log."

"Me too," he confessed, admiring the view with her.

They arrived at the cabin in the small hours of the night. After buying additional supplies, they rode the highway all the way out of town, cautious of any pursuit. For now, it seemed they had slipped out of the city without being followed, though neither Anna nor Dan believed for a moment they were safe. With the resources at Malcolm's disposal, he could still find them, even here.

"How long have you been coming here?" She flicked a strand of brown hair from her face as she regarded him.

"Since I was a kid." Dan tried not to look in her direction when he spoke. Now that things were not so chaotic, he was noticing her far more than he should. It was saying something that she looked gorgeous despite wearing the most unflattering robe he had ever seen.

"It's beautiful." She smiled at him, "And it's nice to have somewhere you can go to just leave the city behind you."

"Yeah," Dan agreed. "Stuart and I were going to...."

Dan paused a moment at the realization he and Stuart would never do anything again. It was only a few weeks ago they talked about another trip out here. A surge of grief for his old friend came upon him so acutely, Dan couldn't breathe. For a moment, just a brief instant of time, Dan had forgotten Stuart was dead. The truth hurt now he remembered it.

"Hey, it's okay to hurt Dan. You know that better than anyone." Anna reached for his hand and held it in hers for a moment. She knew what it was like to lose a loved one and empathized with his pain. Still, she did not intend to let him face his grief alone, not when she suspected he believed what happened to Stuart was his fault.

"I do." He nodded, swallowing the grief at the loss of his best friend. "I really miss him. He's always been there, and I haven't got used to the fact he's gone."

"It will take a while, especially after the way you lost him."

"Yes, it will," Dan conceded and lifted his gaze to meet hers. Once again, the warmth in her eyes soothed thoughts of Stuart's loss. It surprised him how much being with her eased the pain, though incapable of erasing it. "I thought I'm supposed to be the shrink?"

"You are." She looked at him with the same growing affection. "But we cops deal with people dying more often than you do. We live with the possibility every day because of the badge. If not to us, then someone else. All we can do is to suffer the loss and move on. If we let it eat us up inside, it would affect how we do the job."

"Couldn't have said it better myself." Dan smiled, impressed by her insight. Under other circumstances, he would be giving the same advice. "You lose many people in your life?"

"My mother, when I was little, and after my brother died in the line of duty, my dad just slipped away." Anna blinked and looked away because suddenly, the advice she gave him a moment ago seemed hollow.

"I'm sorry."

"Thank you." She faced him again. "They both passed awhile back. I still miss them, but I'm over it."

He did not for one second believe that, but wasn't about to contradict her, either.

"So, how long do we stay here?" He decided a change in subject was prudent since he didn't want to dwell on Stuart's death. He may be a psychiatrist, but he was not ready to discuss the full extent of his grief with anyone, not even to Anna, despite how much he liked her. It was still too fresh. Perhaps when this was over, he would be ready to talk about it, and if Anna was still in his life, he hoped it would be with her. For the moment, he just wanted to get through this mess alive.

"I'm not sure. I was thinking of calling my chief at the precinct, but what do I tell him? As it is, people will be asking questions about why I didn't hand those three to the INS."

Dan sympathized, facing the same dilemma himself. "I'm sure they'll be doing the same at the hospital about what I did with Moses."

"Malcolm's a powerful man." Anna sighed. "It won't take long to track us down. We can't hide forever. He has resources we don't."

"I'm sorry I got you into this."

"I think I was on my way there." Anna patted him on the shoulder. "I was investigating the death of one of his employees and was about to interrogate him. Besides, it's for the best. You and I both have different pieces of the same jigsaw puzzle."

"Speaking of your pieces, where are the other two?" He referred to Syannon and Hadros who were not in the lodge when he awoke. Aeron had taken the duty of keeping a vigil over Moses.

"Communing with nature. They were just itching to go out into the woods. I think they've had enough of the city."

"You notice they don't sleep?" Dan pointed out.

"Tell me about it." Anna rolled her eyes, remembering how she found all three glued to the TV set for hours during the first night of their stay. "I don't think they sleep the way we do."

"Really?"

"Yeah." She nodded. "I wish we could talk to Aeron. I've got a thousand questions."

"I can relate. I get the impression Aeron wants to talk as well, but the language thing is in the way. I'd like to understand his relationship with Moses. It's definitely close because he kept watch over Moses all night so I could get some sleep."

"He's very attached to you," Anna pointed out.

"Yeah, I noticed that." Dan remembered how Aeron reacted at the first sight of him. "I think he and this War Dragon were very close."

It was not an idle supposition. Whoever he was to Aeron in the past, it was clear the elf cared deeply for him.

In another life, Dan suspected they were friends the way he and Stuart had been. Another disturbing detail, which Dan did not reveal to Anna, was his ability to guess what the elf was thinking. Dan would have put it down to his psychiatric training, but it seemed much deeper because Dan had small insights into how Aeron reacted to certain things. The elf appeared to have the same understanding of Dan, too.

Once again, the entire notion of reincarnation left Dan very off balance.

"When I was in college," Anna began, "my philosophy professor said reincarnation wasn't just coming back with the same soul but also to the same people. Your soul recognizes the people from its past. Perhaps that's why this is happening. All this is a cosmic turntable, and we're just playing the same record with a different tune."

Dan grinned at the analogy. "You have too many thoughts."

Anna laughed. "I do, but I've also decided if we're playing highlights from *The Fugitive*, then you need to be able to defend yourself."

Dan did not like the sound of this. "Like how?"

Anna smiled at him. "Trust me."

Aeron sat in the chair watching Tamsyn, unable to imagine the most powerful seraf of his day reduced to a frail and helpless old man.

During the wars, he witnessed the feats the wizard accomplished in his long life. Tamsyn stood against the Primordials in Enphilim's name. In the darkest days of Balfure's occupation of Avalyne, Tamsyn kept hope alive by telling them their best days were yet to come.

That he was here before Aeron, helpless and forgotten after four centuries, his mind in tatters, was an outrage.

During Tamsyn's absence, Aeron feared he was the last of the King's Circle. For so long, grief over the mortal companions who meant so much to him, not just his wife Melia, left him in perpetual mourning. While Aeron missed Dare, the others meant almost as much to him. Kyou the dwarf, Ronen the loyal soldier of Carleon, Kira, the warrior of Angharad. Each of them lived inside his heart but did not fill the emptiness.

The tragedy of being immortal was the continuous grief of losing loved ones.

Fear drove him to embark upon this quest, but not in a million years did he conceive he would find what he had. Not only was Tamsyn alive, but so were Dare and Arianne. True, the duo possessed no memory of the people they once were, but Aeron still recognized them. Everything about Dan was Dare. The way he looked, the stubborn desire to help no matter what the consequences, and even the same self-deprecating manner. Despite their inability to communicate, Aeron could see Dare's fierce desire to protect the weak survived in his latest incarnation.

This was the Dare Aeron knew. As if the last one hundred thousand years had melted away, Aeron stood committed to remaining at Dare's side.

The elf's ruminations ceased when he heard a slight moan and looked up to see Tamsyn stirring in his bed. Aeron remained in his chair, keeping a vigil until the old man came out of his slumber. He remembered what effect saying his name had upon Tamsyn and resolved himself not to speak it. Aeron had seen firsthand what the wizard could do when his power was unleashed.

"Good morning, old friend." Aeron spoke in elvish, recalling that Tamsyn had understood him when they last spoke.

"You are still here," Moses muttered as he looked at Aeron through heavy eyelids. "I thought I dreamed of you."

"I am here, and I came a long way to find you."

"From where?" Moses asked with a little more animation in his speech.

"You do not need to know yet." Aeron decided he would not bombard Tamsyn with too many truths about his past. In his fragile state of mind, the consequences could be another dangerous display of power. "Only that I came to take you home."

Moses sat up in his bed. "I have been lost for a very long time, haven't I?"

"Yes." Aeron nodded. "We feared you dead. I would not believe it until I saw your body for myself."

"How is it that I can understand you?" His brows rose as he waited for an answer.

Aeron smiled at him with affection. "You know several languages. The First Tongue is but one of many you speak."

"Oh." Moses looked confused because he remembered none of it. "It is disconcerting I find nothing odd in your claim to be an elf."

"You are accustomed to being around many races in your time and visited them often."

"Wonderful," Moses snorted. "I was always a vagrant."

"Not quite." Aeron laughed and paused when he heard footsteps approaching the room. A moment later, the door swung open, and Dan stepped through the doorway, followed by Anna. His eyes fixed upon Moses before resting on Aeron.

"You're awake, Moses," Dan declared with genuine relief. "How are you?"

"A good deal better, though I have an elf in my room, and I seem to speak his language."

"So, you can understand him?" Anna gazed at Aeron.

"It appears so." Moses shrugged, too weary to question why.

"Moses, can you ask him who he thinks I am?" Dan glanced at Aeron.

"I can." Moses nodded and relayed the question to Aeron, receiving an answer almost straight away. The old man raised both brows at the response, making Dan a little nervous.

"He says," Moses replied after a pause, "that you were once Alasdare, High King of Carleon, and during the Last War, they called you War Dragon. Your friends in the King's Circle called you Dare."

"Jesus. . . " Anna looked at Dan in astonishment.

"And you were his wife," Moses concluded with an amused smile.

"What?" she exclaimed, staring at Dan, whose initial shock was now giving way to a wide grin.

"You were Queen Arianne, daughter of the High Queen of the Immortals, Lylea."

"Did you say, *wife?*" Anna stammered, a hot flush of embarrassment racing to her cheeks.

"He said wife." Dan smirked.

"Get that smile off your face." Anna frowned, uncertain about how she ought to feel learning her theory of cosmic turntables meant a karmic predisposition to falling for this man.

"It's fate." He continued to smile, his hand lowering onto her shoulder before he got elbowed in the stomach.

Aeron chuckled and commented for Moses to translate.

"He says that you have changed little, Dan."

At that remark, Dan regarded the elf. "How do we know each other?"

Moses relayed the question, and once again received a response.

"He says he knew you for most of your life, that you were friends through many grand adventures. You have saved his life many times, and he has saved yours. When the elves were leaving this world, you were the reason he remained behind for as long as he did. When you passed into death, he could no longer bear to watch any more friends die. That is when he left. You were closer than brothers and more than friends."

Emotion filled Dan as the elf stared at him. Even if there was no way to prove it, Dan couldn't deny sensing the brotherhood Moses described. At this moment, he wished he remembered something of the friendship the elf cherished so much. It didn't matter, Dan told himself, the memories didn't need to be there for him to feel the power of it. Like his friendship with Stuart, the emotion still felt the same.

"Why did he come here?"

"I believe he came looking for me. It appears I have been missing for quite some time."

"Ask him if he knows why *you* came here," Dan inquired further. He didn't want to tax Moses too much by making him act as translator, but unfortunately, there were things they needed to know, and Moses was the only person alive who could understand what Aeron was saying.

Moses relayed the question. The elf turned to Dan for guidance, displaying some trepidation at answering until Dan nodded at him to continue. While they needed the truth about Moses, both were mindful of the old man's fragile state. Neither of them wanted to spark another violent episode by prompting Moses before he was ready.

"I came to find the cause of the darkness." Moses gave Aeron a look of skepticism as he translated the words. "We felt it from across the world; it penetrated the realms."

"And this evil is John Malcolm?"

Anna was still dubious on this point. She could believe the man had too much power, but she had been a cop too long to accept it was all due to his being a supernatural creature. Anna saw evil as a state of mind, not as a living entity. To think supernatural evil could exist, the kind detailed in so many religious texts, made Anna's skin crawl.

"Yes." Moses nodded without even having to translate that question for Aeron. "It is Malcolm."

Aeron reacted to Malcolm's name and continued to explain. Moses absorbed what he said with growing apprehension, and Dan was about to put a stop to it when the old man began speaking again.

"He wants to know if we are speaking of a creature called Maelog?"

"Malcolm?" Dan guessed, understanding why Aeron had brought it up earlier. Malcolm and Maelog, there were similarities in the names. Was it because they were one and the same? "It's possible. Who is this Maelog?"

"We called him Mael the Destroyer," Moses translated Aeron's words. "In his time, he laid waste to much of Avalyne, long before the world as you know it existed. The powers sending me here banished him to the Aeth where they assumed he still remains," Moses concluded, raising his eyes to meet Dan's. "He is Malcolm. I know it."

"And now he wants to kill you because you know his secret,"

"No." Anna shook her head. "He wants to kill us *all*."

## TWELVE
## NEW SKILLS

Dan stared at the gun in his hand and decided the world had gone mad when he agreed to pick up a weapon.

As much as he despised guns of any kind, he hated relying on Anna to protect him, as she had in the parking lot beneath the Monolith. There were dangerous people after them at present. He was a liability if he didn't even know how to shoot a gun. Using a firearm stabbed at his pacifistic core, but in a fight, he needed to have Anna's back.

"This is a terrible idea." Dan frowned as he studied the gun she was teaching him to load.

"Don't be such a baby." Anna gave him a look, sliding the clip into the gun. "Now this is a 9-millimeter Barretta, used by most police officers and military personnel. It has fifteen rounds and is a double-action semi-automatic weapon."

"As in twenty-two bullets?" he questioned her.

"You have a lodge in the woods, and you don't know how to use a gun? Didn't you even go hunting?"

"No," Dan returned defensively. "I come here to fish. If I want meat, I go to a supermarket."

"Look." She gave him a look of infinite patience, aware this was a big leap for him to make. "I don't much like civilians handling guns either. However, the men after us don't have that moral objection and will shoot us on sight if we're not careful. So, you need to learn to use one of these things, even if you never have to fire one."

"All right." Dan conceded the point but shared the same unease with the three brothers who looked just as unhappy at being drafted into this unpleasant exercise. "What do I have to do?"

"Now I've loaded this thing." She handed him the weapon, butt first. "Keep your finger off the trigger unless you're ready to fire. You've seen how I took the safety off. When you don't plan on using it, make sure the safety is on all the time."

Dan took the weapon in his hand, disliking how it sat against his palm. Throughout the years, he'd been in enough hospitals to see the damage these things inflicted upon the human body. It instilled in him a fierce refusal to handle one himself, but the last few days had given him a reality check he hadn't expected. After almost getting killed by Sandra Collins and her people, Dan couldn't rely on others to defend him. He wanted to help when it came time to protect the people he cared for.

"I just point and shoot?"

"Something like that." Anna shook her head, realizing this would be an uphill battle.

Dan lifted his chin to study the target in front of him. The bottles spaced along the wooden fence seemed like such a cliché but he supposed this was because it was beneficial for target shooting. The elves seemed no more eager than he did to handle the guns themselves. Dan offered no comment on their moral high ground since their arsenal included archery weapons and swords almost as deadly as guns.

"Just line up the target with the sight," Anna instructed.

Dan held the weapon the way Anna taught him and took aim. He mused briefly at the innocence of the Coca-Cola bottle, who did nothing to deserve a bullet before realizing he sounded a lot like

Hawkeye Pierce from M*A*S*H. Dan dismissed his wayward thoughts and squeezed the trigger, bracing himself for the noise.

BANG!

To the elves, it cracked the air like thunder. All three jumped, surprised by the powerful explosion of sound, and covered their ears. The shock of the weapon's booming discharge was nothing compared to the effect after the bullet struck its target. The plastic bottle flew off the fence, spinning like a wheel before it landed on the ground smoking, its body split open.

"Sireth!" Syannon exclaimed in horror as they witnessed what those weapons did. "I am glad we were not on the receiving end of that."

"We almost were," Hadros reminded, recalling their encounter with the thieves during their first night in this strange land.

"Its range is considerable," Aeron stated, more interested in the weapon's capability than anything else. "It travels as far as an arrow."

"With greater speed. You cannot chart its progress with the naked eye."

"I suppose." Aeron shrugged, unwilling to admit his bow was a lesser weapon. "I wonder what that small projectile would do, once inside the body."

"Judging by Dan's reluctance to use it, I would say the damage would be considerable," Syannon pointed out.

"Hey, I got it!" Dan said with more enthusiasm than he thought possible. He was sure his novice handling of the gun would prevent him from getting even close to the target, so this was a pleasant surprise.

"Yeah . . ." Anna stared at the mortally wounded bottle, surprised he'd made the shot. *Must be beginner's luck*, she thought. "Try another one."

"Okay." Dan cocked the weapon again, encouraged by his success. "Here goes."

He fired the weapon again and this time with a less dramatic reaction from the elves, although they still reacted to the deafening bang at the weapon's discharge. The second target, this time a Doctor Pepper can, bounced off the fence and landed in the grass nearby.

"Again," Anna ordered, just to see if the doctor could maintain his aim as well as the momentum.

Dan readjusted his stance and squeezed off another round. For the next few minutes, bursts of gunfire disrupted the serene country air. Birds in the nearby trees were frightened into flight, their wings beating a distant retreat as they fled across the sky. After a while, Dan did not even pause to take aim. It was frightening how easy it was for him to grow accustomed to the gun in his hand. He soon lost count of how many rounds he'd fired. By the time there were no more targets to shoot, the weapon no longer seemed so alien.

He couldn't decide if this was a good thing or not.

"You can have it back now." Dan handed the Barretta to her.

Anna saw the uneven trail of bottles lying across the ground, ruined by the doctor's marksmanship, and wondered if he was hustling her. She supposed it could be beginner's luck or a natural talent. It was a skill his educated background probably never exploited until now and judging by his expression, Dan was just as surprised by how well he did as she was.

"You sure you haven't fired a gun before?"

"No." He shrugged, still somewhat bothered by the idea of using one. "Never saw the need for one until now. Did I do alright?"

"Yeah, you weren't bad." Anna headed towards the fence to stack more bottles so they could resume their target practice. "For a beginner."

"A beginner?" Dan burst out, offended by her assessment of his skill. "I shot every one of those things! Those cans and bottles will threaten no one again."

"True." She tossed him a little wink. "If we're at a Seven-Eleven, we'll be completely safe."

"Damn straight."

"Reincarnated or not, they are still the same," Syannon remarked with a smile as he watched the playful banter between the two mortals. While the elves understood nothing being said, the body language between the two was clear enough.

"Fate binds them," Hadros agreed, remembering how hard Dare fell for Arianne the instant he laid eyes on her. It had amused the brothers no end to watch their mortal friend pine after the daughter of the High Queen.

Even for an elf, Arianne took her time to marry. It was tradition for elves to find mates during the first century of their lives. Those who remained unmarried beyond that period rarely wed at all. Since the Immortals viewed the concept of arranged marriages as offensive, the Queen assumed Arianne would find love in her own time. Arianne's friendship with Aeron had created the possibility of an alliance between the two noble houses, but that outcome never became a reality. They were too much like brother and sister for romantic love to form.

When Arianne chose, no one could believe it was a human.

The meeting took place purely by chance. For years, Dare, the future king of Carleon, took refuge in the house of King Halion of Eden Halas. As the last surviving member of House Icara after Balfure sacked Carleon, the elves gave the babe sanctuary and hid him from Balfure. Dare grew to manhood preparing to reclaim his kingdom, and while he was gathering allies, had chanced a visit to Eden Taryn, the home of the High Queen.

There he met Arianne for the first time, and once they laid their eyes upon each other, no one else existed for them in their hearts.

"It will be difficult for me to leave," Aeron admitted.

Syannon turned to him sharply, "Brother, you cannot stay here."

Aeron's silence made Syannon nervous. Syannon remembered the depth of Aeron's friendship with Dare. As older brothers, he and Hadros left Eden Halas first. Aeron, as the youngest, remained the longest in their father's house and grew up with Dare. Syannon did not doubt Aeron considered Dare more his brother than Hadros and himself.

"I am aware of this," Aeron agreed grudgingly. "It is just I have always found it difficult to say goodbye to him."

"He is not the Dare of Avalyne, Aeron," Hadros insisted. "He is a hundred thousand years removed from the War Dragon."

"Yes." Aeron sighed at the weight dragging down his heart. "But it is still good to see him."

"I cannot disagree with you," Syannon confessed, staring at the woman who was family and the man who was once his friend. "I too, will miss them when it is time to leave."

Anna convinced the elves to try their hand at shooting the Barretta but soon concluded that while Aeron showed some ability, none of them were comfortable firing a gun. In a way, she shared their sentiments since it seemed somewhat profane imagining an elf carrying a 9-millimeter handgun. Instead, Syannon convinced Dan to try a sword, since he was supposedly quite good with it once.

Dan's attempts to play Errol Flynn amused Anna. It was strange how fast a bond formed between the four men, even if they could barely exchange a dozen words.

Instead of trying another hypnosis session, Dan allowed Moses the opportunity to recover from the violent episode produced by the previous attempt. Although Moses seemed less disturbed around the elves, the doctor still worried about the patient's wellbeing, considering what they were discovering about him and John Malcolm. After seeing what he could do, Anna was not eager to see another burst of explosive power.

Anna sat on the porch steps, staring at the moon above the mountain. The quiet was allowing her to sift through her thoughts regarding this situation and her growing feelings for Dan. She was fighting her attraction to him because of her belief she was in control of her destiny. Her life unfolded as she willed, not to the whims of fate. The old man claimed they were husband and wife in another life. Back at the precinct, a vision struck Anna when she first saw the elves, and she recalled how incomplete that picture felt because it missed one vital element.

Was that element Dan?

She heard the creak of the door and guessed who it was without turning around to see for herself. While she fought the growing feelings for the doctor, Anna's intuition told her Dan was not facing a similar crisis. He didn't seem to have any trouble with the notion destiny bound them, no matter how outlandish the idea.

"If you'd rather be alone, I'll leave," Dan offered, standing there with mugs of steaming hot chocolate.

"Some psychiatrist. Don't you know you're not supposed to approach a woman with chocolate unless you mean to give it to her?"

Dan chuckled. "Sorry, I slept that day in class."

"You put marshmallows in it," she noted with a warm smile.

"Well, I didn't say I was ignorant." He lowered himself onto the step beside her.

"Thanks." She smiled at him as she nursed the warm mug in her hands.

"What are you doing out here?" Dan asked, although he could guess. She was a strong woman, accustomed to being in control of her situation, but the events of late were enough to shake the foundations of even the most centered person. He could see she was struggling to cope with everything they learned about the world and each other.

"Just taking a breather. It's not every day I teach a bunch of elves and a psychiatrist to shoot a gun."

Dan could sense it was more than that. He was sure her need to catch her breath had to do with learning they were husband and wife in a previous life. As much amusement as Dan drew out of the revelation, he was just as overwhelmed as she was about the whole thing. It was telling that neither of them questioned Moses or Aeron too much about their past relationship. Too much information wasn't necessarily a good thing.

While Dan was drawn to Anna, love was a long way away. Being told they were lovers in the past made it difficult to admit any feelings for each other in the present. If something were to happen between them, Dan wanted it to occur because of how they felt now, not because of some inevitable part of fate.

"Want to talk about it?"

"Is that a professional inquiry?" Anna spoke with a hint of sarcasm.

"Well, I can go find a sofa if you like, but I was just asking as a friend."

"Okay," Anna apologized for being so waspish. "I'll withdraw to the thirty-ninth parallel. I'm sorry, I'm feeling a little displaced now."

"I understand." Dan empathized not just as an analyst but as someone as equally overwhelmed by all that had taken place in the past two days. "Today, I learned to shoot a gun. Do you know how far away that is from who I am?"

"You learned fast," she complimented, aware of how difficult it was for him to set aside his natural aversion to using weapons of any kind. "And you don't have to use it just because you know how."

Anna liked his wanting to do no harm. In the police force, it was brute force that got things done, even more than talking, and Anna wished it were different. It was refreshing to be around someone who didn't think the same way.

"I know. Just like I know we'll get through this. You know why?"

"Why?" she asked, smiling, encouraged by his confidence.

"Because I'm a brilliant doctor and you got more guns in the trunk of your car than the men of Desert Storm."

She laughed and did not resist when his arm draped over her shoulder in a gesture of affection. The touch of him was electric. Her mind raced with the idea of how nice it was to have him so close to her. The shudder rippling through him did not escape her notice, and Anna realized he was just as affected as she. When her eyes met Dan's, she saw the cocky expression melt away to a more intense emotion.

She did not pull away when he lowered his lips to hers, did not resist when he kissed her. Anna closed her eyes and felt her mouth opening beneath his, entering the strange limbo between men and women who crossed the first hurdle of intimacy. Both were undecided on whether this was where they wanted their relationship to go and whether it was possible to pull back before destiny had them in its grip.

All doubt vanished when Dan reacted to the consent given by her parting lips. She was far sweeter than anything he ever tasted in his life, and he wanted to savor every bit of her. Her scent swirled around him and branded itself into his mind. His kiss was exploratory for he wanted to relish every moment. Anything more passionate could come later when they were both ready for it and the psychiatrist in him believed they were not. Instead, Dan basked in the texture of her lips. A soft sigh escaped the back of her throat as she surrendered a little of herself to him.

She tasted like marshmallows.

Anna was reluctant to abandon herself to fate, but she couldn't think, not when his touch was so dizzying. She was not one to fall for a man so quickly. Yet when Anna felt his lips tasting her as if she were something beautiful, she could not deny how wonderful he made her feel. Her pulse quickened as she allowed him to explore her mouth, taking in everything she was in a single intake of breath.

When they pulled away from each other, there was no embarrassment or regret. All that remained was a profound willingness to let those emotions take them where they may, without fear of inevitability. Anna rested her head against his shoulder while they took in the night's beauty. They chose to remain silent, content to bask in their unspoken feelings for now, with Dan concluding that cosmic turntables weren't so bad after all.

It was hope born of desperation that forced Sandra Collins to return to Dan Ellis's apartment again.

Despite her vindication at leaving the McCaughley's home a flaming pyre, Sandra felt the need to issue the same order for the doctor's apartment. So far, there was no sign of where the duo escaped with the patient. With Mr. Malcolm growing more enraged at her continued lack of success, Sandra didn't want to face his wrath again. She needed to find something to avoid more "punishment." As it was, inconvenient questions were being raised about why the respected head of psychiatry at a major city hospital had stolen a patient and fled.

She came to Ellis's apartment hoping to find something and found it as unrevealing as McCaughley's now burning home. Sandra feared this search would be just as futile as the last one. As she walked through the doctor's study, the rest of the apartment was alive with the sound of Barry and his men ransacking the place, trying to find anything that might be a clue to the doctor's whereabouts. Sandra had almost given up when something caught the corner of her eye.

"Barry!"

Within seconds, the tall man was at her side, confusion on his face. "Yes ma'am?"

Sandra did not answer at first. Her eyes fixated on a framed picture of Dan Ellis and the late Stuart Farmer displaying their fishing rods, with the outline of a mountain in the backdrop.

"Find out where this is."

# THIRTEEN
# AVALYNE

With Moses translating, Dan learned from Aeron about the War Dragon and by extension, the age of Avalyne.

Sireth created the universe on the Great Loom, and seeded the world - Avalyne, with its first people, the elves. Like most gods, Sireth departed to fashion the rest of creation, leaving Avalyne and the elves under the care of her children, the Celestials. The Celestials and their servants, the serafs, dedicated themselves to guiding this more fragile form as they explored the bountiful realm Sireth left them all.

Until one of the Celestials, Maelog, decided the best way to guide the elves was to rule them.

Mael enlisted the aid of Sireth's failed creations in the dark limbo of the Aeth. Aware of their deep hatred for Sireth, he offered them the chance to satiate their lust for chaos by laying waste to Avalyne. What became the Primordial War almost brought the elves to the brink of extinction until the Celestials granted them the immortality to continue the fight. To assist them further against the monstrous Primordials, the Celestials breathed life into the dwarfs, master builders and craftsmen who would fashion their weapons in the conflict.

## THE PATIENT

The war continued for centuries, and though the elves no longer need fear a natural death, they could still die in battle. Avalyne became ravaged from the conflict until the Celestials intervened firsthand by sending their servants, the serafs, to help and then confronting Mael directly. After a fierce battle, the Celestials banished their errant sibling to the Aeth with his army. At last, Avalyne settled into the quiet of peace.

Despite Mael's defeat and exile, Sireth revealed her unhappiness upon her return, disapproving of the creation of a second race and the granting of immortality to the elves. Yet she was not so unkind as to rescind the Celestial's gift to Avalyne's first people. Instead, she created a third race to complete her tapestry of the world. These new strands possessed the best qualities of elf and dwarf. They would be thinkers, warriors, builders, and craftsmen, who would soon spread across all Avalyne, forming the many kingdoms of Man.

The greatest of these kingdoms was Carleon.

Peace followed for more than a thousand years under the guidance of the ruling king of its noblest family, House Icara. Carleon forged alliances with elves, dwarves, and other kingdoms, maintaining peace and bringing prosperity to the lands of Avalyne. Majestic cities rose and grand monuments were built to mark the golden age they hoped would last forever.

Then, Mael's most loyal servant returned to the world and brought forward days of ash and darkness.

Balfure, a seraf, fled deep into the realm of Father Death to hide from the Celestials.

In that terrible place, he was twisted beyond all measure and emerged commanding the power of necromancy. With his armies of goblins and monsters, Balfure swarmed across Avalyne. The elves, remembering the brutality of the Primordial Wars, chose not to intervene. Instead, they remained behind the protective enchantment of the Veil, keeping their cities safe from the enemy. The Celestials recalled Sireth's displeasure at their intervention in the previous conflict and left the mortals to their fate.

The King of Carleon, aware his house was about to fall, charged his son's nurse to take the infant out of the capital Sandrine before the end. The loyal maid, pursued by Balfure's agents, fled into the woods of Eden Halas. A vain hope made her believe the forest would protect her and the babe she swore to keep safe from harm. Wounded and desperate, she died where she fell, still clutching the weeping infant in her arms.

If not for his discovery by Queen Syanne, mother to Hadros, Syannon and Aeron, the infant Dare would have died along with his nurse. Instead, the elven queen defied her husband's wishes and brought the child into the safety of the Veil. In Eden Halas, he would have no fear of Balfure while he grew to manhood.

Dan still didn't believe he held the soul of a king who united the land to defeat Balfure and win the hand of the High Queen's daughter. It seemed like a Hollywood fairy-tale. Yet according to Aeron and the others, he and Anna were modern-day versions of Dare and his queen Arianne. His rational mind told him this was insane. He was Dan Ellis, psychiatrist, born in a hospital to parents who would die twenty years later in a car accident. As much as he loved and missed them, they were far from royalty.

Maybe this was the reason the elves insisted on teaching him how to use a sword.

They must have taught Dare when he was growing up in their home and expected the same of him. Although Dan tried to argue the likelihood of him ever needing the skill, Hadros would not be deterred. Thanks to the language barrier, the doctor couldn't explain it wasn't just guns he had a problem with, but all kinds of weapons. Not that Dan thought he would ever get accustomed to using firearms, even if Anna admitted he had a knack for handling them.

As a doctor, taking life was abhorrent to him.

Hadros strode towards him as they continued the lesson. Dan guessed he intended on schooling him on the proper handling of a sword. For an instant, Dan experienced flashbacks to Sister Mary Catherine's classroom, just before he got rapped across the knuckles for screwing around. To this day, Dan got twitchy whenever he saw a wooden ruler or a nun's habit.

The lesson took place on a pleasant shore near a stream, discovered when they explored the woods surrounding the cabin. It seemed a beautiful secluded place to conduct the lesson with an unobstructed view of home in case of trouble.

"Watch," Hadros stated as he took the sword to show him the correct way to wield the well-crafted weapon.

"For a guy who never heard English until a few days ago, you're pretty bossy."

"Syn, show him," Hadros ordered in Elvish before turning to Dan and speaking in English, "Learn."

"Fine." Dan frowned as Syannon took the blade.

The elf handled it with expert skill as if performing an elaborate dance. How anyone looked graceful with a sword was beyond Dan, and yet Syannon did, especially when Dan looked so clumsy. Aeron patted his shoulder in sympathy, and Dan noticed Aeron didn't try to teach him archery skills. He wished they were able to communicate better. The only way to do that at the moment was to use Moses as an intermediary, and Dan sensed the elf would prefer to keep their conversations private.

"You do." Hadros caught his attention again as Syannon handed him the weapon.

Dan had just enough time to clutch the sword's hilt before Hadros lunged. He retreated a few steps before he raised the blade to block the swipe coming at him. Surprisingly, the lessons drilled into his head the last two days quickly resurfaced. While he was not as proficient with it as he was with a gun, Dan succeeded in blocking Hadros's attack. Still, he sensed Hadros was taking it easy on him during this sparring session, and the purpose of the exercise was to make him accustomed to handling a sword.

Dan tried improvising, remembering how Luke Skywalker did this. He soon learned movies lied when his fictional Jedi moves left him unable to defend himself against one of the more straightforward maneuvers of swordplay. He was backtracking again, this time narrowly avoiding the thrusts of Hadros's sword.

Luke Skywalker did not know squat about handling a lightsaber, Dan thought before performing the maneuvers the way he was taught. This time, he fared better, even if the elf had better reflexes than he did. Dan managed to hold his own, but deviations left openings, which Hadros exploited by driving him to the ground.

"Idiot!"

Dan stared at the elf from the dirt. "Let me guess, Anna taught you that one?"

"Do I show, not this!" Hadros repeated one of Luke's more fanciful moves that looked way better than Luke Skywalker ever did it.

"It worked with Darth Vader," Dan defended himself, and then shut up because it just sounded stupid.

"Enough," Aeron spoke up in Elvish as he approached Dan, extending a hand to the fallen doctor.

"He needs to learn how to fight," Hadros stated. "If we are to face Mael, then he must be able to defend himself. He is no good to us in the condition he is in."

"He is a healer." Aeron helped Dan to his feet. "Can you not see how difficult it is for him to pick up a weapon? You have said this is an unfamiliar world from the one we left behind. People do not defend themselves as they once did. They have militia like Anna to do that for them. You told me he is not Darc of Carleon; he is a hundred millennia from being that man."

"I suppose you're right," Hadros conceded the point.

"Besides," Syannon added, "you've seen their weapons. I do not know how useful swordcraft will be to him. Mael will use weapons useful to him, and if those . . . what did Anna call them?"

"Guns," Aeron said.

"If those guns are even half as dangerous as we've seen, then it is likely those are the weapons he would use."

"I know." Hadros gazed at Dan with affection. "I am so

accustomed to seeing Dare wield a sword. He was the best swordsman of his day."

"The greatest," Aeron corrected. "However, that time is past. This may be Dare's soul, but the memory of that man does not exist in him."

"You know it's not polite to speak in another language in front of someone who can't understand a word you're saying?" Dan grumbled.

"Rest now." Hadros came forward and took the blade from him. "Do later more."

"Do more later," Dan corrected snidely, needing vindication after the bruising his ego just took.

"Yes, yes." Hadros dismissed the comment with a wave of his hand.

"Go drink." Aeron turned in the house's direction. "Coke."

"No." Dan shook his head. "Bad for you." He punctuated each word with a translating finger.

Aeron was about to argue when he pivoted sharply away from Dan and stared at the distant cabin. From his expression, Dan guessed something was wrong. Turning to Hadros and Syannon, Dan's insides clenched, seeing them react the same way.

"What is it?" Dan asked while searching for the gun Anna insisted he carry at all times. He had put it down when his lesson began but realized now he might need to use it.

"Danger." Aeron didn't look at Dan when he answered. "Near."

When the gunfire erupted, Dan realized Aeron was right.

Not wishing to interrupt the male bonding session with the boys, Anna opted to remain with Moses. She didn't see the logic in learning to sword fight when it was so much easier to just shoot the enemy. Still, she supposed the elves had their reasons for wishing Dan to master the skill. Watching him learn how to wield a sword would have been entertaining, but she had foresight enough to know her presence would impede his concentration, so she stayed away.

Although Moses remained subdued by his medication, he was lucid enough for conversation. During these talks, Anna grew fond of the old man. The Thorazine kept him from becoming violent but the dosage was just adequate enough to curb his hallucinations to a tolerable state. Anna wondered what John Malcolm did to him. Back where he came from, Moses was a powerful wizard who frequently saved them all. It incensed Anna that the reward for his service was to have his mind tampered with in such a manner.

She supposed she warmed to Moses because of his similarities to her father. He displayed the senior McCaughley's crusty manner and cynical opinion on everything which Anna confessed she shared. It made her see why Dan was willing to risk his life and his career for this one patient.

Anna could say the same about her feelings for the doctor.

The night before saw them cross a line with each other, and Anna sensed there was no going back. If she were not in love with him yet, she soon would be.

It still disturbed her a little, despite how right it felt to be in his arms or taste his lips against hers. She wanted to love him, but she wished it were not some preordained thing written in the stars long before they ever met. The romantic in her should rejoice, but she was a woman of her times, and it was difficult to accept love at first sight.

"You are quiet," Moses observed as they sat across from each other at a stained wooden table playing a hand of gin.

"I thought you would prefer someone who didn't say much instead of someone who's always asking you questions."

"I've grown accustomed to him." Moses smiled as he watched her discarding her cards.

"Yeah," Anna agreed. "He grows on you."

"Apparently so." The old man raised a bushy eyebrow and gave her a knowing wink.

"Have you been eavesdropping?"

"Well, you were out there on the porch for quite some time." Moses's smile was pure innuendo. "One could not help but notice."

"Snoop."

"I have no memories of myself. I must take an interest in the affairs of others." His eyes gleamed with mischief.

"Well, there's no affair. We were just talking." She would sound so much more convincing if her cheeks weren't turning red.

"Elves have good hearing, and they did not hear much speech being conducted."

"You are a malicious old man with too much time on your hands." Anna made a face at him before dropping her cards on the table.

"There is nothing to be ashamed of. I see how he looks at you."

"He hardly knows me."

"Does it matter? Souls know each other."

She opted for an awkward silence instead of an answer as they continued with their game. It embarrassed her to know others were aware of what had transpired between Dan and her the night before, even though their intimacy was only a few exploratory kisses. Anna was still uncertain of her feelings towards the doctor. Everything was moving at a faster pace than she would like. Until she could understand their growing affection for each other, Anna had no desire to discuss it with anyone yet.

A windowpane suddenly shattered, making them both jump. Glass fragments sprayed across the floor as the bullet responsible struck a wall.

"Moses, get down!" she grabbed his arm, dragging him to the floor.

More projectiles tore through the air, shattering objects throughout the living room space as they struck wallpaper, picture frames, furniture, and anything in their path. Anna and Moses stayed close to the floor, with the policewoman upending the table on to its side, shielding them. She pulled out her Glock while she and Moses remained pinned behind the table.

"You should leave me," Moses shouted over the din of breaking objects. "This only came about because of me."

"I would not be so sure about that." Anna peered over the table, prepared to return fire.

This earned her a second barrage that forced her back behind the table. Their strategy was easy enough for her to guess. If Anna did not find a way to get out of this room, the enemy would overwhelm them in a matter of minutes.

"We have to get out of here!"

"That will not be easy considering our present circumstances."

"No kidding." Moses's ability to remain calm amazed Anna. "Look, when I start shooting, I want you to run like hell for the door."

"At my age, that is easier said than done."

"You will try," she snapped. "On the count of three, you go! Understand me?"

"I do this under protest."

"One." Anna shot him a look that ordered him to get ready.

Moses braced himself for the speedy departure even though the action bothered him. This was all on account of him. Dan had already lost a friend because of the doctor's fierce desire to protect him. Moses did not want anyone else to lose their lives on his account.

"Two." Anna's voice hissed in his ear.

"Maybe I should..."

"THREE!" Anna ignored him. "GO!"

He ran forward as Anna stood up from behind her hiding place and emptied an entire magazine through the windows in the direction of their attackers. More glass exploded as Moses crouched low and raced across the debris-covered floor towards the door.

Anna continued to shoot, wincing as bullets hissed past her. She did not stop firing until she was certain Moses had escaped. As soon as he vanished from sight, Anna scrambled back behind the table and released the spent magazine. The shooting ceased, but this was just the eye of the storm. She was empty, and the enemy knew it. With little choice, Anna emerged from her hiding place, crawling towards the chest where she'd stored the rest of her ammunition.

She did not make any more than a few steps when three men in black fatigues smashed through the already broken window. They rolled across the floor after making their dramatic entrance as Anna sprinted towards her spare ammunition. The men moved with surprising speed. One of them launched himself at her in a full-body tackle. Anna let out a quick cry as she hit the floor hard, pain flaring through her side as glass and wooden splinters lacerated her skin. Her gun flew out of her hand, and she made a frantic lunge to retrieve it but was yanked back by her attacker.

Despite the odds, she was prepared to fight them all because she would not go any other way. She only hoped she distracted them long enough for Moses to escape. As they advanced upon her, Anna braced herself for a beating, but instead felt something sharp bite into her neck.

"Ouch!"

Her hand flew to the source of the pain only to find something protruding from her flesh. She pulled the cold metal object from her skin.

"Oh hell," Anna swore when she recognized it.

It was a tranquillizer dart.

Even as the realization formed in her mind, her legs became weak and her head swam. She tossed the dart away, quickly deciding the only option was to try to run. Unfortunately, she managed no more than a few steps before her legs gave out, and she dropped to her knees. A wave of nausea overwhelmed her as the room spun. The faces closing in on her melted into an indistinguishable blur of color. Voices faded, and Anna's last thought before the darkness claimed her was a silent prayer Dan escaped.

Moses did not emerge from the encounter in any better condition than Anna.

They were waiting for him as soon as he stepped out of the lodge, despite Anna's valiant effort to see him away safely. They were led by a handsome blond woman with cold eyes. She appeared familiar to him, though he did not know why. He was sure they had crossed paths before, though he could not remember when that might have been. Moses soon decided that it was a question for another time as the enemy surrounded him.

He thought the men might try to rush him and was thinking of a way to get past them when one of them raised a rifle and fired. The dart struck him in the chest, and Moses could only stare at it in astonishment as the spreading warmth across his body quickly replaced the piercing pain. Despite this, Moses still tried to move, but his limbs became heavy, and he was unaware he was falling until the dirt scraped his cheek.

Through the haze, he heard the woman speak before his world faded into oblivion.

"Take him."

## FOURTEEN
## ARROWS

With Moses and officer McCaughley drugged and restrained in the van behind them, Sandra wanted to return to the Malcolm Building before anything else hampered their progress. If there was one thing she'd learned by now, it was that it was never wise to take chances. Doctor Ellis was a mere annoyance, a person who needed eliminating, nothing more. They could do that anytime. The real prize was his patient. Moses. Along with Anna McCaughley, it was all they needed for now.

The detective impressed Malcolm when she arrived at the Monolith to investigate Richard's death. Sandra supposed if Malcolm wanted another breeder, Detective McCaughley, who was attractive, would suit his purposes. Her master enjoyed beautiful women, even if he did not always use them to create his next body. Sandra had years of practice cleaning up after him when he finished with them. As one who had been on the receiving end of his sexual appetites, Sandra was glad he moved on from her long ago.

"What about Doctor Ellis?" Barry asked Sandra as the limousine left Bear Mountain behind them.

"He'll be along soon."

"Really?" Barry fingered the long, slender piece of wood he'd found on the premises.

"He'll try." Sandra scowled, sparing a brief thought to the doctor who'd brought her so much trouble by his stubbornness. "Doctor Ellis considers himself a hero, and he's just mad enough about Stuart Farmer to do something about it."

"He's just a shrink," Barry snorted with obvious derision. "What's he going to do? Analyze us to death?"

"Probably." She noticed what Barry was holding in his hand. "What is that you're playing with?"

"I found this planted in the trunk of a tree while we were sweeping the place." Barry hoped she would not disapprove because he'd helped himself to a little souvenir. The mercenary, who liked collecting unusual weapons, recognized excellent craftsmanship when he saw it. "There were a few of them, so I figured no one would miss it."

The hint of defensiveness in his voice told Sandra he felt guilty about stealing. However, his moral conundrum was ridiculous since he was presently in charge of abducting two people.

Sandra took the arrow away from him, examining the tapered shaft and the exquisitely forged arrowhead. There were intricate designs on both the wood and the metal, with writing resembling the artifacts Malcolm kept in the private study of his penthouse.

"You found this outside the lodge?" Her brow furrowed, disliking the coincidence.

"Yeah, I figure someone was doing a little target practice. Why?"

"Mr Malcolm needs to have a look at this," she spoke after a pause. Something about the arrow unsettled her, though why eluded her. "I am sure you won't mind. He'll return it once he's done."

Barry doubted it. "Yes, ma'am."

By the time Dan reached the cabin, it was too late.

The gunfire had ceased, and the silence following it spoke volumes. Chances were likely they were waiting for Dan to arrive, but he ignored the instinct for caution and rushed in. After losing

Stuart, the possibility they might take Anna and Moses from him in the same manner made Dan throw caution to the winds. He heard Syannon calling after him, but he did not answer the elf. Not when his worst fears were being realized, like bile forcing its way to his throat.

Aeron kept up with him, refusing to let Dan out of his sight despite his reckless approach. Save being shot by an arrow, the healer would let nothing stand in the way of reaching the people he cared about. Aeron marveled at how easy it was for him to fall into old habits now he was at Dare's side again. True, Dan was not the King of Carleon, but to Aeron, Dan was still the friend with whom he had shared the best days of his life.

While some of Dan Ellis's traits were distinct from Dare of Icara, others remained the same. His affection for Anna for example. It surprised Aeron the couple had not found each other before this because seeing them together was history repeating itself. Though both tried to keep their distance, the great love for each other still existed on a subconscious level. Their passion was as plain today as it was all those years before in Avalyne.

Dan's heart was pounding as he closed the distance between the woods and the cabin. As it came closer into view, he could see the shattered windows and the splintered bullet holes in the paneling. Slowing down, Dan refused to turn back even if he were running into a trap. As he told himself Anna would have tried to protect herself and Moses if need be, the number of bullet holes riddling the walls of the cabin was evidence she had not succeeded.

Nothing was as disturbing as the silence once he reached the cabin.

Dan held his breath peering through the broken windows and seeing the inside just as ravaged as the outside. His instincts told him they were alone. Sandra Collins had taken what she wanted and left. The door to the lodge was ajar, and when Dan pushed it open, he saw shafts of light crisscrossing the room through the holes in the walls. Not much had survived the barrage of ammunition and Dan was careful as he entered, avoiding the broken glass, ceramic, and splintered wood littering the floor.

There was no sign of Anna or Moses.

A quick search of the premises, stepping across the debris and broken furniture, confirmed Dan's worst fears - Anna and Moses were long gone. He should have expected an ambush, but after all the trouble Sandra Collins had gone through to acquire Moses, she would not stick around now that she had her prize. Dan's fears right now were for Anna if they decided they had no use for her.

"They're gone," Dan told Aeron, not caring whether the elf understood or not.

"Yes," Aeron agreed, not needing Dan to speak to know what happened.

"Why did she take Anna?" Dan asked out loud, not expecting an answer. It made little sense Sandra would risk abducting an NYPD cop. While he had no wish to be morbid, it made more sense for them to just kill Anna. Why take her along where she could be witness to whatever John Malcolm intended for Moses?

"They have been taken," Aeron repeated to his brothers when they entered the cabin.

"Taken? Both?" Hadros spoke with the same confusion Dan was experiencing. "Why? It is Tamsyn who is a danger to him, not Anna."

"I do not know." Aeron shook his head, just as puzzled. "It worries me."

Syannon examined the damage done to the house and decided he disliked these guns for a good reason. They required little skill to use and were indiscriminate - it was easy for innocent bystanders to become caught in the barrage. Swords and arrows only harmed one's opponent, not anyone unfortunate enough to be in their path.

"I hope she is still alive. I do not wish her harmed when we just found her."

"We do not know she is dead," Hadros returned, fearing the possibility himself. Even though it was apparent Anna was not Arianne, to them she would always be family.

Through all this discussion, Dan did not speak.

He examined the wreckage of the room in something of a daze. Even though he appeared to be sifting through the damage, his thoughts were far away from the destruction before him. In truth, Dan was on a journey.

It began with a patient who should have been sent to another facility long before he became Dan's personal responsibility.

From there, the journey took Dan beyond the safe boundaries of his comfortable existence, with possibilities that not only shattered his world but everything he knew about himself. Before this, he was a doctor, confident in his ability, the way all doctors were. They always believed life and death were something they could control.

As a psychiatrist, Dan believed healing a damaged mind was to confront the fear making it so, the way one would chase away disease with a vaccine. He wondered how many patients languished in their own private hells because doctors like him were so confident their outlandish tales could not be true. It was easier to say they resulted from a sick mind rather than to admit otherwise. When he first sat across from Moses, he'd also thought that way. He believed Moses was delusional. Now he knew better.

If he were to bring his story to any of his colleagues, Dan was sure they would fit him for his very own straitjacket too.

He had walked into this a complete novice, with no clue what he was facing, bringing Stuart unwittingly into a world so unbelievable they killed him for learning of it. He'd stumbled through this thing like a child scratching away at the dark. Even with the pieces in front of him, Dan had ignored the puzzle until there was no other choice but to believe. Even then, he still acted like a fool. Stuart was dead, and Dan still did not understand what he was facing. All he'd done was run, and he was not even very good at it because it had taken Anna to save his life. Now, Malcolm Industries had both her and Moses in their clutches.

*No more.*

Dan would not let Malcolm, Mael or whatever the hell they

called him, have either Moses or Anna. Dan had been doing nothing but reacting since this all began, running on defense instead of offense. A part of him didn't want to believe Moses wasn't human, that elves could exist, or in another life, he was a king. None of these things seemed real to him, even after Dan saw what Moses could do and met Aeron and the others. Only yesterday, he had awakened thinking this was just an unpleasant dream.

It only became real when he kissed Anna.

When their lips touched for the first time, Dan realized he had been waiting for her all his life. Without understanding how he gained this clarity or caring if it was absurd, Dan loved Anna and perhaps always did, whatever past they had lived. Once he accepted this, it became easy to believe the rest.

And for the first time, he had a plan.

He would get Anna back, and he would cure Moses. Dan would accept no other outcome, and he would tear down the Monolith to see it done.

"We have to go." Dan gestured at the elves to follow him.

Aeron understood the word "go" but their destination was another matter. Even if this was not Dare, he recognized the gleam in the mortal's eyes all too well. This was the look worn by the War Dragon before he charged an army of thousands, with little care whether he would win the day. What mattered was the will to drive his sword into the heart of the enemy.

"Go?" Aeron looked questioningly at Dan.

"We're getting Anna and Moses."

"Danger," Syannon reminded, not understanding everything the healer said but recognizing a call to arms when he saw it.

"Yes." Dan nodded. He understood the reason for their caution, but they had run out of time. "Trust me."

"Trust?" Aeron did not understand.

Once again, Dan cursed his inability to speak the language but decided some gestures were universal, no matter what their differences. He grasped Aeron's hand in his, and staring across their joined fists, he repeated. "Trust."

Aeron grasped his meaning and echoed, "Trust."

Dan turned to Syannon and Hadros, repeating the word because he could not do this without them. If they were going to face the beast that was John Malcolm, they'd have to stand together.

The advantage of being a psychiatrist in a large city hospital with no paying clients was the people he met in his line of work. A sizeable portion of his patients came to him via the New York City Police Department with criminal records behind them.

When a teenager named Luciano "Lucky" Dede knifed a schoolteacher during class after hearing voices, the arresting officers were skeptical he was ill.

The kid came from a family with known links to organized crime. The cops were convinced this was the setup for the basis for an insanity plea. Reluctantly, they brought Lucky to Bellevue for evaluation and were not shy about telling Dan this was a scam, and the boy deserved to be in lockup.

Lucky was a straight-A student who liked books and literature. During their interview, Dan learned the characters were coming alive off the pages of his books and whispering in his ear at night. After three or four sessions, Dan presented the NYPD with his diagnosis, convinced Lucky was suffering the onset of schizophrenia. The boy needed help, not incarceration.

The NYPD balked at his findings, but Dan stood by his report. They transferred Lucky to a private hospital to receive proper treatment, and Dan hoped the boy would learn to manage his condition and live a productive life. Within days of Lucky being removed from his care, Dan received a visit from a man called Vito Andretti. The meeting was brief. Andretti thanked him for Lucky's fair evaluation and declared should Dan ever need a favor, he should not hesitate to call.

Dan thought little of it until he learned Andretti was allegedly the consigliere of the Dede family. The doctor considered himself fortunate to walk away from the encounter unscathed and resolved never to call in that favor.

Until now.

"So, what's a high price college boy like you want with stuff like this?" the overweight man with a balding head and thick Jersey accent asked Dan while leading them through the cavernous warehouse in the Bronx. He'd introduced himself simply as "Nicky."

"Fishing," Dan said, marveling at the illegal merchandise stored there and wondering what kind of clientele this place had.

"Fishing?" He stared at Dan in disbelief.

"Yeah, I'm sick of using flies to lure the fish. I figure a little C4 should bring them up to the surface a lot easier."

The man uttered a laugh through his cigar and Dan saw Aeron wincing at the smells emanating from the place. The elves had an acute sense of smell, and Dan was glad he'd told Syannon and Hadros to watch the car. No point in torturing the three of them. Dan also suspected their esteemed host believed showering daily was optional.

The rows and rows of steel shelves felt like a maze. Since the establishment's operation relied on secrecy, the boarded-up windows and lack of lighting maintained the illusion the warehouse was unoccupied.

"You're real funny Doc." The man sobered up and stared Dan in the eye. "Seriously, not my business why you want this shit, but it won't be on me if you blow yourself up."

"I won't," Dan assured him. "I just want something that will go off without me being near it and when I want it to."

"I don't want to know what you want it for," Nicky stated. "But I can help you. We got remote detonators here. You can set the charges off from a mile away. Watch the fireworks from your penthouse even."

"If that means it will blow up if I press a button, that's good."

Aeron paused at a shelf and reached for something.

"Hey, don't be touching that," Nicky warned, seeing what Aeron was about to pick up. "That stuff's dangerous."

Dan stared at Nicky. "What? Are you kidding? Everything in here is dangerous."

"Well, that's dangerous *and* expensive," Nicky grumbled as he saw the doctor's friend pick up the object anyway and examine it closely.

Dan saw why they fascinated Aeron.

The arrows lying across the shelf were constructed from smooth carbon fiber. The arrowheads were neither the broad nor field type. They were conical and heavier than the shaft itself.

"It just looks like a regular arrow," Dan remarked, "except for the head."

"That's because they're explosive tip," Nicky explained. "You shoot that in somebody's ass and sitting down will be the least of their problems. You're gonna be scraping them off the walls."

"Explosive tips, huh?" Dan was already envisioning just how much damage the archer could do with those arrows in his arsenal. "You might as well put that on the shopping list."

"Are you kidding? You know how much those things cost? I had to ship them all the way from Europe!"

"I thought Mr. Andretti said you would help me," Dan accused, with just enough of an edge to be intimidating. Vito Andretti had sent him to Nicky when the doctor called in his favor. Though surprised by the doctor's request, Andretti made sure Nicky had instructions to provide Dan with everything he needed.

"All right." Nicky frowned, conceding defeat. "You and your girlfriend will send me out of business."

"He's not my girlfriend," Dan bit back.

Nicky shrugged. "Dressed like that, who could tell?"

When she entered John Malcolm's office, Sandra did so with pride at being able to give her master good news. With the capture of Detective McCaughley and Moses, Doctor Ellis was an afterthought she could deal with at her leisure. With his credibility destroyed after kidnapping a patient, Sandra intended to see he never practiced again.

If she let him live, that is.

For the moment, she would relish presenting her success to Malcolm, who had grown impatient with her lack of progress. She knew from experience he would not hesitate to remove her from her vaunted position as his trusted associate if it suited him. At the very least, he could kill her. At the very worst, he might let her live.

Sandra, who endured the punishment for past failures, preferred the former.

"I trust you have pleasant news for me?" Malcolm looked up from his laptop.

"I have them," she said proudly. "It was as I suspected. Doctor Ellis has a cabin, still listed under his maternal grandfather's name, at Bear Mountain. It took a few calls to find out where."

"And did you eliminate the dear doctor?" Malcolm asked, unconcerned with the doctor in any capacity. With the hatchet job Sandra would carry out on his reputation, the man would be lucky if he didn't see the inside of an asylum himself. It was one reason Malcolm loved the twentieth century. Humanity believed in so little.

"No, but we have the Detective and the patient. So, he may be along soon enough."

"And I trust the lady remains pristine?"

"She put up quite a fight before Barry subdued her with a tranquilizer dart. After that, she was no trouble at all."

"You've moved her to my suite upstairs?" Malcolm looked forward to seeing the woman once this meeting ended.

"Yes, but she's still out from the dart so it may be a few hours before she'll be awake. If that matters?"

Malcolm met her gaze with eyes of dark flint. "It is to me. I like the feisty ones."

"I seem to recall. Mr Malcolm, there was something else," she changed the subject. "Barry found this at Doctor Ellis's cabin. He thought it was an Indian artifact."

"And you don't think so?" Malcolm's gaze hadn't strayed from the laptop screen.

"No." Sandra strode to his desk and placed the arrow Barry found on the polished wood. "I'm sure I've seen a similar design on the artifacts you have in your penthouse."

The reaction was unlike anything she'd ever seen from him.

"Where did you get this?" He snatched up the arrow and stared at it in astonishment. For a few seconds, he forgot to breathe. A feeling he had not experienced in centuries rose from the depths of him, like the worst denizens of the Aeth.

Barry found it among the debris," Sandra stammered, shocked to see Malcolm turning white.

"YOU'RE LYING!"

She was flying, and Sandra had a second to process this before the pain flared across her body when she hit the wall. For a second, the pain was so exquisite, she thought perhaps every bone in her body was broken. Sandra landed face-first on the hard floor. Her head spun as she heard his footsteps approaching her. Through the haze of disorientation, Sandra saw him standing above her, enraged.

His eyes were black as infinity.

"Where did you find it?" he demanded, gripping the arrow shaft so tightly his knuckles were white. "Answer me, or I'll tear the skin from you right this minute!"

"I swear to you! We found it at Ellis's cabin! There were a few of them stuck in a tree!"

"Do you know what this is?" He waved it in front of her face as she struggled to get to her feet.

"No." She shook her head, terrified by his rage. "It looked familiar, but I didn't know what it was! I thought you might recognize it!"

"This isn't an engraving! It's a language!"

"A language?" Sandra was becoming more confused by the second. "Whose language?"

"It is a language unspoken for almost a hundred thousand years! It is the language of the Immortals!"

"Who?" Sandra looked at him.

"ELVES!" he shouted. "Elves!"

Sandra tried to hide the disbelief from her voice but could not quite manage it. "How is that possible?"

"I don't know." Malcolm spoke through gritted teeth, forcing himself to calm down. "If this is here, then so are the elves, and our problem with the old fool just became a good deal more complicated."

"How could they hurt you?"

Malcolm turned on her. "That is not for you to know. You will get out there, and you will find Doctor Ellis. It is time he and I met face to face. If you don't find him, I'll find you, and believe me, Sandra, you will regret every second of your last hours on earth. Do you understand me?"

Sandra gulped. "Yes, I understand."

She had to find Dan Ellis. She had to find him, or she would end up as dead as the doctor soon would be.

# FIFTEEN
# MONOLITH

ANNA WAS DREAMING.

On this occasion, her dream was unusually vivid. Its clarity told her she was more than just a spectator but an active participant. Treated to the most beautiful landscape she ever saw, Anna thought she'd strolled into Monet's Water Lily series. Pristine cascades flowed from mountains covered in lush shades of green. Color filled her senses as she gazed at a sky bursting with vibrant shades of blue and amber. The air entering her lungs was fresh, like it felt when you were out in the country.

Anna entered a forest of magnificent trees. Surrounded by shrubs with colorful flowers, she noted the exotic wildlife oblivious to her passage through their domain. Barefoot, she walked across the mossy grass, thinking she was wandering through a fairy tale. Every little girl had this fantasy, she thought with a hint of cynicism.

Anna was still admiring the surreal beauty of the place when she saw a man approaching.

It was Dan.

At least, she thought he was Dan. He was younger, not long out of adolescence, no older than twenty, she estimated. It wasn't easy to tell because he wore his hair long and the five-days stubble masked his youthful face. While his clothes made him look as if he'd stepped out of the pages of a history book, Anna suspected this was no period any modern scholar would recognize. His attire appeared medieval, with a leather tunic and breeches, laced up boots, and a cloak, with vambraces on his arms. At his hip hung a sword. Whatever Dan was in this life, he was no healer.

At the sight of her, he broke into a smile, and her heartbeat quickened when his eyes met hers.

"You honor me, my lady. I did not think you would come."

She opened her mouth to speak, but the words tumbling out of Anna's lips were not her own.

"I did not think I would come either, but I wished to hear more of your plans to fight Balfure."

"Is that the only reason you are here?" The disappointment in his voice was obvious.

"What other reason could there be?"

"I thought perhaps you felt as I did when I looked upon you, Princess."

He dropped his gaze to the verdant ground, embarrassed by the admission.

It dawned on Anna where they were now and who she was in this dream. This was not Dan. He would not be Dan for a hundred thousand years. "My name is Arianne."

"Arianne." He smiled, and when he did, Anna saw the Dan she knew.

"And you, the last son of House Icara, do you prefer I call you Alasdare?"

"To my friends, I am just Dare," he answered, unable to take his eyes off her.

That boyish look of adoration was one she recognized very well. Dan looked at her in the same way, though with not with as much unabashed infatuation. She supposed he had an excellent reason for being so damned cocky about their relationship, Anna thought with a frown. Dan probably felt they were always destined to find each other.

"Dare, then. Tell me why Eden Taryn should ally itself with you? We have no quarrel with Balfure."

"Not yet." The awestruck youth vanished, and in his place was the future king of Carleon.

Dare outlined his hopes for the future, how he intended to unite the people of Avalyne, cowering in fear under the Occupation, fearful of speaking out in case Balfure turned his eye towards them. As he spoke, Anna wondered if this was where it began for the two of them. It seemed her dreams brought her to this place, as if her subconscious mind wanted her to remember Arianne, the Queen of Carleon.

Despite their differences, Arianne had loved Dare enough to die with him. She had sacrificed her place among the Immortals to live out a human existence savagely short in comparison. As Anna saw the way Dare stared at her, so removed from a legend who would bring hope to not just his people, but to all the folk of Avalyne, it pleased her to know Arianne cared just as much for him. Even though in this place, she was not Arianne, Anna reached for him. She brushed the pads of her fingers against his jaw and his chest swelled in elation.

A pang of longing filled her then, not for this future king but for Dan, the psychiatrist who brought her hot chocolate with marshmallows. This boy might look like him, but he wasn't *her* Dan.

She was still thinking this when the world around them faded.

"Arianne..." she heard him cry out with alarm. But he and his voice became distant, and his world evaporated around her.

"Dan!" Anna shouted as she woke up with a start.

For a moment, she could only lie there breathing hard as her mind acclimated to the fact that she was very much in the world she knew and not some fairy-tale past. Once this realization settled in, memories of her last waking moments returned with a vengeance, sweeping through her mind like a tidal wave. Everything from the attack at the cabin to the sting of the dart on her neck, and the blackness following it, flashed through her mind in an instant.

Her first impulse was to jump out of the bed until she took stock of her condition. She was now wearing a pink silk nightgown, and a surge of indignation filled her at being undressed without her knowledge. The effects of the tranquillizer dart had yet to wear off completely, and the heaviness in her limbs was still present when she attempted to ease off the bed. Reluctantly, she surrendered to her situation for now. She was in no shape to attempt an escape. Instead, she took stock of her surroundings and tried to regain her faculties before considering her next move.

As she studied the room, Anna tried to remember when she saw a place furnished in this way. Black marble tiles covered the floor while the décor was very much in the spirit of Dali, with surrealistic paintings and bizarre sculptures. The furniture, what little of it there was, added a further nihilist slant to the place. While some would consider it stylish, Anna found it to be clinical and sterile. That thought sparked a memory, telling Anna exactly where she was.

*The Monolith.*

She had seen the same decor in John Malcolm's office.

"Detective McCaughley."

Anna jumped, startled by his sudden appearance.

She told herself if not for the drug, there was no way he would have snuck up on her. Then again, John Malcolm wasn't what he appeared to be, at least according to Moses and the elves. She turned towards his voice to see him crossing the floor towards her. She wished she had her gun.

The predatory gleam in his eyes reminded her of the murderers and rapists she encountered on the job. Vulnerable but determined not to show him how helpless she felt, she maintained her composure.

"Mr. Malcolm." Anna noticed the arrow in his grip and recognized it as one of Aeron's. Did that mean he had captured Dan and the elves too?

"How did you sleep?" He paused next to the bed and lowered

himself to the mattress, an action which sent dread coursing through her. The comparison to a rapist didn't seem so uncharitable now.

She hid her anxiety with sarcasm. "After being shot by a tranquilizer dart. Not well... Where is Moses?"

"Moses?" He chuckled to himself as if enjoying some private joke. "Is that what you're calling the seraf?"

"Tamsyn?" Anna blurted out and immediately cursed herself for her mistake.

"Now, how could you know that?" Malcolm's eyes narrowed, and his gaze felt sharp enough to pierce her skin and draw blood.

Again, Anna swore under her breath at her own stupidity. "He must have mentioned it while we were playing gin. You know how it is."

"I seriously doubt that," he stated with so much confidence Anna no longer doubted Dan was right. It was Malcolm who had caused Moses's condition.

"Perhaps you learned his name from whoever owns this." He held up the arrow for her to see.

"An arrow?"

"It's an arrow inscribed in the First Tongue," he stated, his gaze boring holes into her. "The language spoken by elves."

"Those little guys working for the shoemaker?"

His hand lashed out so fast, she barely had time to register it, let alone draw away before he grabbed her by the hair and pulled her forward. Their faces were barely an inch apart. He pressed the arrow into her cheek, ensuring the point was on the verge of breaking skin. His eyes were black with menace, and as Anna stared into them, she could very well believe Malcolm was some evil creature born of an ancient world.

"The Immortals crafted this, and I will know how it came to be here. I can make this pleasant for you, Anna, or I can make it agonizing. The choice is yours," he hissed, brushing his knuckles against her bare thigh.

Something inside Anna snapped at his touch. The tranquilizer might have dulled her reflexes, but the rush of adrenaline and her fear compensated. Anna slammed her palm into his face and grabbed the hand holding the arrow, yanking it forward as she used the momentum to jump off the bed. Her limbs still felt heavy, but she recovered enough to sprint for the door. As she raced towards freedom, she was suddenly swatted aside by some unseen force. The power behind it was more than enough to send her sprawling to the hard floor.

She hit the marble painfully, then saw Malcolm climbing off the bed.

"When I am done with all this, Anna, we will have plenty of time for me to show you how much pleasure there can be from pain."

Anna said nothing, but decided she better escape before she learned what he meant by that, firsthand.

The moment it appeared through the cracked window of Anna's horseless carriage, the elves bore no illusions about what it was.

Dan was oblivious to it, as were most of the inhabitants of this city, but for Aeron, Syannon and Hadros, the sight made them shudder. They'd heard tales of it from more ancient members of their race and were grateful they were not yet born when the Destroyer sought to rule the world. Avalyne had not seen its like since Mael's seat of power, Sanhael, fell into ruin during the Primordial Wars.

When the Monolith came into view, the elves knew without doubt this edifice of black glass and steel was the center of Mael's new kingdom. Its darkness filled them like filthy grease and gripped them with dread. Of all the things witnessed by them since their arrival in this realm, this was the first one they feared. Never had they imagined the enemy they would face was Mael, the Celestial banished into the Aeth. It had taken the might of all the Celestials to depose the tyrant aeons ago.

What chance did *they* have?

Oblivious to the thoughts running through the minds of his companions. Dan drove Anna's car towards the Monolith, replaying the specifics of their rescue plan in his head. Aware he was the novice in this situation, Dan crafted his idea out of sheer desperation and the belief that it was just insane enough to work. He suspected Sandra expected him to make some foolhardy attempt at a rescue, but Dan didn't care. After what had been done to the people he cared for, Dan no longer worried about how much damage he caused getting them back.

"Are your seat belts on?" Dan turned to the elves, who were staring wide-eyed at the Monolith. From what little he'd learned about Mael, Dan didn't blame them for their reaction. After what the man had done to Moses, Dan was sure "tyrannical dark lord" was a barely accurate description of John Malcolm's evil.

Aeron tore his eyes away from the structure and turned back to Dan. The healer stopped the carriage in front of the tower. While necessity demanded they travel using these horseless carriages, Aeron found being strapped in quite displeasing. However, it was the thought of facing Mael that fueled his trepidation, not the mechanical carriage.

"Danger." Aeron gestured to the Monolith.

"No kidding." Dan nodded in agreement before leaning over the elf to ensure his seat belt was securely fixed.

Satisfied they were all strapped into their seats, Dan reached for Aeron's hands and placed them on the dashboard.

"Brace yourself," he explained, trying to clarify his request with hand gestures, confident when the time came, the elves' dislike of cars would breach the language barrier.

"You too." He motioned to Syannon and Hadros to do the same.

"Dan, what?" Hadros spoke, unable to stand the suspense any longer. The eldest of Halion's sons had a terrible premonition that Mael was not the only danger they were facing. Dan's insistence that they wear these uncomfortable straps did not bode well for their present circumstances.

"Trust me," Dan muttered under his breath as he faced the wheel again, "you don't want to know."

Eyes facing forward, Dan sat up straighter in his seat as he gripped the steering wheel. Once he started the T-Bird's engines, there would be no going back for any of them. Dan wondered when he went from a respected psychiatrist to a lunatic about to wage seven kinds of hell on a corporate giant believed to be an evil dark lord. Adding to the insanity, he was in the company of elves, in a T-Bird now loaded with a lot of optional "extras."

To hell with all that, Dan told himself. The only thing that mattered was Anna and Moses.

The car rumbled to life, prompting all three elves to grip something when the vehicle surged forward. As the engine's roar climbed towards crescendo, Dan watched the speedometer dial making its steady ascent. It didn't take long for the rumble to become a roar so loud he could feel the powerful revs of the engine through his seat. Beside him, Aeron stared ahead, his jaw tense with anxiety. Dan supposed this would not ease the elves dislike for cars any time soon.

"This is why we wear seat belts!" His voice rose over the roar of the car's engine as he jammed the accelerator and sent the white wall tires jumping over the curb.

The T-Bird sped across the sidewalk, sending pedestrians running out of its path in panic as it raced across the small square. With shouts and curses at his reckless driving exploding behind it like artillery shells, the T-Bird surged forward. It reached the short steps leading to the main doors of the Malcolm Building within seconds. The elves cried out in words he did not understand but suspected were the same as those of the pedestrians swearing at them.

Metal scraped against the concrete as the T-Bird made its journey up the steps. A loud clanking noise preceded the muffler tumbling away, ripped from the underside of the car. At the top of the steps, the tiled pathway was flanked by benches where workers had lunch or fed birds and stopped at the main entrance of the building. The commotion had brought a few bystanders forward to investigate, with one or two using their phones to record the moment.

Once atop the steps, Dan shifted the vehicle into gear and sped up. The T-Bird lurched forward again, two tons of metal racing ahead with a lunatic behind the wheel. As the tires screeched, the onlookers screamed in fright, scattering in all directions to avoid being run over. The car drove across the path, on a collision course with the glass doors. The security guards having been alerted to the commotion the car caused when it sped across the walkway, shouted at the people inside to clear the area.

"Keep your head down!"

The warning came a second before the car smashed through the revolving doors, demolishing them in a spectacular explosion of glass and metal. The car's hood took the brunt of the damage but kept going, smashing its way through. Dan ignored the frightened cries and the screech of metal grinding against metal. Instead, he aimed the T-Bird at the security desk where the guards stared blankly at him in shock.

They unholstered their guns and opened fire as the T-bird sped towards them, crushing glass and debris under its wheels. For a moment, Dan feared they wouldn't get out of the way and he'd end up running them down, but the sight of the car speeding towards them ended that question and Dan was relieved when they ran for cover.

"What in Sireth's name is he doing?" Syannon swore as the carriage continued its destructive course through the front lobby of the Malcolm Building.

"I think he was trying to surprise them!" Hadros decided if he were not free of this accursed vehicle soon, he would not be responsible for his actions.

"It succeeded!"

"He has a plan!" Aeron defended Dan, refusing to think the former king of Carleon had utterly lost his mind. What made Dare such a formidable warrior in those days was his unpredictability. It appeared the trait had survived in his latest incarnation.

Once the security guards dispersed, the car continued across the lobby, heading towards the elevators at the far end of the room. On its way, it demolished chairs, chipped stone columns and shattered glass partitions. Having left a path of destruction in its wake, the T-Bird screeched to a halt, engine rumbling.

"Let's go!" Dan shouted as he unfastened his seat belt and jumped out.

The elves were more than happy to comply and freed themselves without protest. Dan grabbed the knapsack he'd stored in the back seat and searched the ruined lobby for a place to hide it. An upended potted plant at the far end of the room caught his eye, and Dan ran towards it while his companions collected themselves.

They didn't have a lot of time. The security guards had no doubt called for reinforcements and would be back once they arrived.

Finished with his side task, Dan jogged across shards of glass, broken fragments of stone and pieces of crushed furniture. The others were already at the elevators. Pushing the button on the controls, he turned to the elves who were dusting themselves off and looking to him to guide them through this perilous plan.

"Aeron!"

Security guards appeared again, returning to the lobby to confront the intruders. In seconds, they would have a firefight on their hands. Aeron armed his bow with one of Nicky's arrows, nodded in acknowledgment, and took aim as one of the elevators pinged its readiness to accept passengers. The elf retreated into the narrow space with Dan and his brothers, still fixed on his target.

He aimed for the rear section of the wounded T-Bird, at the place where Dan had shown him earlier. As the doors closed, the explosive-tipped arrow flew through the gap.

The explosion flattened them against the rear of the elevator, so loud it felt like thunder erupting within the confined space. Anna's beloved T-Bird disappeared in a fireball that spewed forth rolling clouds of flames before the doors slid to a close and the elevator began its journey upwards. The shock wave rocked the cab, but it continued its ascent without hindrance.

It was a few seconds before any of them could speak.

"Well, that went all right." Dan shrugged, noticing Hadros was visibly shaken, while Aeron and Syannon were frowning at him.

"What? I told you it would be rough."

"You! Danger, driving! Idiot!" Syannon swatted him on the shoulder.

"That's why I told you to wear seat belts." He made a slashing gesture across his body from shoulder to hip.

Aeron replied with the same gesture across his neck. "No more driving."

"Fine," Dan grumbled, then noticed the elves were no longer scowling at him.

The shadow on their faces did not result from the explosion they just escaped. Aeron clutched his bow so tightly his knuckles were white. Syannon and Hadros appeared even more apprehensive than when Dan was ramming the T-Bird through the lobby. The tension in all three betrayed their fear, as if something terrible snared them in its grip.

"What's wrong?"

"Danger," Aeron whispered, his eyes scanning the space within the elevator.

"Where?"

Hadros's eyes dropped to the floor just as the elevator halted and then dropped. Instead of going up, the elevator was now plunging fast.

"Hell!" Dan cursed and began jabbing at buttons to keep the elevator from continuing its perilous plunge.

It refused to stop even after Dan mashed his fingers against every button, lighting up the entire panel. He watched the digitized screen display the floors as they passed. His stomach hollowed as they quickly approached the ground floor. *Security must have override control*, he thought with dismay. He pulled out the gun he had tucked away and prepared himself for a fight. The elves, while still affected by the danger they were sensing, recovered enough to follow suit by brandishing their weapons in readiness.

Except the elevator didn't stop at the lobby.

Instead, it continued its downward journey with the panels no longer registering what floor they were on. Dan sensed they were going down much further than the basement parking lot. The seconds became a minute, then two with the elves growing more anxious as the time passed. Dan could not blame them. He had not foreseen this happening and wondered if it would be necessary to play his trump card a little sooner than expected.

Then the elevator jolted to a stop, dropping everyone to their knees.

"This contraption will kill us far sooner than Mael!" Syannon hissed as he picked himself up from the floor and brushed his hair out of his face.

"Calm down," Aeron barked, more concerned with escaping their confinement than the mechanics of this box. "I do not think this... device is customarily unsafe. If not, Dan would not have led us here."

"You have too much faith in him, Aeron," Hadros bit back while picking himself up from the floor. "This is not Dare."

"Dan has my faith." Aeron's tone turned hard.

"Are you sure that is wise, Princeling?" Hadros insisted, rising to Aeron's challenge.

"Hey!" Dan's voice interrupted their "discussion" before it became any more heated. "Some help here?"

The doctor attempted to pry the door open with his fingers with no success. Ignoring his brother, Aeron stepped forward, produced his dagger, and slid it into the crack between doors, forcing them apart.

"Thanks," Dan added as he helped Aeron widen the gap. From the tone of the argument, Dan assumed Hadros was unimpressed by the turn their plan had taken. Dan couldn't fault his vitriol. He guessed Hadros was questioning the choices leading them here while Aeron defended him. It made him proud knowing this elf would do so vehemently, even against his own brothers.

"Friend." Aeron gave him a brief smile. "Even idiot."

Dan uttered a quick laugh but hid the sentiment's effect on him, especially when Hadros patted him on the back in a conciliatory gesture. The elf looked guilty for doubting him, and Syannon offered Dan a smile, showing solidarity with whatever Dan planned to do next. Touched by their renewed confidence, Dan turned back to the door. "Let's get the hell out of here."

It was time to find Anna and Moses.

# SIXTEEN
## BASEMENT DWELLER

ANNA WAS WONDERING about the cause of the violent tremor rocking the building when the sprinklers came on.

She pressed her face against the glass window, trying to observe what was happening on the lower floors, but smoke obscured her vision. People were running from the base of the structure like ants after someone threw a rock at their anthill. Even though she heard nothing in her prison, the pandemonium erupting in the courtyard below was unmistakable. The activation of the sprinklers meant there was a fire in the building.

As the water sprayed across the room, Anna realized this might be her one chance at escape. She hurried towards the locked door guarded by Malcolm's thugs, watching her step to keep from slipping on the wet marble floor. Her own clothes were nowhere in this room, giving Anna the sinking feeling that Malcolm believed she would need nothing but what she was wearing during her stay in his company. The thought of what he intended for her made the normally unflappable policewoman shudder in disgust and fired her determination to escape at all costs.

Anna reached the door only to pause as the knob turned. She

quickly took up a flanking position just as it swung open. Anna held her ground, aware she had only one chance at this. A tall man in a black suit slipped past, seeking her out through the hiss of water. The distraction gave Anna a minor advantage, and she took it. Striking him across the back of the neck, the blow lacked the power to render him unconscious, but it did knock him off balance. Anna closed the distance and threw a front kick into the small of his back, propelling him forward.

The slippery floor finished the rest of the job when he lost his footing and landed face-first on the smooth marble. In the pool of water forming on the floor, a river of blood gushed from beneath his face. His body had slapped so hard against the floor that she wasn't surprised when he did not move again. There was no point in checking if he was still alive. All she wanted was the .45 in his hand.

By now, she was soaking wet, hair plastered to her face and the silly nightgown clinging to her skin. She swore at the thought of having to fight off an evil lord in a nightgown. If she got herself killed, she prayed they didn't find her like this. The indignity was too much for her feminist sensibilities.

There was no one in the corridor, and Anna suspected everyone was too busy dealing with the fire on the floors below. She needed to get lost in the evacuation process before Malcolm and his people realized she escaped. The only thing saving her from his wrath after her last escape attempt was his desire to find the elves. She could not fathom why the trio worried him so much when it was Moses who was more of a threat. She wondered what kind of danger the elves posed to him, movie star looks notwithstanding. Despite their immortality they could still die.

Why did they frighten him so?

A question for later, Anna decided as she ran past the elevator and made her way to the fire stairs. She had to find out where they were keeping Moses and if possible, rescue him without being caught herself.

When they opened the doors of the elevator, Dan almost wished they hadn't.

A wave of humid air rushed into the cool confines of the elevator, carrying with it a fetid stench, making them all wince in disgust. Dan pitied the elves' superior senses because if he could barely control his own gag reflex he couldn't imagine how they tolerated it. Beyond the bright, fluorescent lights was a dimly lit world of sinister shadows. The tiled floor beyond the doors was only a few slabs wide before turning to dirt.

Dan ventured out of the elevator and surveyed their new surroundings. No ceiling of concrete hung above them like one would expect in a building. Instead, it resembled the roof of a cave. Stalactites hung from above like serrated teeth, and as Dan delved deeper into the cavernous surroundings, he heard what sounded like the swirl of water.

"Dan," Aeron called out.

Dan looked over his shoulder and observed the elves were even tenser than he was. Aeron had armed his bow, while Syannon and Hadros took an attack stance with their swords. Their eyes were hard and set as if they expected to go into battle at any second, and their grim visage prompted him to reach for his gun. After his initial reservations about using one, Dan found the steel within his grip to be reassuring.

"Stay," Aeron spoke further, and the tone of his voice was not a request.

"What is it?" Dan looked around and found it difficult to make anything out. They were in an enormous cave. Its boundaries were so wide that the light coming from the service lamps around the elevator was not enough to illuminate all of it.

"Danger," Aeron stated tautly.

Dan heard the swirling once again. He looked towards the direction it had come and took another step forward without thinking.

"Dan!" Aeron barked sharply. "STAY!"

"We can't stay here," Dan protested, wanting to get out of this place so they could resume their search. "We have to find the others."

Aeron did not answer because like Syannon and Hadros, he knew there was something alive in the darkness, and it was coming for them. Aeron could feel its warm breath carried on the waves of sultry air filling this cavern. The unbearable stench was, without doubt, the rancid smell of rotting flesh. This cave was home to something vile, something needing to feed.

The elves' palpable fear made Dan nervous. All he could hear as he stared into the dimly lit cavern, was that damnable swirling of fluid demanding an explanation. He had taken part in dissections and autopsies in medical school and felt sickened when he recognized the stench. The warmth and humidity in the cavern made him think they were walking down the gullet of something alive.

"Aeron, can you feel it?" Syannon asked.

"Yes." Aeron nodded. "It draws near."

"We should go," Hadros advised.

"Where?" Aeron turned to him. "That contraption brought us here, I doubt it will take us away from it."

*Scrape.*

All four reacted to the scratching sound of something dragging across the ground. The shadows were flickering against the light, and a chill ran up Dan's spine. Warm, moist air washed over him and once again that fetid stench assaulted his nostrils. With a sudden flash of clarity, Dan realized something was breathing in front of him. And it was *big*.

The doctor retreated, intending to join the others when it rushed at him from the darkness.

"DAN!"

Aeron gaped as the creature stepped into the scant light of the cave. It dripped with water, and though there were still too many shadows for the elf to see it in its entirety, there was no mistaking what it was. Aeron had not seen its kind in almost a hundred thousand years, not since their battle in the Starfall Mountains. It was a swamp creature, although lack of a swamp did not affect its mobility in the slightest. It slithered across the ground like a snake, with sturdy front limbs dragging it forward. Thick, slimy tentacles flayed about its misshapen head, and one appendage coiled around Dan, shaking him hard.

"Is that what I think it is?" Syannon exclaimed as they ran towards the beast.

"Yes, yes!" Aeron armed his bow. "It is an avank!"

The avank were dark denizens of the Aeth, freed into the world when Mael sought to use them for his army. During the Primordial Wars, they infested many of Avalyne's waterways and were the bane of the river folk. After the conflict ended, Aeron thought they had vanquished the avank for all time. However, if Mael was here, Aeron supposed he would have brought with him his foul servants to safeguard his new kingdom.

It took Dan a few seconds to come to grips with the possibility of his doom at the hands of a monster resembling an unholy union of Geiger's alien and a rhinoceros. Terrified, he suppressed the urge to scream when it widened those enormous jaws and revealed long, yellow teeth capable of crunching him to a pulp. Panicked, he remembered his gun and opened fire.

Thunderous noise rocked the cavern with each gunshot as Dan fired blindly, emptying an entire clip into the creature's open mouth. The beast reared its massive head and roared in pain when the bullets tore through its flesh, but still maintained his grip on the physician.

In retaliation, it shook Dan about trying to rattle the fight out of him. The gun in his palm threatened to slip out of reach, and Dan knew if that happened, he was as good as dead. Sheer terror disoriented him as he vainly attempted more shots, only to be met with the despairing click of an empty chamber. Then, suddenly, an arrow struck the fleshy appendage trapping him.

The creature bellowed in agony as the arrow bore deep into its gray flesh, and it reacted by shaking Dan even more violently. If he didn't get free soon, every bone in his body would be broken by the time the thing got around to eating him. His gun was empty, but there was no way he could reload it without dropping the clip the way he was being viciously jostled. Instead, he reached for the arrow planted in the creature's limb and twisted hard, driving the point deeper into its wound.

The avank roared with agony again and opened its huge mouth to bite when Syannon jumped into the air, swinging his sword in a wide arc. The blade sank into the tentacle coiled around Dan, severing it completely. Once again, the cavern trembled with a bellow borne of excruciating pain. Dan had only a second to register all this before he was suddenly free and tumbling to the ground.

Black blood spurted from the severed tentacle, creating a spray as the avank swatted another limb at Syannon and sent the elf flying. Hadros was quick to move to his brother's side as the behemoth lumbered towards him. Dan scrambled free of the limb coiled around him while Hadros slashed at a tentacle reaching for Syannon. The elf was on his knees, dazed after the impact with the cave wall.

It was then Dan noticed what Aeron was doing.

The youngest son of Halion was calmly arming his bow with one of Nicky's arrows, oblivious to the furious battle being waged with an enraged monster about to kill them all.

"Dan! Help!" Aeron gestured to Syannon.

Dan nodded, guessing Aeron's plan. He sprinted across the rough ground and reached Syannon. Blood was flowing from a wide gash across his forehead as he tried to stand up. Meanwhile, Hadros was slashing at the avank, protecting his vulnerable brother. Each blow met flesh as Hadros deftly avoided tentacles and limbs threatening to swat him aside or crush him.

"Syannon!" Dan wrapped his hand around the elf's arm and helped him to his feet. His wound looked a good deal worse than it was, but his blood-soaked face still made Dan wince in sympathy. "Go! Now!"

Syannon nodded and stumbled toward the elevator as Dan

reloaded and went to help Hadros. The cavern boomed with gunfire and the creature's angry howls as both men assailed it with bullets and blade. Glancing over his shoulder, Dan saw Aeron running forward, his bow armed and ready. Aware of what Aeron intended to do, Dan grabbed Hadros's arm.

"Come on! We're going!"

Hadros stared at him curiously, but Dan didn't answer, continuing to widen the gap between themselves and the monster. The creature was in pursuit now, heading straight for Aeron who was now the closest prey within its reach.

"Aeron!" Dan called out to the lone archer standing face to face with the creature. "Come on!"

Aeron paid little heed to Dan's call. He was taking aim at the avank's most vulnerable spot, its mouth. The thing was snapping its jaws furiously, expecting a meal. Aeron intended to feed it, though the beast would not find the cuisine palatable.

Once Aeron unleashed the arrow, he did not need to see what came next. Instead, he turned on his heels and sprinted toward his companions.

The explosion was not as fiery as the one responsible for obliterating Anna's car, but it was enough. The blast blew the avank's skull apart with a climactic boom.

Blood and charred flesh splattered the walls of the cavern as the headless beast stopped moving. Its huge tentacles slapped against the ground in the wake of its fiery end. The brief flare of light from the blast flooded the chamber with much-needed illumination and revealed a swampy bog at its center.

Who knew how long the avank had survived in its murky depths until today? As foreboding as the marsh was, even more chilling was the mound of bones scattered around it. How many enemies had Malcolm sent down here? Were they all devoured by the creature now lying on its side, its black blood soaking into the dirt?

Aeron marvelled at the power of Nicky's arrows, grateful for a decisive end to the confrontation with the avank. He headed back to his brothers and his best friend, for there was little time to linger. While they escaped the fight with minor injuries, he still did not like to see the blood on Syannon's face. Dan was tending to the wound, while Hadros hovered close by, trying to hide how worried he was.

Despite the situation, Aeron couldn't help but smile. Hadros still worried about them the same way he had when they were children. Aeron supposed that no matter how old they were, Hadros would always feel it was his responsibility as their oldest brother to protect them.

The avank's demise allowed Aeron the chance to examine the cave. He wanted to find another way out of this place, avoiding the metal contraption that brought them there. Since arriving in this world, Aeron had observed that man's labor-saving devices created opportunities for disaster when things went awry.

Aeron moved past the avank's dead carcass to explore the cavern further. It appeared to be a hollowed space in the earth, with no means of reaching the surface. However, the avank, like most beasts, needed to breathe, so there had to be a way for air to reach the chamber. The fire from the burning carcass was dying, and were it not for his superior eyesight, he might have missed a small aperture at the far end of the chamber.

"Dan!"

Dan had dealt with Syannon's wound as best he could. He joined Aeron.

"What have you found?"

Aeron pointed.

"That my friend," Dan said with a smile as he saw the access way for some ancient and forgotten sewer project, "is our way out of here."

Anna stayed out of sight.

Well, as best as a woman dressed in a sheer nightgown could during an emergency with people tripping over themselves to leave the premises. She hurried down the fire stairs, grateful the only people she saw were Malcolm Industry employees obeying the building procedures during a fire drill. Anna was sure if Moses were being kept anywhere, it would be on the same floor as John Malcolm's office. The bastard would want to keep his prize close to him.

Anna knew how dangerous this was, and if she had any sense, she would get out of there. However, Malcolm's questions about the elves told her Sandra had not captured them after abducting her and Moses. Chances were Dan was safe, too. That thought alone filled her with a deep sense of relief. Losing him would hurt her as badly as losing her father and her brother.

It was a sad but undeniable fact she was fast falling for Dan Ellis.

Why else would she be risking more than just her life to recover the patient he was so determined to protect? She supposed she had been fighting it ever since she met him, but it wasn't *that* much of a fight. Since they kissed two days ago, thoughts of him filled her every moment, even though she had so far refused to play into the hands of fate by falling in love with him.

*Talk about denial.*

For a few minutes, Anna remained hidden in the corner of the corridor, considering her next move. Despite her desire to free Moses, she could not deny Malcolm terrified her. Fear was something she was unaccustomed to experiencing. In her line of work, death was a real consequence of the job, and she accepted it like most police officers. Except this was different. Malcolm wouldn't just kill her. He would make her suffer in ways she dared not imagine, and after seeing humanity at its worst, Anna could imagine quite a lot.

Footsteps against the wet floor made her shrink further into her hiding place. She stayed concealed until she saw one of Malcolm's dark-suited thugs walking past her. Anna waited until he was a few steps ahead before she crept up behind him and jammed the barrel of her gun into the small of his back.

"Move, and I'll see to it you're eligible for disabled parking for the rest of your life."

He tensed, intending to react, but Anna shoved the gun harder against his back, giving him an unspoken warning of what a terrible idea that would be.

"What do you want?"

"You know who I am?" Anna ignored his question.

"Yeah. You're Detective McCaughley."

"Good, then you know I came in with an old man . . . " Anna's eyes continued to scan the corridor to avoid being surprised by anyone coming along. "Where is he?"

"I don't know."

She knew that was a lie.

"Listen," she hissed menacingly, "aside from being drugged, kidnapped, and told I'm going to be the love slave of some Voldemort knockoff, I've had to run around dressed like a Victoria Secret model! So, don't misunderstand me when I say if you don't tell me where he is, I will blow your damn head off!"

Her words were sharp enough to penetrate, and he yielded.

"All right, all right," he submitted unhappily. "I'll take you to him."

"Thank you." She prompted him into movement by jabbing him with the gun barrel. "I'm glad you see things my way."

It felt as if they had been climbing forever, and Dan worried they would never reach the surface again. The access hatch took them through the system of underground water mains, electrical lines and other utilities required for a structure the size of the Monolith. Throughout their exhausting climb, Dan was coming to grips with the knowledge a creature that should not exist had almost eaten him. Worse yet, it had been living for who knows how long beneath New York City and feeding on the helpless victims Malcolm delivered to it.

His limbs were aching by the time they emerged from the long shaft into the basement parking lot. Emergency services were still focused on the ground level where the explosion originated. Dan led the elves to the service elevator, convinced they would be clear since fire safety protocols prohibited their use during an emergency. As reluctant as the elves were to step into another elevator, they didn't have any choice. Their detour into the bowels of the earth had cost them precious time, with the element of surprise gone for good.

"We have to find Moses," Dan spoke, aware the elves understood English a good deal better than they expressed it. "We have to take the fastest way there."

"Tamsyn," Aeron reminded.

"Yeah, Tamsyn." Dan supposed it was time to remember Moses had a name.

"Dan, Mael danger. We must stop," Syannon added, struggling to make himself understood.

"I know." Dan lapsed into silence as he pushed the button, hoping this journey to the top of the Monolith would not be as eventful as their last attempt.

Whether or not they saw it on his face, Dan feared what would happen when they reached Tamsyn. From all accounts, Mael or Malcolm was exceedingly powerful, and none of them could fight him. So why had he kept Tamsyn alive? This was the part Dan understood the least. Why let him wander around for centuries instead of dealing with the threat once and for all? Instead, Malcolm's method for dealing with Tamsyn had been to lock him away forever . . .

The answer came to him like an epiphany, and the rest of the puzzle fell into place. Dan knew how to solve their problem.

He prayed he was right because if he wasn't, he would never forgive himself.

## SEVENTEEN
## REVELATION

In the year 1630, Tamsyn arrived in the fledgling colony of New Amsterdam.

The Dutch West India Company had established the colony two years earlier after purchasing the isle of Manhattan from the natives. With the discovery of the New World, scores of colonists from Europe were sailing across the Atlantic. For those insightful enough to see it, the new continent spoke of opportunities and untold wealth. It was virgin land, untouched with untapped resources. Unlike the rest of the world, already divided into pieces by the dominant powers, the New World was unclaimed territory.

It was also the perfect place for those with something to hide.

For twenty years, he searched. He crossed the cold, imperialistic lands of Europe and entered the dry, parched deserts of Arabia. On the roof of the world, he followed the Silk Road. He witnessed what men did with the world since the days of Avalyne. Tamsyn marveled at their accomplishments, but without the Immortals and the Master Builders, they had become colder and more ruthless. It was a perfect breeding ground for evil.

He traveled many roads and made many acquaintances, but none he trusted with his identity. The men of this world were not ready to believe great kingdoms existed long before their most ancient memories of civilization. They would never accept such information and he decided not to complicate his time in the New World by volunteering it. Instead, he learned their languages and customs while pursuing the darkness that remained beyond his reach.

It was a sheer stroke of luck his search brought him to New Amsterdam.

His sources revealed a secret coven of devil worshippers who fled England twenty years earlier to escape the Inquisition. Since returning to the world of men, the precepts of organized religion confronted Tamsyn, and he found it all somewhat confusing. Despite holding the same fundamental beliefs, the practitioners of the different religions would commit unspeakable atrocities to ensure their interpretation was the one which dominated all others.

It was utter foolishness.

The New World was not only an ideal place for the secret cult who wished to escape the ruthless grip of the Inquisition. It was a place they could practice their faith without suspicion. Unless one lived in the townships, the new frontier provided ample anonymity for those who wished to remain hidden. The order's plan demanded secrecy, and they journeyed across the Atlantic to achieve it.

This Tamsyn learned from the terrified few who returned from the colonies and were grateful to confess to him if only to unburden themselves. From these poor, misguided fools, Tamsyn learned the truth. The cult calling itself the Black Serpent sought to give the devil a human shape through a ritual discovered in an ancient spell book. To Tamsyn, these texts sounded like the ancient magic used by Balfure, presumably lost during the destruction of Astaroth, the seat of his power.

The spell involved the birth of a child. Tamsyn remembered the icy chill listening to the tale told by a poor, ignorant soul who aided in unleashing a monster from his ancient prison. One of the cult's most devout followers, a young woman, had allowed herself to be quickened. The ritual, similar to the ordeal endured by Arianne as she carried Carleon's unborn prince, took place soon after.

The earth had trembled beneath their feet as if screaming out in protest. A shadow fell over the new mother as the evil spirit entered her womb, casting adrift the innocent soul of her unborn babe, and taking possession of its body. When she emerged from her trance, understanding and regret filled her heart. But repentance had come too late; her soul would be denied salvation. The babe slumbering in her womb was no longer a child, but an evil force that had chosen her well.

It understood she was too weak to destroy it.

Through some miracle, Anna and her hostage made it across the floor without being discovered, She kept a close eye on Malcolm's hired thug, and stayed alert to everything around her. Only Malcolm and his inner circle occupied this level, and she doubted they would evacuate because of a fire. Still, the emergency would bring both the NYPD and the NYFD to investigate, so Malcolm and Sandra would be busy for a while. It was the only window of opportunity Anna was likely to get. She hoped it was enough.

She wasn't blind to how vulnerable she was, never more so than when Moses's prison came into view. This, she knew, was the point where things were most likely to fall apart. She was walking a tightrope but would not leave Moses to his fate because Malcolm frightened her. Allowing fear for her own safety to sway her would be to admit defeat, and she had too much pride for that.

"He's in there," the thug grunted.

"Well then, you better open the door." Anna shoved him forward. She had already taken his gun and was aiming both weapons at his back.

He craned his neck far enough to scowl at her before approaching the door. Anna suspected there would be guards inside the room with Moses since there were none outside. Considering all the trouble Malcolm had gone through to capture Moses, she doubted he'd leave his prize unprotected.

The tall man opened the door reluctantly, with Anna shadowing him to ensure he did not warn his comrades inside the room. As expected, there was a man inside. Anna remembered Sandra calling him "Barry" before they shot her with the dart.

Like the rest of the building, the room suffered the effects of the sprinkler system combating the fire. Moses and Barry seemed just as waterlogged as she and her hostage. The old man sat in a wing chair next to the bed, arms folded, seething with annoyance at his incarceration. He glared at Barry as if his gaze alone could incinerate the behemoth of a man where he stood. However, the stormy expression on his wizened features faded into joy and relief when he saw Anna behind Malcolm's henchman.

"Anna!" he exclaimed jubilantly.

"Hey Moses," Anna greeted, just as relieved to see him.

Barry, however, was not so agreeable. The enormous man took a step towards her, and Anna knew if she allowed him the advantage, he could break her in half and give whatever was left to Malcolm.

"I wouldn't try anything Barry." Anna pointed the other gun at him. "I'm ambidextrous, and I'm sure I can take you both out before you even got to your gun. Now drop it on the floor."

"Malcolm will have your head for this, Walters," Barry hissed at his subordinate.

"I didn't have much choice," Walters explained nervously, aware of the untenable situation he was in. If he had not complied with Anna, she would have shot him, and now that he had, Malcolm's punishment would be just as final.

"Hey," Anna barked at them both. "I didn't say you could have a conversation! Drop the damn gun!"

Barry cursed under his breath and relinquished his weapon. Anna kept her eyes fixed on him as she spoke to Moses. "Moses, get it."

Moses did not hesitate. The old man jumped out of the chair and retrieved the gun. "I hope you do not expect me to discharge this thing?" Moses frowned as he examined it with distaste.

Such a crude device, he thought, not at all elegant like a sword or a bow. Actually, so much destructive power in so compact a form was somewhat disquieting.

"No, I'll handle that if he does anything stupid." Anna shot Barry a look before she brought down the butt of the gun against the back of Walter's neck. The man collapsed in a heap, having barely enough time to utter a cry of pain before landing unconscious.

Barry took a step towards her, hoping to take advantage of her momentary distraction, but Anna was too fast for him.

"Stay where you are, Barry." She stepped over Walter's unconscious form and approached him with caution. "I *will* shoot you to get out of here alive."

"The only way you're leaving here is if Mr. Malcolm lets you and I think he plans to get to know you better first," Barry sneered.

Anna felt her cheeks flush with anger, and she would have killed him there and then, but knew it would jeopardize their escape if a gunshot alerted the entire level to her presence.

"That will never happen," Moses growled, furious now he understood why Anna was captured with him.

"I think it will," Malcolm's voice remarked, startling them all.

Anna swung around and pulled the trigger without hesitation, but Malcolm had anticipated her reaction and jumped out of the way. The bullet whizzed by him and impacted on a wall. Before she could squeeze off a second shot, Barry lunged forward and grabbed her arm, wrapping a massive fist around her wrist and veering the gun away from his employer. A trail of bullets riddled the ceiling as Anna and Barry wrestled for the weapon.

"Leave her alone!" Moses shouted as he watched Anna losing her battle

"Or what . . . *Tamsyn?*" Malcolm gloated confident that he was in control of the situation.

"Stop it!" Moses cried out as the name impacted upon his psyche and brought with it pain. "You do not have to harm her! I will go with you and do what you wish but let her go!"

"Oh, *Tamsyn*," Malcolm shook his head in resignation. "You will do it anyway, and I am keeping her." The CEO of Malcolm Industries turned his head towards Anna, who was struggling with Barry.

An unseen force swiped Anna's legs out from under her. She let out a soft cry of pain as she landed hard on the wet marble. The fall was all the advantage Barry needed to subdue her completely. Once he reclaimed his gun, he aimed it at her face, intending to shoot if his master gave the order.

"Thank you, Barry. Now please escort Detective McCaughley back to my suite. I will deal with her later."

He met Anna's eyes and offered her a sadistic smile. Being under this creature's power frightened her more than dying.

"You touch me, and I'll kill you," she hissed.

"I have no doubt you will try, and I shall enjoy you even more for it."

As Moses watched Anna's terrible fate unfold, an image appeared in his mind. He did not know if it was a memory or a hallucination. He saw the face of a woman who took her own life after learning what she'd unleashed into the world. Moses remembered her, seeing the absolute despair in her eyes that even death had not erased. Now here was Anna, who had become the new object of Malcolm's sadistic desires in her attempt to save him.

He would not stand for it! People were suffering because of him!

He had to do something!

"You will not lay a hand on her, you foul creature!" Moses shouted suddenly and startled them all with the fury in his voice. "I won't let you hurt her like you hurt..." Moses struggled to remember.

The name was there . . . buried deep.

"Elizabeth!" It finally wrenched free of his trapped memories. "Like you hurt Elizabeth!"

"I didn't hurt Elizabeth, Tamsyn. *You* did, by telling her the truth."

"NO!" Moses screamed in pain, knowing Malcolm was right. His fury built up and exploded in a surge of power.

Without warning, John Malcolm was flying. He smashed into the wall before tumbling to the marble floor. Something had opened inside of Moses, something he did not quite recognize but was surging through him. He turned his attention to Barry and concentrated hard. He realized he had the power to make things move, and anger and fear brought that power to the surface.

Barry screamed as Moses flung him through a window. The bodyguard shattered the glass, allowing a rush of wind into the room. He uttered a piercing scream as his body plunged downwards.

Anna scrambled to her feet and stared at Moses in shock, unable to believe what had just happened. She retrieved her gun and aimed it at Malcolm.

"Stop!" Moses ordered. "You can't kill him with guns. You need to leave now!"

"Moses..."

"Anna, get out of here!" he ordered before she could finish her sentence. This was a great strain, and already he could see Malcolm starting to recover.

"Not without you!" she cried out, refusing to leave him no matter how frightened she was of Malcolm.

"GO! GO WHILE YOU STILL CAN!"

Anna knew he was right. This was a fight she could not win. She reached for Moses and gave him a quick embrace. "I'll find Dan, and we're coming back for you! No matter what Moses, we'll find you!"

"I know." He nodded with a sad smile. "Now hurry!"

Anguished at having to leave him, Anna knew Moses needed more help than she could provide. She ran out of the room. Malcom was recovering quickly, and Anna knew Moses could not beat him, only give her enough time to escape. She would not squander his sacrifice. She would come back for him, no matter what it took.

Anna would not let him vanish for another four centuries.

# EIGHTEEN
# MAEL

THE GUNSHOTS ECHOED throughout the entire level of the Monolith's penultimate floor.

It was a simple matter to reach this floor with everyone having been evacuated from the building after the explosion in the lobby. Fire crews and police were moving throughout the lower levels of the building and remained unaware of the drama taking place high above them.

The service elevator took them to a few floors shy of the top, so they completed the rest of the journey on foot. Dan wanted to avoid using the main elevators in case Malcolm had another monster waiting in a den somewhere.

When he heard one gunshot, followed by several others in rapid succession, Dan's resolve to remain calm shattered and he was running before he realized he was moving.

"Dan!" Aeron shouted after him. "Stop!"

"Keep him in sight!" Aeron ordered as he chased their wayward companion. After seeing the wounds inflicted by guns, he appreciated why Dan might fear either Anna or Tamsyn being harmed by one.

"Mael is close," Syannon stated as he followed Aeron. "I can feel him."

"So can we all," Hadros agreed, his jaw tensing. "His stink is throughout this place. I still cannot imagine how we are to defeat him. If he overwhelmed Tamsyn, we have no chance against the beast."

"We have to try," Aeron said. Seeing Dan turn a corner, he hastened his own pace until he caught up with the human.

Dan heard voices shouting and followed them to their source, convinced they originated from the same place as the gunfire. He prayed he was not too late. Despite his fears about how much damage Malcolm might inflict on Moses's mind, Dan dreaded even more what Malcolm wanted with Anna. It made no sense for them to take her until he remembered what Moses told him about Malcolm resurrecting himself in a new body when needed.

Who were the mothers of these children whose souls were supplanted by a monster while still in the womb? Something told Dan if he did not find Anna soon, she might find out the hard way.

"Dan!"

Dan stopped dead in his tracks when he saw Anna standing meters in front of him.

There was a moment of dead silence as they faced each other in the corridor. Since her abduction, they had emerged from separate journeys to converge at this singular point in time. For a few seconds, neither reacted. Dan and Anna just stared at each other in a rising wave of astonishment and heart-stopping relief.

When they finally snapped out of their surprise, Anna was running towards him. They met in a fierce embrace followed by a passionate kiss. The emotion surging through him at seeing her safe told Dan he cared nothing about cosmic turntables. He *loved* her. As Anna clung to him, a swell of warmth filled his heart, knowing she was just as thrilled to see him. For those few seconds, it didn't matter whether their love was predestined. How they felt for each other right then was all the compass they needed for the future.

"Are you all right?" He looked at her when they parted. "Did he hurt you?"

"No." Anna smiled, genuinely happy to see him. "Moses got me out of there. We have to go back for him!"

At that moment, the elves appeared. Syannon and Hadros reached Anna, showing their affection at seeing her again with warm embraces.

"Safe Anna." Syannon smiled. "Very good."

"Come on." Anna prompted them into moving as she started hurrying back the way she had come. "We have to go help Moses!"

As the group continued down the corridor, Dan noticed the wet nightgown plastered to her body. "What are you *wearing?*"

"Don't start with me." Anna shot him a look of utter contempt. "You have no idea what I've been through today."

"Oh, yeah?" Dan countered. "You should see what he keeps in his basement."

The chair broke beneath Moses's body when he was thrown against it. Sharp fragments tore into his flesh through the damp clothes and his body flared with pain. He took a deep breath and forced himself to his knees, steeling himself for the next assault. He raised his eyes to Malcolm, lacking the power to fight this malevolent evil who had stolen his life and made the memory of his name an agony. His strength was dwindling, and he would soon be incapable of sustaining a prolonged battle with Malcolm.

"Your delusions are boundless, Tamsyn," Malcolm growled, using the name as a weapon, and relishing it when he saw his quarry flinch. "You think because you helped bring down Balfure, you can pit yourself against *me*? Do you think I learned nothing while I was in the Aeth? They trapped me in a prison where I witnessed everything but could do nothing! Can you imagine the torture of being without form and shape and yet aware?"

"I don't have the least idea, but if they imprisoned you, then I wager it was for a compelling reason!"

A table flew at Malcolm, but he was ready for it. Just short of a few inches from him, Malcolm changed its direction so that it crashed against a wall, sending it to the floor in jagged pieces.

"You know nothing of why they locked me away." Malcolm dusted himself off and approached Moses. "My brethren and the rest of them rule from behind their curtain like cowards. Sireth charged us with governance over this world! All they did was sit back and allow inferiors to run loose over it. I gave Avalyne challenge! I made darkness that will be remembered long after Enphilim and all those fools have vanished into the End of Days. This world is ripe for a second Primordial Age. You have walked among them for four centuries. Their capacity for destruction is on a scale I never dreamed possible. Did you think mankind would survive on its own once you and the elves abandoned them?"

His words made no sense to Moses, but he knew one thing, there was still hope for man. "They have managed quite well without anyone."

"You think so, do you? They see suspicion in everything, and they revel in decadence. Even when they are pious, they twist the message of hope into restraints. Those who do not conform are made outcast or killed outright! They place their religion so loftily; it is a joy to destroy and murder in its name. Not even my armies were so bloodthirsty! The destructions these creations of Sireth can accomplish is what I love about them. I will help them reduce this world to a graveyard. When they are a memory, I will build my kingdom on their broken bones!"

"No!" Moses screamed and hurled another piece of furniture at Malcolm. Like before, Malcolm swatted it away, bashing it against the floor into a pile of fragments. Dismayed, Moses knew he did not have the strength to keep fighting. He dropped to his knees, his body weak and exhausted.

"I give you the chance I offered you four centuries ago." Malcolm approached Moses as he panted on the floor. "Join me and take your place by my side. You can show your true face, Tamsyn, not the one Enphilim and the others force you to wear to walk among men. You are not an old man despite the shape of your flesh. If you wish order, at my side, you will have it. We will put them under the same yoke, and you can see just how glorious it can be to serve me."

"I suspected I refused that offer before." Moses glared at him. "So it should not surprise you my answer remains unchanged. To hell with you!"

"Hell?" Malcolm shook his head, unsurprised by the answer. "There is no hell for us, Tamsyn, but I can make you wish for one."

Moses groaned in pain as he felt Malcolm's power crushing him in a tightening grip. His bones cracked, and the pain became so intense he screamed. The seraf's cries pierced the air as Malcolm watched his face contort with agony. Moses felt the air forced from lungs that slowly collapsed as he curled into a ball on the floor, writhing in excruciating pain.

With despair, Moses realized Malcolm might finally be prepared to kill him.

"Is that Moses?" Dan demanded as they reached the place Anna left the old man. He hoped they might snatch him and get out of there before the entire building was alerted to their presence, but it was always a slim hope. If Malcolm's thugs had not converged upon them already, they soon would.

Dan entered the room to lay eyes on John Malcolm for the first time.

His first instinct was to shoot him. Moses was screaming in agony, and even though Dan was uncertain how, he knew Malcolm was the cause. Just like Malcolm killed Stuart.

Dan raised his gun to fire when Malcolm turned quickly on him, and an instant later, he was spinning in mid-air before being flung hard against the floor. His weapon slid beyond his reach on impact.

"Dan!" Anna cried out, hurrying to his side.

"Mael!" Aeron shouted, distracting Malcom from Dan as he unleashed an arrow in the dark lord's direction.

Malcolm caught it by the shaft before the arrow could pierce the skin. Aeron reached for his dagger and flung it in swift retaliation, but

Malcolm waved it away harmlessly before it could reach him. Reacting with equal speed, Syannon hurled his sword at Malcolm while the dark lord was dealing with Aeron. However, Malcolm easily fended off the attack, seemingly invincible.

Behind them, the door slammed shut, locking them inside the room.

"How nice to meet you, Doctor Ellis." Malcolm sneered at Dan as Anna helped him to his feet.

"Stop! You're killing him!" Dan shouted.

"I would be more concerned about your own life, Doctor Ellis. You have caused me a great deal of inconvenience. I am tempted to keep you alive just to torture you for the rest of your existence, but I suppose I should be grateful. You brought me the elves *and* the lovely Detective McCaughley."

With that, he ceased torturing Moses. Moses stopped screaming, his body flopping against the floor in exhaustion when the pain abruptly left him. Anna hurried to his side, ignoring the threat Malcolm had just made on her life.

"You're never getting your hands on her," Dan hissed, wishing he had told Anna to leave instead of placing her in Malcolm's crosshairs.

"The arrogance of humankind never ceases to amaze me. How do you propose to stop me? The elves would have told you by now who I am."

"No," Dan bit back. "I can't understand a word they say, but I don't have to, to know you're on parole from wherever it is they locked you up."

"Oh?" Malcolm glanced at Aeron. "Which one are you?"

"I am Aeron," Aeron answered, trying to decide what to do. It was clear Mael was toying with them. He heard the enemy's men approaching in the background and knew time had run out for them. "Your return to this world will not go unnoticed. Enphilim knows there is darkness here. It is only a matter of time before he and the Celestials come for you. If you kill us, you will only accomplish bringing about the inevitable far sooner."

"Oh, elf, you are a fool," Malcolm replied in the First Tongue. "If I wanted to kill any of you, you would not be here. I could have ended this worthless seraf long ago, but I could not risk his spirit crawling back to his masters with news of my rebirth. Why do you think I have allowed him to live?"

"What are you saying?" Dan asked, not understanding anything being said.

"This is tiresome." Malcolm looked over his shoulder at Dan.

A flare of white-hot pain ripped through both Dan and Anna's skulls as if a dagger had pierced them. The agony was beyond comprehension, waves and waves of unrelenting pain. Dan was hardly aware of Anna's suffering because he was screaming from his own.

"What are you doing to them?" Syannon demanded and took a step towards Anna.

Malcolm swatted him aside before he took another step. In retaliation, Hadros flung his sword at the dark lord, but Malcolm deflected the blade, sending it spinning towards its owner. The blade sank into the centre of Hadros's thigh, drawing a cry of pain from the elf.

"Hadros!" Aeron rushed to this brother, now driven to his knees, impaled by his own sword. As much as Aeron wanted to attack, he knew it was pointless and seethed with impotent fury at their helplessness.

Hadros was bleeding onto the marble floor, his face etched in pain as he tried to remove the blade from his flesh. Both Dan and Anna had stopped screaming as Aeron tried to attend his brother.

"You foul beast!" Aeron cursed at Malcolm. "We will defeat you. I swear it!"

"That's for sure," Dan muttered as he stood up.

Aeron stared at the doctor, realizing Dan not only heard his words but understood them.

"You understand me?" Aeron asked.

Dan looked at him, mystified, before shooting a glare at Malcolm. "What did you do to me?"

"You need not sound so ungrateful. I found it tiresome to explain myself twice. You have an old soul, Doctor Ellis, you, and Detective McCaughley. I recognized it the first time I met her. As I made Tamsyn forget who he was, I can make you both remember you once spoke the language of the elves. Consider it a parting gift, like a last meal."

"Son of a bitch," Dan swore and turned to Anna. "Are you all right?"

"Yes," she nodded, still at Moses's side. "I feel like I have a hangover, but I'm okay."

"How touching," Malcolm snorted in derision. "Anna, say goodbye to the doctor."

"Not just yet." Dan picked up his gun without any interference from Malcolm. The doctor suspected the dark lord allowed it because he was arrogant enough to believe Dan posed no threat. "You know I've been trying to figure all this out, and finally I understand. You can kill me, and it won't make one bit of difference, will it?"

"Dan be silent." While it pleased Aeron that he could communicate with his old friend, Dan did not understand who he was dealing with. "He will kill you, make no mistake on that."

"I would listen to the advice of your elvish friend." Malcolm stared at him hard. "Provoking me will only make your death more painful."

"You know, the funny thing is," Dan continued to speak, confusing everyone around him with his insistence to be heard, "all this time, I couldn't figure out why you just didn't kill Moses. I mean, he's been wandering around for four centuries. You had plenty of time to end his life, and no one would even care. Look at him . . ." Dan gestured to Moses, who was sitting up, having finally emerged from his unconscious state. "He's just a waste."

"So far you are saying nothing compelling me to keep you alive," Malcolm scoffed, bored by the doctor's sudden diatribe.

"Dan," Syannon warned. "Please be quiet. Do not provoke him any further. He does not lie when he claims he can make your death an agony."

"Dan, what are you doing?" Anna hissed, thinking this was the worst time to psychoanalyze this guy.

Dan ignored them all and resumed, "All this time, I was trying conventional therapy and drugs to stop supernatural forces from turning this guy's mind into swiss cheese. I didn't understand what I was dealing with. You tampered with his brain so much I will never fix it, even if I had him in sessions for the next hundred years. As one of my interns put it, it's the wiring that's the problem. You messed up the part of his brain that allows him to remember."

"Goodbye, Doctor Ellis," Malcolm snorted impatiently.

Dan continued unafraid, "But then you made it all so clear."

"I did?" Malcolm was curious enough to ask.

"You did. You could have killed Moses anytime, and you didn't. Maybe that's the cure. *Death*."

And without saying another word, Dan turned to Moses and fired a bullet into his skull.

## NINETEEN
# ELIZABETH

Elizabeth Malcolm's son was already eighteen years old by the time Tamsyn found her.

She hid well. Tamsyn doubted anyone other than those with his powers would have discovered her sanctuary. The cultists gave up after a decade of searching, certain by now that if the child were still alive, he would have sought them out. As Tamsyn traveled throughout New Amsterdam, he could only imagine what effect the infant must have had on his mother.

Despite the wicked deed she committed by allowing her body to be used to birth such evil, Tamsyn held no malice towards her. Before even meeting Elizabeth, he learned of her noble lineage and the rebellious streak leading to her unfortunate situation. The coven, calling itself the Cult of the Black Serpent, exploited the sixteen-year-old's naïve spirit, filling her head with dreams of manifest destiny. Desperate to escape the duties of her life, Elizabeth embraced the fantasy with the same open arms she welcomed her lover. She never knew him, only that he was a faceless member of the cult she would never meet again.

Once pregnant, Elizabeth was sequestered away, attended to

hand and foot by the apostates of the coven. They were determined to ensure the health of the child slumbering within her. She did not understand until too late the child inside her body was a fatted calf intended for sacrifice. In the dark ritual that followed, Elizabeth knew something terrible happened to her unborn child, but what, exactly, was beyond her.

To save them both, Elizabeth stole him away, determined to raise her son in the light. She sought refuge with her family to discover their only thought was to rid themselves of her and the scandal her bastard would bring to their aristocratic name. Their help was only given after she promised to take the stipend provided and never come home again. Elizabeth accepted their terms and vanished.

Until Tamsyn found her.

When he entered the village of Kittery, the community had only kind words to say about the Widow Malcolm, who worked as a seamstress, raising her only son David. While the boy was a bit of a wayward soul, Widow Malcolm's reputation was inviolate. When he met Elizabeth face to face, Tamsyn couldn't deny being a little enamored.

Even though he wore the skin of an old man, Tamsyn appreciated beauty and Elizabeth was a lovely creature. With gold-colored hair and peach cream skin, her fragile manner hid her strength. Tamsyn could tell that the guilt of her sins weighed on her each time he stared into the reflective pools of her blue eyes. The determination to provide for her and her son despite this impressed him.

Elizabeth spent her days as the local seamstress, darning socks, and mending clothes for a pittance, in a life far removed from her aristocratic origins. She lived in a small home of rock and timber with a leaky roof and occupied her time with the books she borrowed from the local pastor. In this simple life, Elizabeth tried to instill good Christian values in her son, hoping God would save him from the evil of his conception.

She wanted to save her David's soul, unaware it had been destroyed in the womb.

Tamsyn entered her life, playing the part of a recent arrival to Kittery. He introduced himself to her and struck up a friendship. Over the coming weeks, both discovered a mutual love of books, because despite her current circumstances, Elizabeth possessed an educated mind. They would discuss William Bradford's *Of Plymouth Plantation* and poems by Anne Bradstreet. Other times he would join her for breakfast and sometimes for supper, talking about the world and the way it was.

It was impatience that forced Tamsyn's hand.

After waiting weeks for David to return from his travels, Tamsyn revealed his knowledge of her sordid past. Although Elizabeth felt betrayed by Tamsyn's duplicity, he assured her he was no worshipper of Black Serpent. Instead, Tamsyn claimed to be the father of a daughter who, like her, had been tricked into joining the evil coven.

It had taken much to convince her of his noble intentions, but finally she confided the truth about David, perhaps needing to expunge herself of the secrets she had kept for so long. She knew there was a seed of evil in her son, despite her desire to raise him as a good Christian. Elizabeth believed God might yet save his soul.

Until Tamsyn told her there was no soul to save.

Black Serpent had destroyed it the instant the Ritual of Transference took place. What entered her child's body was Mael, the great destroyer, who now had a foothold in the world. Tamsyn thought she took it rather well and wondered if, on some level, Elizabeth always suspected the truth. It did not occur to Tamsyn his revelation would destroy any expectation she had for redemption and for saving her son.

They found her a day later, drowned in the river.

Tamsyn saw her body floating in the murky water, her hair spread out like a crown, her lovely features finding peace at last while staring into nothingness. He did not know how long he stood by the embankment wallowing in the depths of his guilt, even after they took her body away. He had no doubt his callousness had killed her. In all his years of existence, Tamsyn had never suffered such shame.

Duty to his masters had made him forget the fragile heart trying valiantly to redeem itself for past sins.

With his truth, he'd taken away her hope.

It was in this state that he met David Malcolm. David, or Mael in his new skin, recognized Tamsyn instantly and knew the part the seraf played in his mother's death. David was not bereft of all feeling for the woman who had been mother to him for the past eighteen years. In learning of her death, he felt genuine sorrow at her passing.

Perhaps this was why he attacked Tamsyn with such ferocity and why the seraf was incapable of defending himself on any level.

By the time David finished with him, the mage once called Tamsyn was no more. In his place was a frail old man with no memory of who he was or what he had done.

It was almost merciful.

The back of Moses's skull exploded outward, spraying Anna with blood and gray matter. She uttered a cry of horror and shock as the gore splattered over her, stunned by what Dan had just done.

Dan saw surprise on Moses's face a split second before his features disappeared in a bloody mess of ruined flesh. He knew he would never rid himself of that terrible image. For Dan, the entire scene slowed to a crawl, and every second of the grisly vision played out in vivid detail. The power behind the .45 caliber bullet caused Moses's head to snap backwards, cracking his neck so violently Dan thought it might have broken. There was no time for Moses to utter a sound as his body fell against the floor in a heap. Blood pooled around what was left of his skull in a tide of expanding crimson.

"NO!"

Malcolm screamed in absolute fury at what Dan did, an instant before flinging him across the room like a rag doll. Dan landed against the opposite wall, his body forcing a protest from his lips in reaction to the pain.

Malcolm seethed with rage, fists clenched and waving in fury as he regarded the dead man before him. Dan tasted blood in his mouth as fell prone to the floor, a wave of dizziness rushing through him as he saw Anna standing over Moses's dead body.

Syannon and Hadros gaped at him in horror, doubt creeping into their eyes as they tried to understand what it was Dan had just done. Only Aeron didn't stare at him accusingly. Instead, the elf's brows furrowed as if trying to work out a problem in his head. Dan hoped Aeron would grasp the truth and not condemn him, any more than Dan would condemn himself if he were wrong.

At that moment, the door swung open, and Sandra ran into the room with more of Malcolm's men in tow. The woman surveyed the scene before barking orders at her subordinates to secure the area.

"What happened?" Sandra looked at Malcolm in confusion.

"KILL THEM!" Malcolm was so angry he barely managed to get the words out. "KILL THEM ALL!" He pointed a shaking finger at Dan. **"STARTING WITH HIM!"**

"I wouldn't do that if I were you." Dan shot Sandra a look of contempt. "If you know what's good for you Sandra, I'd start running now. *They'll* be coming."

"SILENCE!" Malcolm strode towards Dan, picking up the sword Syannon had thrown at him. "I will tear the heart out of you myself!"

"Who's *they*?" Anna demanded, wanting an explanation. She had to believe there was a reason for Dan's actions and that he had not just murdered Moses in cold blood.

"You released him," Aeron answered, grasping Dan's intentions. "You sent Tamsyn's spirit to the High Castle so he could warn Enphilim about Mael..."

"Yeah. It's the same reason he couldn't kill you three. You'd go to the same place, wouldn't you?"

"Yes," Syannon nodded, recovering from the shock of Tamsyn's death now that he understood Dan's reasoning. "We would join them in the High Castle."

"What are you waiting for?" Malcolm barked at Sandra as he stormed towards Dan, preparing to swing his blade. "Kill them!"

It quickly dawned on Malcom what Dan had done. He would

not use his formidable powers to kill the doctor swiftly. He would do it slowly, with his bare hands. As he moved in for the kill, Dan kicked out, striking Malcolm on the knee cap. The blow caught the dark lord by surprise, and he tumbled to the floor, the dark lord on dark marble.

Dan aimed for his head and pulled the trigger. For the second time that day, he emptied his full clip into the target.

While the entity called Mael could use his abilities to prevent swords and arrows from reaching him, bullets at point-blank range took greater effort. Some of them reached their target and sent Malcolm staggering backwards. He registered pain as they struck, and his body convulsed spasmodically as the barrage did its worst.

"You bastard!" Sandra screamed, flinging herself at Dan.

Anna dropped her in a full-body tackle before she reached him.

Both women rolled across the floor with Sandra shrieking like a banshee. As a cop on the force, Anna had experience subduing violent offenders and was more than able to handle one insane corporate executive. Straddling Sandra, the detective grabbed the blonde's head with both hands and slammed the back of her skull against the marble floor.

Sandra went limp without further protest.

Malcolm's men, reluctant to open fire with their employer and his associate in the crossfire, rushed the elves instead. Aeron reached for his arrows while Syannon retrieved his sword to battle Mael's human agents. With the speed that had earned him the reputation as the best archer in the realm, Aeron put three of them down in quick succession. Meanwhile, his older brother charged the remaining mortals, injuring one with a crippling strike and forcing the others to retreat or call for reinforcements.

Dan got to his feet and approached Moses, the gun hanging limp in his hand. He noticed Anna tying Sandra up with the electrical cord she'd ripped away from a damaged lamp. If Dan were not so sick from the surrounding violence, he would have ended Sandra's life for what she did to Stuart. She was just as guilty as Malcolm for his best friend's death.

Despite how well the others might think he conducted himself, Dan fought nausea at the sight of what he'd done to Moses. *Do no harm*, he thought, looking at Moses's dead body. He had done plenty. It didn't matter if Moses wasn't human, Dan had taken a life, an action flying in the face of everything he was. He never wanted this and wished there were some other way to free Moses from his prison.

Yet it was a truth undeniable that despite his moral objections, Moses's body was a trap, a far more effective prison than any fashioned out of steel or stone. Dan promised to help Moses and consoled himself with the knowledge he'd kept that promise, even if he'd committed murder to do it.

"Dan . . ." Aeron appeared at his side, acknowledging his dismayed expression. "You did the right thing. It is not something any one of us could have done. If Tamsyn were here, he would be the first to agree."

"I've never taken a life before, Aeron." Dan met the elf's gaze, grateful they could speak to each other now. He didn't presume to understand what trickery Malcolm had used, but the words came naturally, as if he wasn't speaking a second language. "I wish there was some other way and I'm not even sure I'm right."

"You are," Aeron assured him. "Tamsyn is a seraf of the Celestials. They chose the form in which he arrived in this realm. When he is at the High Castle, he is not flesh. He is spirit, and you cannot kill a spirit. You freed him Dan. I do not think it is an act that my brothers or I could have done in your place. Tamsyn will now do what is necessary and return to us, I am certain of it."

While it did not leave him absolved completely, Dan appreciated the effort. "I'm glad we can finally talk to each other Aeron. Thank you."

Aeron opened his mouth to respond in kind, but the desire to do so melted away when the threat of danger speared through his consciousness. The elf's gaze swung away from Dan as a wave of terrible dread swept through him.

Dan saw the sudden change in Aeron's mood and followed his

eyes when Aeron spun around. Even if he lacked the elves superior senses, he perceived the room becoming colder, with evil shadows forming around them. During his first session with Moses, Dan experienced something similar. For a second, he almost sensed Moses's powerful spirit, even if he didn't understand how to articulate it.

"Dan! Aeron!" Syannon shouted a warning from where he still attended Hadros.

John Malcolm had been lying motionless since Dan emptied a full clip into his human body. He should have been dead. But as Aeron and Dan turned around, something rose out of Malcolm's corpse. It emerged like rising smoke, in wispy tendrils swirling into a shape. Something not quite a man materialized before them. All light bled out of the room, strangled out of existence by the black form in front of them.

"What is it?" Anna demanded, horror overcoming her senses.

Neither Dan nor Aeron answered, but both suspected it was not Malcolm.

John Malcolm was the empty shell lying on the floor. The silhouette taking shape before them with its wraithlike tangibility was the essence inhabiting the bodies of Elizabeth Malcolm's descendants for the past four hundred years.

This was Mael, in his original state, lacking the body he had used to wage war across Avalyne. In his pure form, he possessed the power of a Celestial and like them existed as energy. Only Sireth could end him. Before them was the malignant form unleashed so many centuries ago in the Ritual of Transference. It was in this form he had supplanted the soul of Elizabeth's baby in the womb.

Once Aeron and the elves snapped out of their stupor at the peril unfolding before them, the elf fumbled to arm his bow. A great arm, like a curtain of black, lashed out at him, swatting the elf aside as if he were nothing. Aeron sailed across the room, slamming hard against a wall.

"Aeron!" Dan shouted, forgetting he was in as much danger when he saw Aeron sprawled across the floor, unconscious.

Dan managed a few steps towards Aeron before something hoisted him off the floor. Icy fingers tightened their grip around his neck as he dangled in the air. Struggling to breathe, Dan stared into the black cloud in front of him. It glared back with yellow eyes filled with hatred and menace. He gasped painfully as his windpipe was crushed against his spine.

Mael's evil soaked into his skin as Dan struggled helplessly within the dark lord's clutches. As his vision blurred, he reached the sad realization that his victory against Mael might be a pyrrhic one. The Celestials would get the son of a bitch, but not before he killed Dan first.

"Doom me to the Aeth will you, human?" Mael's voice was like the low rumble of a quake, just before it tore the world apart. "I will not go alone. You will pay for my destruction with your death. Perhaps I will not kill you, but pull you apart, like the wings off a fly! How would you like that doctor? Do you think your precious whore will look at you with anything but revulsion if I tear the arms and legs from your body and leave you a limbless cripple?"

Dan was incapable of speaking. The invisible talons around his throat made it impossible. He heard Anna screaming, but the lack of oxygen was making it difficult to focus. The only thing he saw was the hatred in Mael's eyes as he fought to stay conscious, trying to pry the iron grip from his throat without success. Anguish overwhelmed him, and his struggles weakened as the world turned dark.

Anna watched Mael strangling Dan with no idea how to help him. In desperation, she retrieved Sandra's gun and rushed forward, uncertain if bullets would do any good in stopping the monster hell-bent on killing the man she loved.

"Let him go, you bastard!" She fired into the thickest part of the cloud. The explosions of gunfire ripped through the air, but Anna's heart sank when she saw the bullets passing straight through Mael as she feared they would. She looked around for Aeron's dagger. Once in her grasp, she slashed at Mael's black form, frantically trying to hurt him. Dan's struggles were weakening, and Anna knew if he didn't escape Mael's grip soon, he would die.

Anna couldn't lose Dan! Not now, not after she found him!

"Watch him die," Mael spoke, his gravelly voice booming with triumph. "Watch me crush his body and devour his soul. I will not go alone into the Aeth!"

By now Syannon retrieved his sword and was rushing to help Anna. Meanwhile, Hadros had crawled across the floor towards his unconscious brother, ignoring the pain of his own injury to reach Aeron. Syannon did not know if he would be any more effective against Mael than Anna had been, but he would die trying to stop this enemy. Like Aeron, Syannon deduced Dan's plan had been to free the seraf, so he would bring word of Mael's presence to Enphilim. It was a solution none of the elves would have considered.

Dan should not have to die for his insight.

Before Syannon could enter the battle, a sudden burst of bright white light in the middle of the room halted him in his steps. Like a bolt of lightning, it struck the floor and spread out, swallowing everyone in its brilliant white glare, blinding them. A deafening roar, not unlike the blare of trumpets, filled the air and without warning, the ceiling above them tore away with a tremendous shudder.

Debris rained down on them as the unseen force ripped away stone and steel from the building's superstructure. Syannon had just enough time to pull Anna to safety. Over his shoulder, he saw Hadros trying to do the same with Aeron who was still unconscious.

"What is happening?" Hadros demanded as the wind from their lofty height rushed into the room. There was no place for shelter as the top of the building was torn away, leaving a gaping wound at the mercy of the elements. Overhead, the ominous gathering of clouds and the flashes of lightning told Syannon something was about to happen.

And it had nothing to do with Mael.

# TWENTY
## CELESTIALS

Dan had stopped moving.

From where she stood, Anna guessed if he were not dead yet, he soon would be. However, Mael's grip on him slackened with the evil entity's realization of the phenomenon taking place around them. Malevolent yellow eyes fixed on the skies above, dark even though it was hours away from dusk. The thick cumulus promised a storm of extreme ferocity as spidery webs of lightning flashed across the sky.

For the first time since their confrontation with John Malcolm, Anna sensed fear from the errant Celestial. Perhaps understanding what was coming, he uttered a loud bellow that shook the walls of the ruined building. Anna was forced to clap her palms over her ears to protect her eardrums from the deafening roar.

"NO!"

Mael's scream of indignation was followed by his release of Dan.

The doctor tumbled to the debris-covered floor and Anna bolted towards him, hardly noticing the stinging pain caused by the glass shards and jagged fragments of rock against her bare feet. When she reached him, she skidded to his side, praying frantically he was still alive.

"Dan!" She rolled him onto her lap and winced at the discolored flesh around his neck. "Wake up!"

The doctor didn't stir, and when she lowered her ear to his face, his breathing was thready. Determined to stave off the panic threatening to overcome her, Anna told herself he wasn't dead yet and rolled him on to his back. While he was still alive, she could save him.

"Come on, Doc!" She checked his airway was clear, running through the steps for administering CPR in her mind. All the while, she ignored the rising fear in her heart when Dan didn't react to her touch.

He should be doing this!

She was the cop, the one who handled the guns and fended off the thugs chasing them! His job was to be the funny smart ass, who took everything in stride and brought her hot chocolate with marshmallows. All they shared so far was this bizarre adventure. She refused to accept this was the end for them. Why did he have to be so maddening by ending up like this!

Tears of frustration ran down Anna's cheeks without her being aware of it. She pressed her lips to his and blew into his mouth, refusing to let him go. It was too soon! She refused to believe the Fates would be so unkind as to let them find each other only to split them apart a short three days later.

"Please Dan," she begged as she took a deep breath and resumed the resuscitation procedure. "Don't do this! You can't leave now!"

Dan remained motionless.

"Aeron!" Syannon tried to revive his younger brother as Hadros secured the makeshift bandage around his thigh. "Wake up!"

The side of Aeron's face was a deep shade of purple, a stark contrast to his fair skin. Syannon feared he sustained an injury too severe for either he or Hadros to attend. They were too far from home to bring their youngest brother to a healer, and neither of them trusted the physicians of this world, no matter how capable Dan seemed.

His brother's anxiety prompted Aeron to awaken from the limbo his unconscious mind occupied at present. Aeron opened his eyes as the pain from his injury reminded him of its presence, and he uttered a loud groan of pain. He recalled his last memory and sat upright, remembering they were still in danger.

The distant screaming became louder in his ears and when he raised his eyes upward, seeing sky where there should have been a ceiling. For a second, Aeron gaped at the cracks of lightning tearing through the gray clouds with spidery tendrils of blue followed by deafening bursts of thunder.

"What is happening?"

"I cannot say," Syannon was grateful Aeron was conscious again. "But I think Dan's plan to send Tamsyn to the High Castle might have succeeded."

Mael's roar of fury ended suddenly, taking with it the thunder and the lashing winds. The world seemed to drain of every sound. For a second, there was a stillness not seen since Sireth began weaving the fabric of the universe on the Great Loom.

The sky remained black, but the clouds dispersed, and the black canvas left behind glittered with the diamond dust of the cosmos.

"They are here," Aeron whispered.

The sky came alive with color, like the most magnificent firework ever unleashed. For a second, it seemed like a star exploded, brightening the darkness with vibrant sapphire light. It bloomed like a flower before it was joined by another burst of color. Like a drop of sunlight splattering across the sky, others followed, each as dazzling as the first. It covered every inch of the heavens until anyone who saw it became lost in the beauty of the canvas being painted above them.

No one who saw it, save the elves, understood what they were seeing.

Every elf learned from birth the history of their creation. In a time before the universe had shape, Sireth the Creator gave life to the Void. With her Great Loom, she began weaving the tapestry of the cosmos, creating the first thread with its distinct color and purpose.

Each thread would intertwine to form the fabric of creation. The first of these was Enphilim, and as her First Born, he was her most loyal son.

Together, he would guide the others who followed, aiding Sireth in creating the cosmos.

Not since the Primordial Wars had the Celestials appeared like this. Their threads stretched across the sky beyond the Monolith, reaching across the city like banners of color. People paused in the streets, staring in wonder, captivated by the vibrant display and the beauty that made everything hard disappear for a brief time.

It lifted them to a place beyond the flesh, where they glimpsed something more significant than their mortal existence. The starlight that had vanished from their hearts when the Immortals left Avalyne, burned brief for a time. Tears came, smiles stretched across jaded faces and hope came alive in everyone.

Later, there would be scientific explanations for what took place this day, but not one person wouldn't long to see the phenomena again.

The elves were just as transfixed by the Celestials return to the world. Dan's plan had succeeded. In ending Tamsyn's mortal life, he enabled the Celestials to come here to end the threat of Mael once and for all.

Amid all of this, a voice spoke in Aeron's mind.

*You must leave now.*

Through the fog of his unconscious mind, Dan Ellis was being surrounded by ribbons of colour.

In the dismal place he was struggling to escape, the magnificence of it shredded the darkness until Dan turned away from it for fear of blindness. Yet when it chased away the fog, shades of creation swirled around him, bursting with unique light. It was the most beautiful thing he had ever seen in his life, and he would dream of it until the day he died.

"Doctor, you must wake up."

"Moses!" Dan exclaimed at the sight of the man stepping out of the rainbow clouds.

At least he thought it was Moses. The face was the same, but he was no longer an old man of seventy. Now he was closer to his late fifties. His hair and beard were more brown than gray, and the injuries inflicted by Malcolm's men and himself were absent. Seeing him alive and well, even in the middle of this vortex of light, filled Dan with more joy than he could express.

"It appears I do not need further therapy." Tamsyn grinned as both men embraced briefly.

"What is all this?" Dan asked, his gaze sweeping over their surroundings once he pulled away.

"It's how your mind is perceiving my masters," Moses explained, admiring at the vortex with affection. "There's much excitement taking place in the waking world Dan, so you need to wake up."

"My mind?" Dan didn't understand, but it mattered little in the face of Moses's presence before him. "Moses, was I right? I didn't kill you?"

"Of course not." Tamsyn allayed his fears immediately, feeling great affection for this mortal who risked everything, including his soul, to save him. "You undertook what you did at great expense to your conscience, and I grieve the pain it caused you, but you saved me, Dan. In fact, you saved us all."

Dan's smile faded a little as he allowed Tamsyn to see his relief knowing he killed no one. "I was praying I wasn't wrong. Even after I pulled the trigger, it terrified me I made a mistake."

"You did not." Tamsyn clutched his shoulder. "You freed me Dan, and I am most grateful for that."

Emotion churned inside Dan, but he responded sedately. "I promised you we would find your past together, no matter what. I couldn't do anything less. You were my patient."

"Thank you." Tamsyn smiled at him. "Now, it is time for me to help you. Dan, you must wake. The Celestials are here, and you cannot remain where you are."

"I don't understand..." Dan said when he heard someone else calling him through the cosmic storm in his mind. It was a voice of desperation, tugging at his heart. "Tamsyn, what's going on..."

But Tamsyn had vanished, and Dan was once again alone, alone in the wilderness with only one voice left to guide him out of this place.

*"Please Dan, don't do this to me! You can't leave me now!"*

It was Anna.

"Anna!"

Dan gasped at the sight of her kneeling over him, and behind her was a vision no words could describe. Tamsyn was right. The Celestials were here.

Dan realized his head was being cradled in Anna's arms, and when he stared into her face, there were tears of relief. She embraced him hard, planting soft kisses over his face as she expressed her relief with more emotion than he ever saw her display. When their lips met, it was the sweetest kiss he had ever had in his life because the scene above them made it even more beautiful.

"Anna, Dan," Aeron's voice broke the tender moment. "We must leave."

Both Dan and Anna looked up at the elf to see the urgency in his eyes. Aeron nodded towards Mael, who was still standing in the middle of the room, struggling against the threads of energy binding him. They enveloped him until the darkness of his form became thin creases of black against their brilliance. His screams became muffled, silenced by the ribbons of Celestial power, his strands joining their threads again.

As the radiance from the threads expanded, the walls of the building quaked once more. Unlike the tremors caused by the explosion, this one increased in intensity and Dan agreed it was an excellent idea to vacate the premises.

Dan allowed Aeron and Anna to help him to his feet, with Syannon doing the same with Hadros. They made their way across the debris-covered floor and noticed Sandra's unconscious form where Anna had left her. Anna looked at Dan, questioning whether they should take her with them. Dan thought of Stuart, who had died so needlessly because of this woman, and reached his decision.

Let her face judgement with her master.

With the structural failure of the building imminent, they avoided the elevators and so the journey to the ground was long and arduous with Hadros suffering the worst of it. On the way down, Dan recovered enough to support himself, allowing Aeron to help with his brother's descent. The tremors were becoming more violent with each floor they passed.

Dan thanked God building management evacuated the place earlier. Most of Malcolm's employees did not know their master was an ancient god from beyond. They were innocent workers, going about their day-to-day lives with no notion of Malcolm's ambitions to create a second hell on earth.

The building continued to quake all the way to the lobby. Once they emerged into the hall, the effects of the C4 explosion were apparent from the utter destruction.

Outside, people had gathered on the street when Dan, Anna and the elves left the Monolith. Whether they were watching the light show across the sky or the impending doom of the Malcolm building, Dan could not say. Most seemed mesmerized by the dazzling aerial display, basking in the cosmic fireworks coming out of nowhere like magic.

What the elves could not perceive but Mael could, was his brothers and sisters, all children of Sireth surrounding him. He had seen none of them since the end of the Primordial Wars when they intervened to put an end to his warmongering. The world before him vanished from view as the threads binding him swallowed him whole. Their light exploded outwards like a star being born, and Mael knew it was over.

They had come for him.

From a distance, Dan and the others watched the Malcolm Building collapsed almost as chillingly as the Twin Towers. The

Monolith disintegrated, starting from the remains of the top floor before working its way down to the ground. People regained their senses at that point, all too familiar with what was coming after the tragedy of 9/11. They scattered beyond the reach of the blast, running as fast as they could to reach minimum safe distance.

When the deafening blast of the building's destruction tore through the air, the spectacle compelled everyone to look as the Monolith collapsed on itself. The building disappeared before their eyes, the ball of dust and smoke shrinking into a cone-shaped pile. In the aftermath, the phenomena above vanished. The skies cleared and became as sunny as a late New York afternoon could be.

It was over.

"Where they...?" Anna asked, looking at the elves for an answer.

"They did what they came to do," Syannon spoke while staring at the sky, wearing a slight smile.

"It was so beautiful," Anna whispered. She closed her eyes and revisited the memory in her mind. "It was like the universe was being born."

"You are not far wrong," Hadros agreed. "We are told that is how it came to be."

Anna could see the elves were just as affected by this as she. She felt a wave of affection for the trio and knew it didn't matter if she didn't remember being Arianne. Anna and the queen of Carleon shared the same love for them. Anna hugged Hadros and felt for the first time in too long that she was not alone. They were her family.

Dan was still staring at the ruins of the Monolith in deep thought. This nightmare was over, but Moses was not here. He wondered if he would ever see the man again.

"Dan . . ." Aeron placed a hand on his shoulder, noting the sadness on Dan's face. "Are you well?"

"Moses - I mean, Tamsyn, should be here."

"He should be," Aeron nodded in agreement. "But this task was the Celestials alone to undertake. They could not send him to accomplish it in their stead."

"I know." Dan remembered the strange dream where Tamsyn reached out to him. "I think he came to me. I think he wanted me to know he was all right."

Aeron did not doubt it. "He spoke to me, too."

Dan's eyes widened. "He did?"

"Yes. He told me we had to flee Mael's tower. I believe Tamsyn is now in the High Castle because you ended his task here. All you did by killing the body was send him on his way much faster."

"So, he is really alive? Back in this High Castle?"

"Yes. No doubt when we return, Tamsyn will be full of stories."

"I'm glad." Dan grinned at Anna, pleased to hear this. "You can take him my bill."

# THE VEIL

### Three Weeks Later

Dan stared across the pier at the boat where Anna was waving at him.

He offered her a smile and returned the gesture before resuming his journey across the deck. The Anemone was a motor yacht he and Anna bought almost a week ago. She was a trawler-style vessel, seventy-five feet with a twenty-foot beam and a top speed of twelve knots. The Anemone came complete with spacious living areas and cost Anna and Dan every cent they possessed. In less than a day, it would be ready to sail from its dock at Point Pleasant Borough where it had spent the last week.

Anna received a hefty insurance settlement for her house, razed to the ground by Sandra Collins during the woman's rabid pursuit of them. Finding out what she'd done made Anna feel a little less conflicted about leaving the woman behind. Dan sold his apartment, wishing to leave New York as soon as possible. The Malcolm Building's destruction left him in serious trouble. Too many people saw him drive into the lobby of the tower. While they had yet to put a name to his face, Dan suspected it was only a matter of time before someone came after him.

Dan wanted to be away from New York before that happened.

Not that he had anything to leave behind. Sandra had made good on her promise to see his career in ruins. The day after the Monolith's destruction, Dan discovered he was out of a job.

The hospital board, pressured days earlier by John Malcolm, fired him for his unauthorized removal of Moses from the premises. Since Dan couldn't reveal what became of the old man, they saw no reason to rescind the decision. Anna took a leave of absence from the force without too many questions being asked. Since she and Dan had no connection, she remained unscathed by the fallout of the Monolith's destruction.

Dan converted almost everything he owned into cash and departed New York for Point Pleasant, with Anna and the elves joining him to decide their next move. Pooling their resources, they bought the boat and still had enough money to remain at large for quite some time. The yacht had been a priority since the elves would need to return to the Veil now their quest was complete. Although Aeron wanted to stay, it was clear this age was no place for the Immortals. They were too different, and the modern world too alien.

As much as Dan hated to admit it, it was not safe for the elves to remain.

With no way to recover their ship still sitting in impound somewhere in Bay Shore, Halion's sons had to rely on the modern equivalent to make the journey home. Dan's plan was to see the elves away from these shores before he and Anna headed for Canada. He wished she did not have to give up her life in New York, but Anna was adamant about being with him. A part of Dan couldn't help being thrilled Anna cared enough to make the sacrifice. Whatever happened, they would face it together.

"Hey Doc," Anna greeted as he made his way across the gangplank onto the Anemone's main deck. "You bring me Oreos?"

"How do you keep that gorgeous body with the junk you eat?"

Dan teased as he reached into the box of supplies he carried and handed Anna her favorite snack.

"I shoot people. It's great exercise."

"Then I think I better get you a thigh master instead." Dan gave her a look, never able to tell whether she was kidding about things like that.

"That better be because of some medical need to save my life and not because I need it." She eyed him through narrowed eyes as she tore open the Oreos. "Besides, it's not my fault I've run out. We have elves who have never had chocolate in their lives, and they're making up for the lost time."

Dan didn't ask her to elaborate as he followed Anna into the main cabin.

The elves were staring at the inbuilt TV set in the Anemone's recreation area, complete with a small video library. Dan, who was a decent sailor, ensured the Anemone came well equipped. There were GPS units and solar panels attached to rechargeable batteries capable of generating sufficient power to run the electrical appliances on board for an indeterminate length of time. None of these was as important as the ten cases of Coke in the galley.

Coca-Cola had a hell of an untapped market waiting behind the Veil.

The elves might spend months on the ocean, and Dan wanted them to do so with creature comforts. He taught them how to handle the yacht and was confident they could sail the craft on their own once it came time for them to part company. It astonished him what fast learners they were, and he suspected this applied to everything they attempted.

"Any word on whether there's a warrant out for me yet?"

"I'm not sure," Anna confessed. "I can't make too many inquiries without someone wondering why I'm so interested. At the moment, it makes things simpler if people think I don't know you. They won't look to me as a lead to finding you."

"I know. I never thought it would end like this."

"It's not an end." Anna leaned over and kissed him, trying to make him feel better. "It's a beginning."

"In Canada," Dan shrugged, not at all looking forward to the idea. "You'd think that bastard could have fixed it so I could speak French as well as elvish."

"Well, your average evil lord is very nearsighted," Anna pointed out, wishing there was more she could do for him than offer unconditional support.

Anna regretted Dan was being punished in this way. If only people understood John Malcolm was a monster intending to conquer the world, then Dan would have nothing to fear. He'd saved them all because of what he'd done, but instead of being hailed as a hero, Dan was fast becoming a suspected terrorist. She knew the net was closing, far more than she made Dan aware. It was only a matter of time before the identification on him was complete, and she dreaded to think what would happen then.

Either way, they had to leave for Canada *soon*.

"Hey guys." Dan greeted the elves and noted their eyes were fixed on the television.

"Hello Dan," Hadros greeted from the sofa, his attention not moving from the screen. "We were watching the tales of Xena. She is a brilliant warrior in battle, though they do not reveal what kingdom she is a princess of."

Dan eyed Anna critically. "You let them watch that?"

"It was on Netflix," Anna liberated the box of groceries from him on her way to the galley.

"You guys know none of that is real right? I explained TV to you."

"But the tales of her adventures cannot be lies," Syannon insisted. "These tales are recreations of real events, are they not?"

"Yes, they're recreations of stories." Dan wondered if he failed in explaining the concept of television. "However, those stories are no more real than the rest of it."

"Then what about the beasts?" Aeron asked. "Would you have us believe the creatures the lady is battling are falsehoods as well? I do not think this enormous worm is a creation."

Dan decided at this point, explaining CGI was far more trouble than it was worth, and let the matter go. Besides, he was not getting into a philosophical debate about Xena with a bunch of elves. The entire thing was absurd enough as it was.

"Never mind." He conceded defeat.

"Have you completed your preparations to leave?" Aeron asked Dan, aware the healer was facing severe consequences for his actions against Mael. Aeron didn't fully understand why Dan was being brought to account for ending the threat of the wayward Celestial, and it pained him Dan would suffer for it.

"More or less." Dan nodded. "When you are ready to leave tomorrow, Anna and I will head up north."

"You did a great service to your people," Syannon was just as displeased by Dan's precarious situation. "They should not punish you for it."

"I'll be fine," Dan assured them, touched by their concern. He knew he would survive this if Anna was with him. Besides, saving Moses had been the right thing to do, and Dan did not regret any of it, even if it meant life as he knew it was over.

Suddenly, Aeron's eyes hardened, and his jaw tensed with concern. "Something draws near."

"What?" Dan blurted. "What do you mean something draws near?"

There should be nothing drawing near!

They had destroyed Mael. Sandra Collins was dead, her body recovered within the debris of the Monolith, and Malcolm Industries was in turmoil. Yet it wasn't just Aeron sensing the danger. Syannon and Hadros were now on their feet, having detected the same threat. Almost on cue, Anna's running footsteps across the deck told Dan something was going on.

"Dan, I just saw at least three suits asking questions across the wharf. They look like FBI."

Dan had to leave right now. If he didn't, he would endanger all of them, especially the elves who could not afford to be captured by the Feds. If he let them go without him, he'd get arrested in a day, followed by a life sentence for terrorism.

Aeron saw Dan's worry and decided for once, he would decide what came next. The idle thought he had been nursing in his mind since learning of Dan's outcast state now became the best solution possible.

"Anna, we have everything we need to depart, do we not?"

"Yes." Anna nodded, her eyes showing her anguish at what was about to happen to Dan. "We have everything we need."

"Good." Aeron turned to his brother. "Syannon cast us off. Hadros start this vessel. We are leaving."

Syannon's face filled with understanding as all three brothers agreed in silence Aeron's decision was the only course before them and left the cabin to do as instructed. Both Dan and Anna looked at Aeron, wondering what the elf had in mind.

"You are coming with us."

"What?" Dan stared. "Coming with you where?"

"Home." Aeron met both Dan and Anna's eyes in quick succession to show he would accept no argument in this matter.

"As in, the Veil?" Anna gasped in similar shock. "Aeron, you can't be serious."

"Why not? You are both forced to flee because of us. In our realm, we can offer you sanctuary for as long as you live with no fear of pursuit. Let us offer you protection for a time. Your stay need not be permanent. As possible as it was for us to journey here, you can return home when your people no longer hunt you. With us, you are beyond their reach. Can you say this solution is any less promising than your decision to live as fugitives?"

Aeron was right.

If the Feds were here, then they had connected him to the Monolith's destruction. Even if he fled to another country, there was no guarantee they still wouldn't come after him. Extradition laws could be flexible when it came to terrorism. Dan couldn't be sure he would be any safer in Canada than staying here.

He had expected to go to ground, but this was hardly what he had in mind. Yet the more Dan considered it, the more he became enthused by the idea. Since meeting Aeron and his brothers, Dan wondered about the world they came from, a place where magic and gods walked among them. Besides, the chance to see Tamsyn was inviting. Still, he couldn't expect Anna to come with him.

"What do you say, Anna?" Dan looked at her, seeing the emotions on her face as she wrestled with the same question. "Want to sail away with me?"

There was never any doubt in her mind that she wouldn't. Anna left her life in New York, her career, to be with Dan. She was done fighting how she felt about him. In her dreams, she witnessed the people they'd been. Two souls who loved each other through all the ages of the world. How could she walk away from that?

"Yes." She nodded, her eyes glistening with affection. "How can I let you go anywhere without me when I love you?"

Dan broke into a grin, deciding he would never tire of hearing her say those words to him. He took her face in his hands and kissed her before responding in kind. "I love you too. I couldn't imagine doing this without you."

"We can come back, right?" he asked, turning back to Aeron. "This isn't a one-way deal?"

Aeron was unclear what a one-way deal was, but he took an educated guess. "Yes, you may return whenever you wish."

Dan faced Anna again and knew this was right. Perhaps they were always destined to take this journey together. He didn't know how much of their lives was theirs to choose, if there was any choice at all.

One thing was undeniable. Dan had waited for Anna all his life. Whatever lay before them, they could weather it if they were together.

Behind the Veil.

**THE END**

Dear reader,

We hope you enjoyed reading *The Patient* Please take a moment to leave a review, even if it's a short one. Your opinion is important to us.

Discover more books by Linda Thackeray at https://www.nextchapter.pub/authors/linda-thackeray-science-fiction-fantasy-author-australia

Want to know when one of our books is free or discounted? Join the newsletter at http://eepurl.com/bqqB3H

Best regards,

Linda Thackeray and the Next Chapter Team

# ABOUT THE AUTHOR

Born in a village in Malaysia to Ann, an irritable new mother (who wouldn't be after 48 hours in labor?), and an underpaid midwife, X was named by a deranged grandmother, with dementia. Once out of her pain-induced stupor, Ann decided to give her new daughter a proper middle name to avoid the risk of being put into a home later in life.

And so, she was called Linda.

Linda was an unremarkable child, save a few notable incidents. For example, a pot lid is not a substitute for Wonder Woman's tiara (five stitches), four-year-olds don't need to shave (no stitches but lots of toilet paper), and utility truck drivers are not necessarily qualified operators of their vehicles (seventy stitches).

At eight, Linda received religious enlightenment when she saw Star Wars at the Odeon Theatre and hence began her writing career.

For many years, the cages of various pets in the Thackeray household were littered with pages from Linda's scribblings. Subjects usually ranged from whatever science fiction show was on television or at the movies. There were a lot of Star Wars.

At 17, Linda moved to Sydney, Australia. She was disappointed it was not occupied by Paul Hogan types with big knives and croc skin jackets but pot-bellied blokes with zinc cream and terry towel hats. Linda's father (also known as that bloke who buys me stuff to piss mum off when she's mad at him) settled in the town of Young, a community of 6000 people and no movie theatre.

Linda survived this period in the wilderness by raising kangaroos and writing original works but eventually got saddled down with the necessities of life. Though she continued to write, work came first. Work, HBO, comic books, and rent. It's a kaleidoscope.

Even the kangaroos left out of boredom.

In 2014, Linda decided to start writing seriously again. Mostly because Australia's strict gun laws make it very difficult to 'go postal' in the workplace. Moving to Woy Woy, which is Aboriginal for 'Big Water', she's dipped her toes into the Indie pool and found she needs a pedicure. Her books are labors of love, and she is pitied by her friends on Facebook.

Supported by two cats Newt and Humphrey, she spends her days trying to write novels, while having unclean thoughts about Michael Fassbender and Jason Statham. Sometimes together.

Author Page: https://www.lthackeray.com/

Amazon Central Author Page: https://www.amazon.com/Linda-Thackeray/e/B00NE63G76/

Facebook: https://www.facebook.com/Scribee310z/

Twitter: https://twitter.com/Scribe310z

Goodreads: https://www.goodreads.com/author/show/8331182.Linda_Thackeray

CPSIA information can be obtained
at www.ICGtesting.com
Printed in the USA
BVHW070420290121
599074BV00003B/412